# THE
# Exceptionals

## ERIN
## CASHMAN

Holiday House / New York

To my father, Tim, for sharing with me his love of books,
and my mother, Josie, for teaching me to believe

To my husband, John, and our children, Sean, Maggie, and
Danny, for their enduring love, encouragement, and support

## ACKNOWLEDGMENTS

I am so grateful to my truly *exceptional* editor, Pamela Glauber, whose ideas
and guidance were invaluable in shaping *The Exceptionals*. She worked tire-
lessly in editing this book, and the result is a far better novel. Thank you to
Erica Silverman for all of her hard work, support, advice, and truly excellent
agenting, and to her dedicated team at Trident Media Group, including Alex-
andra Bicks (who was the first to read the manuscript) and Sarah Smith.

A special thanks to Cornell Lab of Ornithology for answering all of my
hawk questions and sending me spectacular photos. I spent many an hour on
their informative website.

Thanks and love to Sean, Maggie, and Danny Cashman for listening to
all of my wild ideas, and to Maggie and Danny for reading (and rereading!) the
manuscript and for their careful editing. A special thank-you to Maggie for
being the authority on all things teen! Thank you to Kelly Ryder, Charlotte
Arnold, Sally Mielke, Jill Faber, Leigh Hesler, Jan Rejto, Janet Maxwell, Barbara Loblundo, Linda Caroll, Micheala Barth, Kim Forshay, Jennifer McDon-
ald, Stephanie Leydon, and my sister Kathy Thornton for their friendship,
laughter, encouragement, and/or reading of the manuscript.

Thank you to my husband, John, for reining my imagination in at times,
for his constant support and encouragement, and for his spelling and punc-
tuation help! And last but not least, thanks and love to my father, Tim Hef-
fernan, for sharing with me his love of reading and a good story and to my
mother, Josie, for her belief in the unbelievable.

Library of Congress Cataloging-in-Publication Data

Cashman, Erin (Erin Theresa), 1965-
The exceptionals / by Erin Cashman. — 1st ed.
p. cm.
Summary: Fifteen-year-old Claire, apparently the only normal student at a school for people with
supernatural powers, learns that she is the subject of a famous prophecy, and when fellow students
start disappearing, she must use her ability to communicate with animals to help them.
ISBN 978-0-8234-2335-4 (hardcover)
[1. Supernatural—Fiction.  2. Ability—Fiction.  3. Human-animal communication—Fiction.
4. Schools—Fiction.  5. Prophecies—Fiction.  6. Missing persons—Fiction.  7. Family life—
Fiction.]  I. Title.
PZ7.C2682223Exc 2012
[Fic]—dc22
2011010877

# Contents

# PROLOGUE

I only hesitated for a moment. I wrapped my hands around the thick black wire and pulled with all of my strength. I felt the energy surge through my body. Everything went from blindingly bright, to gray, then slowly faded to black. I knew this was how it was going to end; in truth, I was glad to have it finally over with.

They say your life flashes before your eyes when you are about to die. Mine didn't—well, not exactly, anyway. My story played out in my head, at least the part that led me to where I am now, lying peacefully on the forest floor.

Tom, a boy I had a crush on for years, finally asked me to the Spring Fling last March. We went with Tom's best friend, Joey, and Joey's girlfriend, Amber. Not the brightest bulb, Joey tried to sneak beer into the dance when everyone knew the police would be checking the cars. Surprise, surprise, we got caught.

The police were actually reasonably nice, and let me, Tom, and Amber go home. But they did call our parents. Tom and Amber probably got a lecture. I knew I wouldn't get off so easy. My parents were tough—especially my mother. I thought they would ground me for a month. Actually, I wasn't grounded at all. But I *was* punished, and the severity of it shocked even me. It's strange how your life can change in a second—a pivotal moment—and yet, you only realize it looking back. If I hadn't got caught that night, I would have finished up my sophomore year at Lakeville High a few days ago, and I would not be dying right now. And yet, if I had to do it over, I wouldn't change a thing. Well, maybe one thing. I wish I had written it all down so everyone would know how I ended up like this and, more importantly, that I had no regrets.

I would begin on that blustery March night, and this is what I'd write....

# CHAPTER 1
# a Fateful Night

My parents drove me home from the police station without speaking. This in itself was a miracle. My mother usually had to know everything. I'm sure there were FBI agents not as thorough. The silence was unnerving.

We drove through the town center, with its wide, tree-lined streets and tidy shops and restaurants. I wasn't going to be the first one to speak. I had plenty to say, but I wanted to begin from a position of strength. My father turned left, down the long, dark, winding road that hugged the shores of the lake. My parents continued to look straight ahead, as if their eyes were fixed on a fascinating sight instead of the dense woods that surrounded Lakeville.

I looked out the window at the darkness that enveloped us. I could see my pale reflection staring back at me like a ghost. My dark auburn hair was piled up in an uncomfortable but elaborate "updo," as the hairdresser had called it. I had on the most beautiful green silk dress; when I twirled, the hem floated up around me. It was a dress to dance in, not that I'd gotten a chance to. In fact—I checked my cell phone—I'd worn it for three hours, most of the time sitting down, either in a car or at the police station. I had imagined this night a hundred times—but never like this.

"I know I'm in trouble," I began, unable to stand the oppressive quiet a minute longer, "but I didn't know Joey was going to bring beer. I mean, we knew they were going to search cars. What kind of an idiot hides beer under his seat when he knows the police will be checking?"

"Oh, I see, Claire," my mother, Maura, said sarcastically. "So the real problem isn't the underage drinking—it's being stupid about it?"

I sighed. "Mom," I said evenly, "the policeman already told you, I wasn't drinking. In fact, no one was drinking. Joey admitted to bringing the beer, and the rest of us didn't know it was in the car. What's the big deal?"

She and my father exchanged knowing looks. She turned her head back toward the fascinating night again and didn't answer.

"So, can we just get it over with? How long am I grounded for?"

"We'll talk about it in the morning," my father said softly.

"Dad? You're starting to freak me out." I wished my mother would just turn around and yell at me—her favorite pastime. Not knowing was making me insane.

"Please?" I begged. So much for my position of strength.

Finally we pulled off the country road and up to the entrance of Cambial Academy. Even in the dark I could see the lights from Crane Hall twinkling in the distance, the imposing brick building silhouetted against the night sky.

My father rolled down the window and waved to John, the security guard sitting inside the small booth next to the gate.

John peered into the window. "Good evening, Professor Walker, Professor Crane, Claire." A moment later I was welcomed home by the loud creak of the heavy iron gate swinging open. We continued down the main road into campus, turning before we reached the dorms. We passed Principal Grogan's house with its inviting front porch, not that anyone would want to visit him, then finally came to ours, set apart by a multitude of trees. We all got out in silence.

I trailed behind my parents into the house—a large white Victorian with a wide wraparound porch. The only one to greet me was Darwin, our golden retriever, since both my brother and sister board at Cambial.

I threw my silver, sequined clutch—the one I had carefully chosen to match my shoes—onto the kitchen table. "Can we *please* just get this over with?"

Again, the meaningful looks. "All right. Have a seat."

With mounting dread, I sat down across from my parents.

My father, Charles, lightly drummed his fingers on the table. He was a tall man with broad shoulders and, usually, a kind face. Now he wasn't meeting my eye—not a good sign. "You know that we have allowed you to attend Lakeville High School—"

"Allowed?" I snorted. "What choice did you have? I couldn't go to Cambial, and besides, I didn't even want to. I like my normal friends from school, thank you very much. And do you know what they all call Cambial? Freakial, because it's a school for freaks."

"The conditions were," he continued calmly, ignoring my remark, "you get good grades and at all times handle yourself appropriately." He paused, his clear blue eyes brimming with disappointment. "I'm very surprised by what happened, Claire."

It was my turn to look away. I always disappointed my mother, so I was desensitized to that, but I hated letting my father down. "I have good grades, I am number two in my class, and I have never been in any trouble."

"Until now," my mother snapped.

With an awful flash of intuition, I knew where this was going. "Mom, listen—"

"No, you listen," she seethed, her dark eyes penetrating my every thought. She couldn't, of course—at least not yet—but she could tell if I was lying, with less margin of error than a polygraph test.

"You are fifteen years old, a sophomore in high school. I have tried to indulge your"—she threw her hands up, searching for the appropriate word—"adolescent wallowing, but this has gone on long enough. You were in a car with people of poor character who had every intention of drinking and supplying you with alcohol. And if this Tom person were to ask you if you wanted a drink, what would you have said?"

I concentrated on closing my mind. It didn't work as well when I was upset or angry—which, unfortunately, was usually when I lied.

She frowned. "I suspected as much. You leave us no choice. You will be transferring to Cambial. Principal Grogan will allow you to attend classes with the other students until they go to their afternoon sessions. At that time, you will work independently, and I will review your work."

Although I saw it coming, a part of me never believed she would actually do it. She thought nothing of ruining my life! As her words sank in, the room began to spin—I had to grip the edge of the kitchen table to steady myself. "You can't! I won't go! You can't make me!" I screamed, well aware I sounded like a two-year-old.

"We did, and you will go," she said evenly, and with that, she swept out of the room.

# CHAPTER 2
# Cambial Academy

I awoke Monday to the constant *tap tap tap* of the rain against my window. The weather matched my mood. I looked in the tarnished mirror that sat above my bureau, surveying my puffy blue eyes. I had cried myself to sleep, again, as I had every night since my parents handed down the edict. In fact, I had barely left my room and had even canceled my shopping plans with my friends Tori and Lexi. They would have asked if I'd gotten in trouble, and I couldn't bear to tell them what my parents had done; saying it out loud made it more real somehow. Of course the incident at the dance—and the aftermath—would be all over school very soon. *"Claire Walker transferred to Cambial! Can you believe it?"* I could almost hear the whispers being passed around Lakeview High right now; Monday morning before homeroom was prime gossip time. The jockeying to take my place in the elaborate social strata would have already begun.

I looked at my alarm clock, its stern face reminding me that if I didn't get a move on I was going to be late on—I could hardly stand to think it—my first day. I got dressed quickly: jeans, a blue sweater, and sneakers. I had walked around campus enough to know that some of the students here dressed very differently from the kids at Lakeville, but this outfit should fit in anywhere—even when I didn't. I sighed, resigned to the inevitable, and went downstairs.

My father sat at the table drinking coffee. Since my mother, assistant principal of Cambial, left before him, it had always been his job to get me to school. He looked up from the paper and smiled at me nervously—clearly worried I would pitch another temper tantrum. I didn't have it in me.

"What can I get you for breakfast, honey?"

Without answering him, I opened the refrigerator. Why make it easy? I knew my mother was the driving force behind the decision, but he went along with her, and that made him just as guilty.

I sank into the farthest chair from him and picked at my granola bar.

"Well, we better get going. Your mother dropped off your schedule this morning, so you don't need to go to Crane Hall. You have English first, and I'm headed that way. We can walk together."

"I've lived on campus my whole life. I'm pretty sure I can find it myself," I snapped. Although I dreaded the journey across the quad alone, I was sure walking to class with my dad was not cool, even here. I grabbed my empty backpack and stormed out, letting the screen door slam behind me.

I trudged through the cold drizzle, eyes planted firmly on the ground until I reached my classroom. My uncle Dan, who wasn't really my uncle but my parents' closest friend and my godfather, was my teacher. He mostly taught science and engineering, but he loved literature, so he always taught one English class a term. There were about a dozen kids in the class, all of different ages—the classes were often mixed, based on interest and ability rather than age—but all of them turned around to stare at me.

Uncle Dan, or Professor McAllister now, smiled in welcome. "Anywhere you want, Claire," he said, motioning with his hand to the three empty chairs that were upholstered, like the other ones, in a mishmash of styles and fabrics. I quickly picked the closest one, which just happened to be one of our old family-room chairs.

As soon as I slinked into my seat, the girl next to me turned around and flashed a huge smile. "I'm Winona Stargazer, but everyone calls me Winny. Well, everyone except my brother—he calls me Nona. I'm sooo happy to meet you!"

Winona Stargazer? Why did that not surprise me. She had

long, curly hair that fell in ringlets and huge chocolate-brown eyes. Her skin was beautiful, a golden honey color. She was wearing a billowing white blouse and several beaded necklaces, and long earrings that almost grazed her shoulders. She looked like something out of a bad '70s movie.

"Hi." I smiled slightly and quickly looked away. I already knew she wasn't someone I wanted to hang out with.

"I'm part Native American, on my dad's side—not that I ever met him. My mom moved us around a lot until we finally settled in a commune in Vermont. She's a fortune-teller."

Way too much information. I nodded and gave her another halfhearted smile, hoping she'd get the hint.

"Everyone, this is Claire Walker. Introductions, please," Uncle Dan said with a little flourish of his hand.

The boy next to me smiled. "Hey, Clay-er. I'm Pete," he said with a thick drawl.

A boy across from me nodded. "Sam."

The girl on the other side of Winny waved slightly. "I'm Ally," she said shyly. If she were an animal, she'd be a swan; she was tall and thin with long, straight blond hair.

My new classmates continued to yell out names that I couldn't remember, staring at me curiously the whole time. I was sure they all knew who I was already: an abnormality at Cambial, since everyone believed I was normal.

"Here you go." Uncle Dan handed me a well-used copy of *Wuthering Heights*, which I had already covered at my old school and read several times on my own.

Despite myself, I soon got caught up in the discussion—not enough to talk, but I was listening intently.

"Claire, what do you think of Heathcliff?" Uncle Dan asked, running his fingers through his wavy brown hair.

I felt every eye in the room on me. I fought the urge to slide down in the chair. "Heathcliff," I began, trying to keep my voice from shaking, "is his own worst enemy. He loves Cathy, but doesn't think he's worthy, so he sabotages his chance with her rather than risk rejection."

Uncle Dan smiled encouragingly at me. Ever since I was a little girl I wanted his approval, and I could see my classmates felt the same way. He was everyone's favorite teacher—it made me feel a little sad for my dad, who, rumor had it, was nice but boring. Dan McAllister was anything but.

"But he's also so arrogant—like he thinks he's superior to everyone," Pete said. Apparently no one raised their hands at Cambial. "I mean, what's there to like about 'im? He's always pissed off, lashin' out at everyone. And Cathy? She's so selfish. And she didn't have the sense God gave a gopher. They totally deserve what they got."

Dan nodded again. "What do you say to that, Claire?"

"Well, of course he's superior; they're all a bunch of idiots!"

Everyone in the class giggled, especially the girl named Ally. "Linton is a wimp," she said. "Who would take him over Heathcliff? And he was a total snob, too."

Winny chimed in. "No, it was Heathcliff who didn't give anyone a chance. He preferred to isolate himself, hiding behind the mask of superiority he wore like armor so he wouldn't get hurt. He was the true coward."

Was she for real? Who talked like that?

The bell rang, and he turned back to the class. "For homework—think—think about what we talked about, and about what makes someone a villain and whether Heathcliff fits the bill. People aren't all good or all bad—and neither are great literary characters. I want a lively discussion tomorrow!"

*Think?* That was homework? And I had to admit that class wasn't terrible. School might not be so bad after all.

"Good luck today. I'm sure this isn't easy," Uncle Dan said softly as everyone filed past.

I shrugged. "Not that *she* cares." Just thinking about my mother made me furious.

He smiled sympathetically, but didn't comment. He was an attractive man; it was obvious he must have been very handsome when he was younger. I always wondered why he never got married. My father said he loved a girl once, a long time ago, but she died. He often seemed so lonely; I wished he would find someone.

"You'll do fine, I'm sure of it," he said as he put his hand on my shoulder. "If you have any problems or there's anything you want to talk about, you know where to find me."

"Thanks."

I walked down the steps to the quad, putting my one book in my bag and removing my schedule.

"Where to next?" Winny asked, peering over my paper.

Great, she had waited for me. "Uh, math," I groaned.

"I have math, too. I can walk with you!" She beamed.

Oh great. If I wasn't an oddity to begin with, now I had to walk with the school kook.

"I'm headed that way, too," Ally said, to my immense relief. "But don't worry, math isn't bad; they just cover the basics. If your special *is* math, forget it," she said, shaking her head.

I knew all about that. The kids whose special was math spent most of their time with my dad in the Think Tank, as Grove Hall was called. There were labs and computers for the math and science kids to "think outside the box."

"So what's your special?" Ally asked.

Winny looked at her and shook her head ever so slightly, her huge brown eyes narrowing.

I just assumed everyone would know. "I don't have one," I said overconfidently, like I was bragging.

"Oh, no big deal. It doesn't matter," she said quickly.

But it did matter. It mattered more than anything to the kids at Cambial.

The school was founded by William Crane, my great-grandfather who had a PhD in both math and physics. He believed that he was able to utilize a greater percentage of his brain than most people. He sought out others like himself and eventually founded the school, hoping to encourage and train young minds. What he discovered surprised him. There were many students gifted in math and science, but others had more unusual abilities.

To the world Cambial was a highly selective, very eclectic school. Its students went on to graduate from top colleges, make major discoveries in math and science, found new companies, and work for the government and law enforcement agencies across the country. But the entrance interview had nothing to do with academics. The admission staff was looking for something else entirely.

My grandparents on both sides met at the school. My mother's mom, Marie, was a truth seeker—she could tell if someone was lying and read their emotions. My mother's dad, Paul, was highly skilled at telekinesis—moving objects with his mind. They were employed by the government at various times, especially during the Cold War. Together they infiltrated spy rings and fed the government crucial information. They were legends at the school. They often worked with my dad's parents, Jillian and Edmund, who were both mediums—they could communicate with the dead. Several years ago, they were all on a secret mission when their small plane crashed, killing all four.

Like my Nana Marie, my mother is a truth seeker. The FBI has requested her services on many occasions. My dad is a mathematician, and a brilliant one at that, and a code breaker. He can break codes—any code—faster than a supercomputer.

My brother, William, or Billy to everyone except my mother, is telekinetic. Not particularly talented, though. He can only move small objects. He works hard at it, but hasn't improved much. His teachers say he's unable to free his mind.

My sister, Charlotte—otherwise known as Miss Perfect— can also communicate with the dead when they choose to appear. She's so gifted that she started school this year at age ten, a year before everyone else. The problem is, she never refuses a request from a ghost—especially if it's to tattle on Billy and me. We try to nip that in the bud, but she's such a goody-two-shoes that she just can't help ratting us out.

My great-grandfather, William Crane, used to visit her often, passing on advice to my mother about running the school, but he hasn't appeared since my grandparents died. Strangely,

Charlotte has never seen any of our grandparents, even though we were very close to them.

What's my "special"? I can hear animals talk. Actually *talk* is too grand a word. I can hear their thoughts—usually just *thirsty, hungry, tired, frightened*—but I can't communicate with them. So although I can do something unusual (lame, but unusual), I can't prove it. Anyone can say they hear animals in their mind. Even my parents were dismissive of my ability, never offering to help me like they did Billy and Charlotte. I decided long ago, I would not humiliate my family by attending the school where everyone would think I was a fraud. So when I was in fifth grade (Cambial starts in sixth), I told my parents I couldn't hear animals anymore. I saw the looks on their faces—it wasn't disappointment; it was relief.

On the way to math, Winny prattled on and on about her brother, Chetan, who was a senior, bragging about how amazing he was at telekinesis. Fortunately, I didn't really have to participate in the conversation; all that was required of me was an occasional nod.

After math I had history, and then science. Naturally, Winny was in all of my classes. When the double bell rang signaling lunch, I was finally free. I rushed across the brown, mushy grass of the quad—before Winny could follow me—and exhaled. I had made it through day one. I looked up at the gray-green sky and saw a few rays of sunlight trying to break through the clouds. Their fingers reached through the trees, casting a mottled pattern on the grass.

The other kids headed for the cafeteria, but I preferred to eat at home, alone. When I opened the side door, I was greeted with the most delicious smell: Tony's pizza. My dad must have bought it as a peace offering. I was trying to decide whether to go easy on him when, to my surprise, I found my mother sitting at the table, my favorite pineapple pizza in front of her.

"Can I talk to you for a minute?" she said. It was more of a demand than a request.

Reluctantly, I slid into the chair across from her.

"Claire, I understand that you're angry with me. But as your mother, I have to make choices that I believe are best for you. You need to be at Cambial. I need to know what's going on in your life."

"Best for me? Give me a break. This sucks for me."

Her lips tightened into a thin, straight line. "Do you think I wanted to do this? I was stunned when the police called. I would never have believed you were in a car with friends like that—friends who drink. I realized then, I don't even know your friends. I met Tom once; I never even met the other two. You never brought friends home—"

"Oh, please. I couldn't."

She sighed. "I know. But I want you to know—despite what happened—I do trust you. I know how hard this has been for you. Frankly, I worry about the choices you will make because of this."

I rolled my eyes. *This*, which we never spoke of, was the fact that I'm not special. How dare she make it about Cambial? Just because her world revolved around the school didn't mean mine did. I clenched my teeth, trying to contain my anger.

"I know I've said this before," she continued, looking up at me with pain in her eyes, "but you are special. This school can only measure certain talents, those that are quantifiable. You're a wonderful writer. Shakespeare wouldn't have been accepted at Cambial either, and he certainly was special."

"Mom, I'm not going to make bad decisions because I didn't go to this stupid school. I loved Lakeview High! I was happy there, but you had to go and ruin that. I think you're the one who can't let *this* go. Sorry to disappoint you, but I'm ordinary."

"Claire, you are not—"

"I am, and I'm fine with it. It's *you* who can't stand the fact that the great Maura Crane gave birth to an average girl. Well, get over it. And for the last time, I didn't drink! I don't think I would have. But if I did, and that's a big *if*, it would have had nothing to do with this school because—guess what?—I don't care about Cambial. Maybe it would be because you drive me crazy."

She exhaled loudly. "You may not see it now, but you were on a self-destructive path—"

"Please! I'm like the model teenager! I get good grades, I'm on the track team—"

"I'm talking about the drinking!"

*"There was no drinking!"*

She covered her mouth with her hands. After a long minute she continued. "I don't want to fight with you."

I leaned back in my chair, my arms folded tightly across my chest. "Really? Seems like your favorite hobby."

"Claire, I wanted to have lunch with you today to tell you that I love you. I hope someday you will understand why I moved you here." She paused. "There is nothing ordinary about you. You are a very special young woman."

I could hear the tenderness in her voice, which caught me by surprise. I looked away from her. "Maybe your expectations are too high."

She sighed.

The silence seemed to stretch on and on. Finally she opened the box and placed a piece of pizza on my plate, and then took one herself. I didn't touch mine. I wouldn't give her the satisfaction.

"I have my special to teach, so I'll see you later today," she said, getting up from the table.

"Wait—what am I supposed to do during specials? You haven't told me yet."

She looked back over her shoulder and smiled at me tentatively. "You figure it out. Do what you enjoy. We'll meet in a few weeks to go over your progress."

I continued to stare at the spot where she had stood long after she left. This was not my controlling mother talking. Figure it out? No list of assignments and expectations? I'd half expected a rubric. I sat back in my chair and ate the pizza.

I climbed the squeaky stairs to my room, followed closely by Darwin, who promptly curled up on my rug—old and worn like everything around here. This house had belonged to my great-grandfather, the legendary William Crane himself. Most people probably would have found it creepy, but I loved it. Under a steep slate roof were all of the usual rooms, but the basement housed a lab, a bomb shelter, and a secret tunnel leading to a large shed in the woods. In the middle of the attic was a circular staircase to a widow's walk, built for my great-grandmother Barbara, who fancied she could read the stars.

For the hundredth time I picked up the handle of the antique black phone—we had to be the only family in America who still had a rotary phone—and tried to reach Tom, but he didn't pick up. Then I tried Amber, Lexi, and Tori, to no avail. I palmed the sleek silver cell phone I got for Christmas, now obsolete in my new life (or lack thereof). There was no cell phone coverage at Cambial; my mother and Principal Grogan thought it was way too risky after someone took a cell phone picture of dancing potato chips and posted it on Facebook. My mother had made a contest out of it, challenging the science and engineering departments to figure out a way to block the reception for two miles surrounding Cambial. Only at Cambial would that be considered fun.

After that, Facebook was banned, too, then even more websites. The kids can use the Internet, but only on school computers, which are equipped with tons of security features—and no photos can be posted whatsoever. So Cambial is basically a dead zone. It's like living in the Dark Ages. I tossed my phone in the drawer and slammed it shut, then plopped down on the lumpy mattress, put Neil Young on my iPod, and cried.

# CHAPTER 3
# Specials

The next day was miserable. And the next, and the next. Despite the fact that I completely ignored both my parents, barely ate, and locked myself in my room, my mother didn't have a change of heart. In fact, it just confirmed what I had long suspected—she didn't have one.

After a week of self-pity and overwhelming boredom, I resigned myself to the fact that this was my new life, so I better make the best of it.

The following week things slowly improved. With each passing day I got ready for school with a little less dread. I really liked Ally, and despite Winny's odd appearance, she was growing on me. She was smart, funny without trying to be, insightful, and extremely honest. She was like an overeager puppy dog; it was hard *not* to like her.

It had been over two weeks since I started at Cambial, and today, believe it or not, I was actually looking forward to school. We were going to watch *Wuthering Heights* in English, and in science—which I've always hated—we were doing a lab on the senses, which actually sounded like fun.

I walked with my dad to English, our new morning routine. Although I was still furious with my mother, he and I had reached an unspoken truce. No one here seemed to care if I walked with my father, or what I wore, or what I said. At Cambial, where everyone was a misfit of some sort, anything went. I found it strangely liberating.

Today was a glorious spring day, so Uncle Dan let us out about twenty minutes early. I sat outside with Winny and Ally on the freshly mowed grass and inhaled deeply—I loved that smell. Ally lay down on her side, her head propped up by her hand. Her skin looked almost translucent in the sun. Winny sat cross-legged, her bronze ringlets twirling around her in the breeze. As she talked, her hands moved in a flurry, and the multitude of colored bracelets adorning her wrists clattered like cymbals.

As I sat there with my new friends it struck me how much things had changed. A few weeks ago I was excited to go to the Spring Fling with Tom. Now I was in a new school, and Tom hadn't returned any of my calls. Apart from a few emails, I hadn't heard from any of my friends, either. Lakeville High seemed like a lifetime ago, and I hadn't missed it nearly as much as I thought I would.

I wondered what Winny and Ally's specials were. I realized I'd been so caught up in myself, I'd never even asked them. "What's your special, Winny?" I was sure, given her fashion sense, it would be clairvoyance.

"Telekinesis," she said dreamily. She sat with her face turned up to the sky and her eyes closed, palms up, as if she were worshipping some sun goddess.

Ally looked at me, one eyebrow raised. "I thought you knew. She's one of the best in the school. She can move large objects pretty far," she said, sounding a little awed by her.

"That's my brother's special, too."

Winny nodded her head and grinned sheepishly. "I know. Billy's really nice."

"Pretty cute, too, huh, Winny?" Ally said, smirking.

Winny shrugged in response, but her golden skin flushed.

"What's your special?" I asked Ally.

Ally looked away, her fine, straight hair draping like a curtain in front of her face. "I'm a code breaker, but I'm not that good."

I smiled, trying to hide my own embarrassment. "I'm sure you're fine. Anyway—look who you're talking to."

The rest of the day flew by, ending with science, where Professor Higgins blindfolded us for the whole period so we could work on developing our other senses. Our homework was to spend half an hour a day blindfolded. I had to admit, homework at Cambial was a lot better than at Lakeville.

When the double bell rang for lunch, Winny and Ally once again asked me to join them in the cafeteria. Today, for the first time, I said yes.

I'd been in Crane Hall dozens of times, but never as a student. In fact, this was the first time I'd been here during the school year. It was a towering brick building at the top of the hill, the oldest one on campus. The dining hall and auditorium were on the first floor, admissions and my mother's office were upstairs, and the gym—Billy's second home—was in the basement.

I walked up the uneven brick path to the cafeteria with my new friends, feeling both nervous and excited. Maybe, just maybe, there was a place for me here at Cambial. Winny pushed open the double doors to reveal a cavernous two-story room. Floor-to-ceiling windows and French doors opened to a wide brick patio, where students were chatting at wrought-iron tables around a fountain. And the food! There was a line for hot lunch, tables with sandwich fixings, a long salad bar, panini makers, fruit, and more dessert than I'd ever imagined.

I followed Ally over to the sandwiches and was just grabbing a muffin when a velvety voice asked, "What are *you* doing here?"

I looked up abruptly, knocking the muffin onto the floor. Jane Morse stood in front of me wearing a hollow smile.

Jane was a very gifted clairvoyant, my mother said the best in the school. She occasionally met with my mother at the house, so I had already met her, but she was so dismissive of me that I was shocked she remembered who I was.

Jane was stunning, and she knew it. Her lustrous, short dark hair emphasized her creamy skin and lazy hazel eyes. If she were an animal, she'd definitely be a fox, I thought.

"O-Oh," I stammered, leaning over to pick up the muffin. "Eating."

She batted her ridiculously long eyelashes. "Obviously," she said, still smiling. "I meant—what are you doing *here*? You don't really *belong* here, do you?"

I felt myself go tomato-red. I was well aware that I didn't belong at Cambial, but who was she to tell me that? I swallowed and took a deep breath, but before I could tell Jane where she could go, Ally did.

"Belong? What do you mean? This school was founded by Claire's great-grandfather. She's lived here her whole life. If anyone belongs here, she does. I don't see *your* name on any of the statues outside."

Jane cocked her head to the side. "Well, thank you for explaining it to me. Of course that's why she's here. Glad to see nepotism is alive and well at Cambial. Good luck, Claire, you'll need it. And Ally, I hear you're just about the worst code breaker in school, so smart move befriending Claire—maybe it'll keep you from getting thrown out." She smiled as if she had just complimented our outfits, turned, and strutted outside with a quick glance back to survey who was watching her.

"Oooh, I can't stand her. She thinks she's God's gift to Cambial," Ally said. "Just ignore her."

Although I was perfectly capable of standing up for myself, it felt nice that Ally was willing to. Still, I couldn't help but wonder how many people felt exactly the same way as Jane. Oh, who was I kidding? Jane was right.

Suddenly I felt a shove from behind. What now? I wished more than anything I had just eaten at home. I summoned my courage and spun around.

"Hey," Billy said. "I keep looking for you. Where've you been?"

He was standing with two of his friends. I knew one of them, Mike Jones, a short, chubby kid who had been friends with Billy for a long time. The other guy was kind of nerdy looking but cute at the same time—tall and thin, with sandy-brown hair and thick glasses covering his light blue eyes.

"Well?" Billy asked.

"Classes and then home," I said, looking down at the floor. He knew full well I had nowhere to go after lunch.

"Food's much better here." He laughed.

"True." I smiled. "Hi, Mike."

"Hi, Claire!" He pulled himself up to his full height, but I still towered over him.

Billy nodded his head toward the taller boy. "This is Henry Moore."

"Hi." I had heard of Henry Moore, of course, everyone here had. By all accounts, he was a science genius. At the end of the school year, Cambial had school-wide tournaments—the kids in each special competed in challenges. Cambial's version of final exams. Henry had won the science challenge every year since he was in eighth grade. The winners of the competitions were initiated into Cambial's most prestigious society—the Exceptional Society.

"Hi." He smiled easily. "How's it going? It must be tough having to change schools in the middle of sophomore year."

I shrugged. "Not as bad as I thought," I answered truthfully.

"A bunch of people are coming over to my room tonight, including your brother," he said, punching him on the arm, "if you guys want to come." He smiled shyly at me.

I looked quickly up at Billy to gauge if he'd be okay with me tagging along.

"Yeah, you should come. It's gotta beat sitting home with Mom and Dad."

Mike nodded enthusiastically. "Definitely, you should come."

Ugh. Mike would follow me around the entire night, like he did whenever he was over. "Maybe," I said.

There was something about Henry—I certainly wouldn't mind getting to know him better, but I wasn't sure I was ready for a room full of strangers who all knew about me.

"I can't tonight," Ally frowned. "I have to practice. Code breakers have a competition tomorrow."

Throughout the year there were small competitions in each special leading up to the final one. I really wished Ally could go—it would be a lot easier with her there.

"Oh, come on," Henry said.

She sighed. "Nope, can't do it."

Winny waved to us from a patio table. I waved back and picked up my tray. "See you guys later."

"Hope you come," Henry said, "and bring Winny."

Mike nodded so earnestly, he looked like a bobble head.

"Thanks, we'll see," I answered, looking up at Henry. He held my gaze, a smile playing at the corner of his lips. I could feel his eyes on me as I crossed the cafeteria to the patio.

Winny was sitting at a table in front of the fountain; at its center a statue of my grandfather Paul looked down at me. "Is Billy sitting with us?" she asked hopefully.

I glanced back over at them, but they were already sitting down. "I guess not."

"Oh," she said, sounding disappointed. "Billy's really nice…," She paused. "And cute."

I tried to hide my grin—that was the second time she'd said that. I knew a lot of girls liked Billy, with his straight dark hair and huge biceps.

When I told her about going to Henry's, Winny shook her head. "I can't, my mom's in town visiting, so Chey and I are meeting her for dinner. He's even coming back early from his hiking trip."

"I didn't know there was a hiking trip."

"There isn't. Chey goes off by himself to meditate. He says it helps with his special."

As if on cue, a very handsome guy walked over to the table. "Hi, Ally. Hey there, Nona."

A wide smile spread across Winny's face. "You're back already! Chey, this is Claire!"

He didn't look much like Winny—both of them had wide smiles, high cheekbones, and big, brown doe eyes, but that's where the similarities ended. Chey was tall and lanky, darker skinned than Winny, with spikey jet-black hair. He was toned and sleek, like a jaguar.

"Well, Claire, I've heard a lot about you, but I've never seen you around. It's great to finally meet you."

"You've heard a lot about me?" I laughed. "Winny brags about you all the time."

"What can I say? It's all true." He winked. "Nona, I'll come by to get you around six. Mom's picking us up at the gate. See you guys later."

\* \* \*

22

When the bell for specials rang, I watched as Winny and Ally hurried off, each in a different direction. Despite the rocky start, I was glad I had lunch with my friends. Other than Jane, everyone I met was pretty nice, and for the first time in what seemed like forever, I might even have plans on a Friday night.

I sat alone on the hard edge of the fountain watching the water ripple out from the center. The patio, filled with students a few minutes ago, was now completely empty. Everyone was at specials but me, and I had to admit I was jealous. But since I was the only one who could hear the thoughts of animals, even if I'd been honest about it, it's not like anyone could train me.

I glanced up at the stone figure of my grandfather in his wheelchair. It looked just like him—the same mischievous smile and scruffy beard (as opposed to the godlike statue of William Crane dominating the entrance).

I thought about Grandpa Paul, and how he almost died fighting Timothy Wilder, a former professor and a seriously mad scientist. The clairvoyants had visions of Wilder recruiting followers and building powerful weapons in his lab, so Grandpa Paul and Nana Marie, along with Grandpa Edmund and Grandma Jillian, my parents, and Uncle Dan, all went to stop him. There was a big fight, and the lab blew up, along with Wilder and all his followers. The force of the explosion threw Grandpa Paul, and he never walked again.

I wished I could still go to him for advice. Another beautiful afternoon was ahead of me, and I had nothing to do. But as I looked up at him I knew exactly what he would have said to me: "Claire, stop your moping and do something useful. The measure of a person is not in her accomplishments but in her pursuit of a worthwhile goal."

I sighed. He was right. Wallowing in self-pity wasn't going to get me anywhere. "Well, Grandpa, I better go work on *my* special." Today, for the first time, I knew what I would do. Instead of going home, I took the path at the back of Crane Hall that led into the woods. I was going to write.

*  *  *

I meandered down the path until I was deep in the forest. The farther I went from Cambial, the more overgrown the trail became, the ferns, moss, budding leaves, and undergrowth surrounding me with infinite shades of green.

I could hear the thoughts of the animals around me, a low humming noise, and if I stopped and concentrated, I could hear individual thoughts or feelings. A red cardinal flew directly in front of me and thought *thirsty*. Curious, I veered off the path and followed him.

The branches scratched at my face as I climbed through the dense underbrush. After a few minutes I came to a shadowy area filled with large, thick trees. Their leafy canopy blocked most of the sunlight, making it impossible for many plants to grow. Feeling a bit uneasy, I stopped and listened to the creatures surrounding me; there was no sign of danger.

I couldn't see the cardinal anymore, but I saw a large hawk swoop overhead. *Thirsty and hungry*, she thought. As she glided downward her strong wings seemed to span the entire sky. I followed beneath her, jogging to keep up. The trees thinned, and soon I found myself on the edge of a field. It was so quiet and peaceful, a little oasis in the middle of the forest. Pussy willows and wild flowers swayed gently on the banks of a winding stream. Lured by the melody of gently flowing water, I climbed up on a large rock that overlooked the brook.

I tried to sit *very* still so the animals would go back to what they were doing before my intrusion. A turtle basking in the sun eyed me cautiously. *Fear*.

I knew if I stayed still long enough, the animals would forget me, since most don't have long attention spans. I sat with my notebook on my knee, waiting for the story, for *their* story. After a few minutes they started to ignore me, but then they unexpectedly returned to me—*person! danger! fear!*—the thoughts jumbled together at an incredible speed and then abruptly stopped. Some animals scampered off; others froze. *That's strange*, I thought; I hadn't even moved.

Suddenly, I heard the tall grass rustling behind me. I whipped around, my heart racing. I was not alone.

# CHAPTER 4
# a Stranger in the Woods

A boy was striding through the clearing, oblivious to me. He was exceptionally handsome, tall with dark, wavy hair that curled lightly around his neck. Despite the spring chill, he wore a T-shirt that exposed his muscular arms. I held my breath, hoping he wouldn't notice me. He seemed preoccupied as he walked along the banks of the stream not ten feet from me, and then he suddenly stopped.

He looked shocked to see me sitting there, but he quickly recovered. An easy smile spread across his face, although his eyes regarded me cautiously. "Hi there," he said.

"Hi," I breathed, feeling my face flush.

"I'm Dylan," he said, coming toward me. He walked with the ease of someone who was good at everything.

He was even more gorgeous up close, with long, dark eyelashes framing beautiful green eyes. I swallowed. "Claire."

"May I join you, Claire?"

I felt my heart beat faster. I shrugged.

He hesitated for a moment and then agilely climbed up next to me. The rock was just large enough to hold the two of us, so he was sitting very close to me, his leg almost touching mine, and it seemed as if there was an electric current between us. He glanced down at the notebook resting on my legs.

"A writer," he said. A statement, not a question.

I couldn't think of a response. I wasn't a writer, not really, more of a chronicler of stories that weren't even mine.

Dylan leaned back against his elbows. "I'm a wanderer, I

guess," he chuckled, as if I had asked. "I walk in the woods to think, clear my head."

"These are the school grounds, you know," I said. Why? I had no idea.

The smile faded from his face, and he sat up abruptly. "I'm sorry, I thought I was still in conservation land. It was nice meeting you." He gracefully leaped off the rock.

"N-No, its fine—the school isn't even close by," I stammered. *Shoot!* I hadn't meant to chase him away.

He turned back to me and grinned. "You go to Cambial?"

Oh no—how to answer that one. Yes and no. I knew Lakeville teenagers thought the kids from Cambial were all strange. "I went to Lakeview High until recently," I said, only partially answering his question. "What about you?"

Dylan leaned against the rock. "I'm taking some time right now—trying to figure out what to do with my life. Why aren't you in s-school?" he stuttered.

"Um…I'm doing an independent study."

The wind blew lightly, catching my hair and tumbling it out behind me. I gathered it with my hand and smoothed it back behind my ear. He was watching me intently. I quickly looked down at my notebook, trying not to appear so self-conscious.

"What do you write about?"

"Animals."

This seemed to intrigue him. "May I?" he asked, peering at the paper.

It took me a moment to realize what he was asking. "Oh! Uh…" was all I could say as I covered it with my hands. "No, I'm just fooling around."

He laughed. "Come on, can't I read a little bit?"

"I really don't like people reading my stories. So what about you? Are you in college?"

Dylan's eyes flickered quickly to mine, and then away. "I was, but then a friend approached me with a really interesting opportunity, so now I'm working with him."

"You're lucky your parents are okay with that; mine would kill me."

"My parents are dead," he said flatly. "Well, I better get going."

"Oh, I'm sorry. I didn't mean to—"

"Don't worry about it. They died when I was a baby. I don't even remember them." He paused. "It really was nice to meet you, Claire."

"You, too. Maybe I'll see you here again," I said a little too hopefully.

"I wouldn't want to trespass. Of course, maybe you're a trespasser, too?" He looked up at me, his expression teasing but his eyes guarded.

"I live on the grounds. My parents work here."

He stared at me, a mixture of surprise and apprehension.

I shrugged. "So I think you're allowed to wander here, as my—" *My what?*

"Friend," he mercifully finished my sentence. "I'd like that. Maybe I'll see you around."

"Sure." I shrugged casually. From the glimmer in his eye, I knew I didn't have him fooled. He leaped over the stream and walked through the tall pussy willows until he disappeared into the line of trees on the opposite bank.

I heard the animals chattering on after he left. Then it hit me: I hadn't heard them while he was there—at least I didn't remember hearing them. Was I that distracted? I'd have to pay more attention next time. And I did hope there would be a next time.

By the time I returned home, I barely had enough time to shower and eat before I was due at Henry's. I wanted to go, I really did, but the thought of walking into the room alone terrified me. What if Billy hadn't shown up yet? What if Jane was there?

I fed Darwin, who was following me around thinking *hungry, hungry, hungry,* and took a quick shower. As I changed and combed my thick mass of tangled hair my mind kept wandering to Dylan. I wondered if (and really hoped!) I would see him again.

"Claire! I got Chinese!" my dad yelled.

As if on cue, my stomach rumbled. I went into the kitchen and was surprised to find Billy piling crab rangoon on an already heaping plate of food.

"Hey, what are you doing here?"

He shrugged. "I love Chinese food. Hurry up and eat. I'll walk over to Henry's with you."

I tried to keep myself from smiling. That's why he came home, to escort me over, knowing I'd feel awkward. I guess I was going, after all.

"Where are you two going, William?" I hadn't heard my mother come in.

"Henry's—a couple of us are hanging out tonight."

My mother raised her eyebrows. I knew she now saw me as a beacon for trouble. "Who'll be there?" she said, trying unsuccessfully to sound casual.

Darwin ran over to her, thinking *hungry, hungry, hungry.*

"Nice try, but I already fed you," I said.

My father turned around and looked at me appraisingly. "What?"

I could feel my mother watching me as well.

*Damn.* "Oh, Darwin's obviously trying to get a second dinner out of Mom." I quickly changed the subject. "Did you get spring rolls, Dad?"

"Of course, and vegetable lo mein."

Billy shook his head. "I don't know how you gave this up," he said, gnawing at a sparerib.

I had to look away. I was a vegetarian; since I could hear the thoughts of animals, there was no way I could eat them. I scooped some food on my plate and sat down as far as possible from Billy.

"And who did you say would be at Henry's?" my mother asked.

He hadn't. "Uh—I don't know, probably Maggie, Mike...," he

paused, "and Nik." Billy, who liked almost everyone, couldn't stand Nik Patel. He was very talented at telekinesis, and pretty conceited. When they were younger, Nik used to tease Billy mercilessly about his lack of skill. That stopped a few years ago when Billy caught up to him in size, but they were far from friends. Since Ally wasn't going, I only knew Mike, and he drove me crazy. Maybe this wasn't such a great idea.

"Hmm…" She paused. "Aren't most of these children seniors?"

Only my mother would call seventeen- and eighteen-year-olds children.

Billy sighed, clearly irritated. "Some are."

"Mike Johnston is a junior, though, and such a nice boy. Don't you think so, Claire?"

Was she kidding me? Now she was trying to pick my boyfriend? "Ah, yup, he's nice. He's also extremely annoying."

Billy burst out laughing, and even my dad chuckled. "I think he has a crush on you."

I rolled my eyes as my mother shot my father a warning glare. "Well, he is a nice boy, very smart and closer to your age, Claire."

And here we had it. She didn't trust my judgment. I wish I could ignore her like Billy, but I just couldn't. "Actually, I find I have more in common with the other *children*," I said sharply. Let her think about that all night.

"Okay, let's get going," Billy said, grabbing my jacket.

My mother opened her mouth to say something, but Billy shoved me out the door before she got the chance. He had witnessed enough of our "discussions" to know how it was going to end—both of us screaming and me grounded for the night.

"Be home by eleven, Claire!" my father called after me. Cambial had a curfew, ten o'clock during the week, eleven on weekends.

"I know!" I yelled as I stormed down the porch steps. It was chillier than I expected, and brighter. The full moon hung just above the horizon like a crystal ball surrounded by thousands of stars. Just breathing in the crisp night air helped me relax.

"How do you stand living there with Mom?" Billy said as we cut through the trees to the quad. "You should board now that you go to school here. She's so annoying."

"No kidding. But at least she's not home much. I can't board, though; I don't have a special, remember?"

Billy stopped abruptly and looked at me. "Nobody really cares—except for you."

I just shrugged. Maybe no one cared, but the fact was that I was only allowed to attend Cambial because of my lineage, and everyone knew it. I'm sure it didn't hurt that my mother was assistant principal, either.

Billy shook his head, exasperated. "Come on, everyone going tonight's really nice. Well, almost everyone."

"If you still don't like Nik, why are you hanging out with him?"

He frowned. "Well, he's not *that* bad anymore. Chey owns him when it comes to telekinesis, so that helped deflate his ego, and besides, he's dating Ally Faber now."

I was surprised that Ally, who was so down-to-earth, was dating Nik. I really wished she was going to be at Henry's.

"I don't know what she sees in him," he added, shaking his head.

I did—Nik Patel was hot. Tall, with smoldering dark eyes and olive skin. But I wasn't about to tell Billy that.

Despite living on campus my whole life, I had only been in the dorms in summer—when they were empty. I had always refused Billy's and Charlotte's invitations to visit; I didn't need a peek at what I was missing. I looked up at the imposing ivy-covered brick buildings and stopped. All of a sudden, I felt like I was in quicksand.

I couldn't shake the feeling that I should turn around and run home as fast as possible, but I couldn't turn back now.

# CHAPTER 5
# an almost-Normal Gathering

When we reached the fourth-floor landing, I could already hear the music drifting down the hall. Billy didn't even knock—he just threw open the door to Henry's room, so I followed him in. It was large—seniors' rooms generally were—with a bed arranged as a sofa, two old chairs that looked like they'd been rescued from the dump, and a long beat-up table overflowing with liquids festering in glass cylinders, which explained the room's slightly putrid smell. An enormous whiteboard leaned against the table, every space scribbled with formulas and notations.

Henry was standing in the middle of a group of kids, showing them some green, slimy stuff. They were all looking up at him in awe.

"Hey," he said, looking genuinely pleased to see me. "Glad you could come. This is Maggie Cullinane and Nik Patel—this is Claire, Billy's sister."

I recognized Maggie from science class. She seemed okay.

"Hi again, Claire," Maggie said in a thick brogue. She was a petite girl with shoulder-length red hair and a smattering of freckles across her nose. "I have to run, but I'm sure I'll be seein' ya around."

"Let me guess—practicing for the TT?" Billy said.

"Chey wins every year, and he'll be picking his partner soon." She smiled slyly.

Billy nodded. "It might just be you, Mags."

Nik shook his head and laughed. "No way—he's picking me. Everyone knows I'm a close second to Chey—no offense, Billy."

I could practically hear Billy grit his teeth, but he didn't say anything.

"I better be off—ya know, you should be practicing, too, Billy. Oh, and Henry, congratulations!"

I winced. Billy had been practicing for the telekinesis tournament—or the TT, as everyone called it—since last summer, but watching him play, you'd never know it. The TT was a huge deal; everyone went. Teams of two compete on a football-sized field, but in place of goalposts were two huge boards, each with holes of different sizes. Each team had twenty balls, ranging from small five-pounders to huge two-hundred-pound ones. The object was to get all of your balls in the corresponding holes before the other team did.

For a game that used your mind, it was surprisingly active, with players running, jumping, and blocking down the field. The cool part was that teams could bring anything they wanted to the tournament to help them, as long as they moved it with their minds. So there were bats, rackets, poles—you name it. It was fun to see the different contraptions the players came up with. The teams were always pretty well matched; so no matter what, it was always exciting. This year, for the first time, Billy made it to the first round of playoffs. He was really accurate and a good defenseman, but despite hours of practice, he still couldn't move the heavy balls. So he'd get frustrated and work out. It was ironic, really, that despite being in the best shape physically, the heavier balls eluded him.

As Maggie darted out the door I was thrilled to see Ally walk in.

"Hi, guys. Hey, Claire."

"I'm glad you came!" I said a bit too enthusiastically.

"So am I. What happened to the studying?" Nik looked just as thrilled to see her as I was.

She shook her head. "Your dad's been working with me almost every day, Claire, and I still stink. I could study and practice from now until tomorrow morning, but I know it as well as I'm going to. I'll never be a top code breaker; life goes on." She shrugged her narrow shoulders. "Hey—did Maggie say congratulations? It finally works?"

I was clearly missing something. "What works?"

Henry held out a glass test tube filled with green goop. "This."

"And that is?"

"Well, I combined several different organic materials," he began, his eyes blazing with excitement, "and then I introduced some different herbs and roots that were reputed to have medicinal properties. You see I hypothesized…"

He lost me there. I kept looking at his cute face and lopsided grin as he futilely tried to explain it to me.

"Well, Claire, want to give it a try?"

From the looks on everyone's faces, it was clear some sort of honor was being bestowed upon me. "You want me to eat it?"

"You weren't listening," he said, but not in a mean way.

"I was, but you might as well have been speaking Chinese."

He laughed, and I couldn't help but join him.

"All right, I'll show you." He removed a pocket knife—which I was quite sure was on the list of forbidden items I was given with my admission packet—and cut a thin, straight line on his palm.

I caught my breath as I watched a streak of red blood run down his hand. "Behold," he said, scooping up a dollop of the green goop and spreading it across his hand. A minute later he wiped it away and held his palm out for me to examine. I looked at it, amazed. The only evidence of the cut was a small, thin line. I traced my finger along the depression in his skin.

"Wow."

"The compound is a cell accelerator. It speeds up the healing process significantly. I assume larger and deeper wounds will take a lot longer to heal, but I haven't tested that out yet." It was obvious from his voice he couldn't wait to test it. The bloodier, the better.

"Cool, you finally got the right formula," Billy said.

"It's about time, too," Ally laughed. "I don't think the rug could handle any more experiments!"

I took in the large burn holes scattered across the floor. "What will you do with it?"

"Oh, I'll tell Professor Higgins about it. He'll be almost as excited as I am!"

"He knows you experiment in your room?" As soon as the words tumbled out of my mouth, I regretted it. I sounded like a hall monitor or something. Why couldn't I learn to filter my thoughts?

"Not exactly," Henry frowned.

The room went silent.

"I just—things are different here. I'm not really used to what's okay and what isn't, but I'm not going to tell or anything. I..." I just let my voice trail off, well aware that I sounded like an idiot.

Henry cocked his head to one side, wearing a conspiratorial smile. "We're not supposed to experiment in our rooms, of course, but professors don't really ask."

"Just like we're not supposed to do telekinesis unsupervised," Billy said as Henry's iPod zoomed across the room into his outstretched hand. "You have the worst taste in music—let me pick."

Ally threw a pillow at him. "Show-off!" she yelled. She was sitting on the sofa next to Nik, his arm casually draped around her shoulder.

I sat down on a huge floor pillow, and Henry sat next to me. As everyone talked and laughed, it started to feel like a normal get-together, that is until Ally's favorite song came on. She started singing, and Billy made the pillows, along with several textbooks, dance along.

"Hey, watch out for my experiments!" Henry yelled when one of the books came dangerously close to a cylinder filled with something purple.

Not to be outdone, Nik sent the armchair sailing through the room, swaying in time to the music while everyone laughed (except for Billy).

At first I sat amazed, but I couldn't help but smile at the

absurdity of it all. Of course I had seen my grandfather and brother make objects move, but always in a very serious, educational manner. This was surreal.

Eleven o'clock came all too soon. "All right, Claire, let's go," Billy said when the song ended.

"I can manage a five-minute walk," I snorted.

"Mom's orders. You don't want to blow curfew."

Reluctantly, I got up. "Thanks, Henry. I'll see you guys later."

Ally gave me a hug good-bye. "Come to my room tomorrow; we can hang out."

"Sure."

Henry smiled shyly and opened the door, his arm brushing against mine. "See ya."

That night when I climbed into bed, I felt happier than I had in a long time.

# CHAPTER 6
# Forbidden Talents

The next week was relatively uneventful except that I almost broke my nose walking into a wall while I was practicing being blind. I braved lunch in the cafeteria a couple more times, and to my surprise, no one seemed to notice or care. It rained every day, keeping me from practicing my "special" in the woods and, worse still, dashing my hopes of meeting Dylan again. The more time that passed, the more it seemed like I had imagined him.

On Friday I went home at lunch and baked a cake in honor of Charlotte's eleventh birthday, since my mother was a disaster in the kitchen. After I finished, I ran upstairs to wrap Charlotte's presents. When I came back down, I was surprised to find Uncle Dan sitting in my mother's office. I knew he was coming for dinner, but I didn't expect him so early.

He was so absorbed by the newspaper he was reading that he didn't notice me. I looked again and saw that the paper was actually hiding a file. It was a plain, thick manila folder, but pretty worn and ratty. Quietly I took a step closer to him, straining to read the label—ANIP—when he looked up and quickly folded the paper with the file still in it.

"Hi, Claire." He smiled.

"Hi, Uncle Dan. What are you reading?"

He shrugged. "Just the paper. No one answered the door, so I let myself in—I didn't want Charlotte's gift to get wet," he said, motioning to the package at his feet. "I was sure your mother said five."

I shrugged. "You know my mother." She had a mind like a steel trap, but small details like dinner plans and doctor appointments often eluded her.

He laughed. "That I do. She's one of a kind."

"Are you all right?" I asked, sitting down across from him. He seemed like he was trying very hard not to be miserable. I wondered if something in the file upset him.

"Oh, I'm fine—it's just…I was reminded of someone today, someone I miss very much."

I didn't know what to say. I figured he must be thinking about the woman he had loved who had died.

"But enough of that, tonight is a celebration!" he said with forced cheer. "So how are you enjoying school?"

"It's okay. It's different here. Everyone fits in."

He smiled, but once again there was a hint of sadness in his eyes. "I wish that were true. You only go to classes—you see the students when they're relaxed. At specials, well…" He paused, searching for the right words. "Let's just say things can get pretty intense."

"How do you mean?"

"It's hard for some students to control their minds. It can be very frustrating, and we, as professors, can be very demanding. The clairvoyants, for example, at times all see a different future. Some visions are…," he paused again, "alarming. What to do with that information? When should authorities be notified? These are all tough decisions, and sometimes students don't understand."

I had envisioned specials so differently—as groups of students and teachers embarking on a great adventure, testing their powers and controlling them, giddy with their developing abilities.

"Then there are those with…"—he paused, lowering his voice—"unique or forbidden talents."

"Forbidden? Why would something be forbidden?" I had never heard of that before.

"Claire?" I heard my mother call from the kitchen.

"In here, Mom."

"Claire, I really shouldn't have said anything about forbidden talents—let's keep that between us," he whispered urgently.

It was amazing—even he was afraid of my mother, and they'd been friends since they went to Cambial together.

"The cake is beautiful," she said as she walked into the study. "Oh, hello, Dan, you're early."

"I'm sure you said five."

My mother raised her eyebrow, but didn't answer. "So, what are you two talking about?"

Oh, no. How was I going to keep that from my mother? Now that he said not to tell her, it was all I could think about, and when I didn't tell her, she would know I was lying. I knew from experience my best shot was a quick exit. "Wow, it's getting late. I gotta go get Charlotte's presents. Be down soon," I said, rushing out of the room.

As I climbed the stairs—two at a time—I saw Uncle Dan lean back in the chair. "We were discussing how she's adjusting to school. She's doing very well in my class."

"I'm glad to hear it."

He, of course, had learned how to close his mind. I had to figure out how to do that.

"Maura, I know we've talked about this time and time again, but I really think you should tell her."

"That's entirely out of the question."

"If she knew—"

I froze at the top of the stairs, listening intently, but the door closed.

Was I the "she"? And what did he think my mother should tell me? I sighed. More puzzling still, what were forbidden talents? Why would a power be forbidden—and why would it be a secret?

By the time I returned to the kitchen, everyone was home. My father was busy at the stove making Charlotte's favorite dinner, shrimp scampi, while my mother and Uncle Dan were sitting at the table with Billy and Charlotte. I couldn't wait to get Billy or Uncle Dan alone to ask them about forbidden talents.

"And Professor Shade says I might even be elected to the

Exceptional Society this year! I'd be the youngest in the history of Cambial!" Charlotte bragged.

Billy looked over at me, and I rolled my eyes.

Charlotte turned, spotting me in the doorway, and clapped her hands. "Finally! Can I pleeeease open my presents now? Everyone's here. I don't want to wait until after dinner," she pouted.

My father laughed. "Oh, go ahead." My parents always gave in to Charlotte.

"Happy birthday," Uncle Dan said, handing her a beautiful silver box tied with a gold ribbon. I recognized it immediately from the expensive jewelry store in town.

She ripped through the paper, her heart-shaped face flushed with anticipation. She opened the small box and removed a delicate gold watch. "Oh, it's beautiful! Thank you," she said, hugging him.

"Maybe you'll get to class on time," he laughed. Then he exchanged a quick look with my mother. "Actually, I'll be going away soon—I'm not sure for how long. Since I may miss both of your birthdays as well, here you go, a little early." He removed two more silver boxes from the bag and handed one to me and the other to Billy.

"But our birthdays aren't for a couple of months. You'll be gone that long? Where are you going?" I asked.

He smiled, but his eyes were guarded. "I'm really not sure how long it will take or where, exactly, I'll be. You know, sometimes we teachers are needed—top secret."

I did know, all too well. My parents had been called upon to help the government before, always very mysteriously.

My brother opened his gift—a handsome silver watch. I opened mine, a watch identical to my sister's. "Thank you," I said, giving him a hug.

"Look on the back," he said.

I turned it over, and it was engraved: To CLAIRE, LOVE ALWAYS, UNCLE DAN. Billy's and Charlotte's were, too. I suddenly had a sinking feeling that he was giving us the watches to remember him by. "Is what you're doing dangerous?" I asked, knowing he wouldn't tell me if it was.

"No." He chuckled, but I could tell he was lying.

"Great-Grandma Barbara says you should be very careful," Charlotte warned, looking over her shoulder.

Uncle Dan smiled. "I always am."

This was another thing Charlotte did that irritated me. She constantly had conversations with ghosts no one else could see. "And she doesn't think you should wander in the woods alone, Claire."

I felt like throwing the cake at her face.

"What?" my mother said, as we both knew she would. "What does that mean? Where are you going, Claire?"

I bit the inside of my lip to keep from screaming. "When everyone's in specials, I sometimes walk in the woods when the weather's nice. I always have, nothing new there."

"How far do you walk?" my mother asked, staring at me intently.

"What does it matter? What do you think I'm doing there? I can't get into much trouble alone in the woods."

"Great-Grandma Barbara says—"

I shot Charlotte a warning look, and she finally stopped talking.

My mother was still watching me, frowning. "Claire—"

"Why don't you set the table?" my father mercifully interrupted.

While everyone ate dinner my thoughts kept wandering. I wondered if Uncle Dan's sudden trip and forbidden talents were connected. I sat next to him, hoping to talk to him about it, but he seemed distracted. I wanted to pump Billy for information, but he inhaled a piece of cake and then rushed out to practice for the TT.

I went to bed frustrated, unable to fall asleep, my mind filled with unanswered questions.

The next morning I trudged through the rain in search of Billy. He wasn't in his room or the cafeteria. I almost went to the library—a long shot, at best—when I realized he must be in the gym practicing for the TT. I pushed open the heavy wood doors and quickly ducked just as a ball came hurtling at my head. It crashed to the floor not two feet in front of me.

"Jeez, Claire! What the hell!" Billy screamed, his voice echoing in the cavernous room.

It took me a minute to catch my breath. "You might want to work on that."

"That's what you get for distracting me! Try knocking next time." He sat down on the worn wooden floor. "Aw, what's the use. I suck."

"You don't. That was a good-sized ball."

He sighed. "Twenty pounds. I can't even budge the hundred-pound one—so how am I gonna move the two-hundred-pounder?"

I knew it shouldn't matter if an object was one pound or a thousand pounds—the principle was the same. Unfortunately, in Billy's mind there was a difference.

"So why are you here?" he said irritably.

I sat down across from him and looked him straight in the eye. "What are forbidden talents?"

His eyes widened, but he didn't answer.

"Well?"

"I don't know what you're talking about it," he said dismissively.

"Give me a break."

His eyebrows knitted together as he looked at me warily. "Where'd you even hear that?"

"Last night from Uncle Dan. He started to tell me about them, but then Mom came home and he shut up."

"I bet he did," he snorted. "Come on, let's get out of here. Maggie will be here any second. As if she needs more practice."

We walked in silence up the stairs and out the back door. The rain had slowed to a cold drizzle. I tied my jacket around me tightly, but even so I was freezing. We traveled down the muddy path behind the library and into the woods. At least the tree canopy offered some shelter from the rain. I could hear the animals all around us—I had to focus to tune them out.

Billy leaned against a large maple tree. "So you know about Crane's Commandments. Well, there are other rules, too."

Crane's Rules of Conduct, or Crane's Commandments as everyone called them, were a list of rules to protect the students, professors, and the school itself. Infractions were severely punished and grounds for expulsion. Most rules were obvious, like don't tell outsiders about specials and don't use your gifts to harm anyone—powers were only to be used to better mankind. So, for example, the kids from the Think Tank had to promise never to use their abilities to create bombs or weapons.

"So what are the other rules?" I asked.

"Well, some powers can't be developed at all; they're forbidden. Usually it's not a problem, because they're really rare gifts; but every once in a while someone comes along with a unique ability."

Rare powers, like mine. So other people had them? Why were they forbidden? I started to feel the anger rise up inside me. Would I have made a different choice had I known? "What are they?" I snapped.

Billy looked at me curiously. "A few people can kind of project themselves—sort of appear to others. That's forbidden."

"Why?"

Billy frowned, the lines across his forehead forming deep creases. "I guess things can go wrong—very wrong. I don't know a lot about it—like I said, these powers are very rare." He shook his head impatiently. "It's not like this place is a controlled environment. The professors try to make it safe, that's why there are rules. Each special has its own. Like mediums can't ask ghosts to spy on anyone. And in telekinesis you can't move a person—I couldn't send you sailing across the room, even though it'd be tempting."

I smirked. "Can some people?"

He shrugged. "I've never seen it, but I've heard rumors. It's insanely hard to move anything living, even something small. But if anyone tries to move a person—automatically expelled."

That seemed reasonable—no one would want to fly around a room against their will. "So why are we out here? Why couldn't you tell me this inside?"

Even though we were in the middle of the woods, he still kept looking around as if he was worried we were being followed. I knew we weren't. The animals would've told me.

"Well, you know one of the reasons we have Crane's Commandments is to keep the students from being exploited. Like when Timothy Wilder was a professor, he started recruiting kids while he was still at Cambial. He taught telekinesis and Think Tank, and he was head of the Exceptional Society, so he knew who the most gifted students were. Well, Grandpa Paul caught him red-handed—practicing forbidden stuff with some of those kids—so he fired him."

"Of course I know that. Then Wilder tried to kill Grandpa and take over the school, but Grandpa beat him and he went into hiding. Then Wilder built that lab and died along with all of his followers when it blew up. So?"

Billy sighed, clearly weighing how much to tell me.

"Billy—come on, what's that have to do with anything?"

"You can't tell anyone what I'm about to tell you."

"You know I won't."

"All right. Henry knows Jay, a kid from the Think Tank who was approached. He's at MIT—or at least he was. Anyway, he told Henry that some powerful people wanted to meet him, and Henry, too, but it had to be a secret. Henry said no. Then Jay disappeared. Henry asked Uncle Dan to look into it, so I think that's where Uncle Dan's going—to find out what happened to Jay. I'm worried that something's going on, and it isn't good. Someone's recruiting—or kidnapping—the most talented kids."

I gasped. "Do Mom and Dad know?"

"Henry told them." He paused. "They've heard rumors, too."

"That's where Uncle Dan's going? To investigate? Who else knows?"

Billy shrugged, his dark brown eyes troubled. "Hardly anyone besides me and Henry. I think just Uncle Dan, Mom, and

Dad. I'm sure they know a lot more than I do. Mom specifically told me not to tell *anyone*."

"Is that why you dragged me out to the woods—so no one would overhear us?"

"Yeah, and because…not many people know what we can do here. Just people associated with Cambial—present and former students and teachers. Even if a student broke Crane's Commandments and told an outsider, who would believe them?"

"So," I said, putting the pieces together, "you think someone connected to Cambial could be involved in Jay's disappearance."

Billy nodded, his eyebrows knitted together. "Someone powerful wanted to meet with Jay *and* Henry—two science geniuses from Cambial—and how would this person have even heard of Henry? It could be a former student or teacher, but it also could be someone here now."

"Does Principal Grogan know?"

He shrugged. "I don't know."

"Wow. This could get pretty dangerous." My heart was pounding. If Uncle Dan didn't get to the bottom of this soon, I knew my parents would get involved. "I'm worried about Uncle Dan."

Billy looked up at me, fear in his eyes. "I am, too. If someone knows about the school and what we can do—I'm worried about all of us."

The thoughts of the animals suddenly became frenzied. *Danger, person, run, hide.* And just as suddenly, they stopped.

I looked around frantically, but I couldn't see anyone. "Someone's here—let's go," I whispered.

Billy's eyes darted from tree to tree. "Where? I don't—"

I grabbed his arm, dragging him toward the path. "Just trust me," I said as we hurried through the woods. As I pushed the wet, scraggly branches out of my way one snapped back, scratching my cheek. Once we reached the lawn, I looked quickly over my shoulder. I don't know if I was imagining it or not, but I thought I saw a figure dart behind a large pine. I was sure we were being watched—or followed.

44

# CHAPTER 7
# The Secret Special

The rain picked up, beating down on us as we hurried home. Neither of us talked; we would have had to yell to be heard over the howling wind. We burst through the back door—dripping wet—and heard Principal Grogan's booming voice coming from my mother's study.

I quietly removed my jacket while Billy slid out of his squeaky sneakers, and we tiptoed down the hall. Even though the glass door to her study was shut, we could hear their raised voices.

I was surprised he was there, since there was no love lost between him and my parents. When my grandfather Paul died, George Grogan became principal. He and my parents had been very good friends before then, but they had a falling-out soon after. My parents accused Grogan of not taking security at the school seriously enough. Personally, I think my control freak mother couldn't stand not being in charge.

Billy and I stood in the hall, peering through the glass panes of the French door from a distance, hoping we wouldn't be seen. Thankfully, my mother's back was to us.

"As assistant principal, Maura, you have a duty to tell me anything you know about Jay Burke's disappearance."

"As I have said, twice, I do not know anything about it. I heard he was missing—"

"How?" he demanded, shifting his portly body on the formal wooden chair that wasn't large enough to contain him. Principal Grogan always reminded me of a walrus. He was narrow through the shoulders and wide around the middle, with a few strands of hair he combed across his otherwise bald head. His brown eyes drooped and were often red and watery due to allergies.

There was a long pause before she answered. "His mother called the school to see if anyone here had heard from him." Her tone was calm and even, but the underlying hostility was apparent.

"And why wasn't I notified of this?" he accused.

"You were. I put a memo on your desk yesterday morning."

"I never received it."

"That's a shame," she said curtly. "Is there anything else I can help you with?"

"No. In the future, please talk to me in person. And let me remind you—no electronic communications of any sort."

"I am well aware of the rule, having been the one to implement it," she seethed. "I do hope you are keeping student records safe."

"Of course I am."

"I would hate to discover that someone could access student files. I do not need to tell you how dire that information could be in the wrong hands," she warned.

"Maura, I don't require assistance running this school."

"I believe we're done," she said, standing up.

Billy and I hurried back down the hall, shutting the side door and talking as if we had just come in.

I heard the front door slam, and then my mother came into the kitchen, quickly followed by my dad.

"Where were you two? You're soaked. And what happened to your face?" my mother asked.

I absentmindedly touched my cheek. "I walked into a branch."

She frowned, turning my face to the side to survey the damage (and likely assess the truth of my story). "Well, I was getting worried about you. You should have left a note."

I pointed to the chalkboard I had hung next to the back door, where I always left messages and where my mother never looked.

"Ah," was all she said.

"Who was here?" I asked, trying to sound nonchalant.

She turned away to pour herself a cup of coffee.

"Principal Grogan was here on *private* school business," my father answered in a firm tone.

"Does it have anything to do with Uncle Dan going away?"

I could see my mother's body stiffen.

My father gave me a sharp, sideways glance. "Dan should not have announced that."

I sat down at the kitchen table to let them know I was not going anywhere. My wet jeans made a squishy noise on the wooden seat.

"Is what he's doing dangerous?"

My parents exchanged a quick look. "I don't know," my mother sighed. "But it is imperative that you keep anything you've heard to yourselves, both of you."

"I know the drill," Billy said.

"Why don't you take a shower?" my father said to me, signaling the end of our conversation.

I did what I was told and let the hot water cascade over me, but so many questions ran through my mind—why did Uncle Dan tell me about forbidden talents if it was such a big secret? What happened to Jay Burke, the science whiz kid—and what was he working on? And more disturbing still—was his disappearance connected to Cambial?

When I went back downstairs, my parents had gone out, but Billy was sitting impatiently at the table.

"All right—I want the truth. Can you still hear animals?" His voice was heavy with accusation.

I was stunned. I sat down across from him. "No."

He stared at me intently, his eyes boring into me. "I don't believe you. I think the animals told you someone was in the woods with us. What I can't figure out is how you were able to lie to mom."

It was amazing how easy it was to fool someone who wanted to be fooled.

"Let's say, hypothetically, that I can hear animals. No one else here can, so what does it matter? Who could even teach me?"

"Someone would have tried, and you could have at least practiced closing and opening your mind."

I looked up at him, feeling the weight of my decision to lie. Maybe it wasn't entirely irreversible. "Couldn't you teach me that?" I asked softly.

The corners of his mouth turned up in a very small grin. "I could if you told me the truth."

I smiled now. I couldn't help myself; I felt almost giddy. "Let's say, for argument's sake, I still hear them. Can I trust you not to tell a soul—not anyone?"

He nodded. Billy, like my dad, never broke a promise.

I took in a sharp breath. I hadn't admitted it to anyone in five years. "I can."

He grinned and pounded the table. "I knew it! I never bought that you stopped hearing them, but after this morning I knew."

"So what do I do? How do I control it?"

And with that, my lessons began. Darwin, naturally, was my guinea pig. For the first week I didn't improve at all. It was so frustrating, I almost quit, but Billy urged me on. The hardest part was learning to meditate so that I was almost in a trance— totally relaxed, focusing only on the rhythm of my heart. Who would have thought total relaxation would be so damn difficult!

But after hours and hours of practice, Darwin's voice became clearer. *Play with me. I want a cookie. Where's my ball? When's dinner?* The thoughts were more complex than I usually heard.

Blocking his thoughts was much harder. I had to close my mind, visualize door after door shutting, no thoughts escaping. Billy assured me this would help me block other people's talents as well, like my mother's—and that, I knew, would definitely come in handy. I was utterly exhausted when Billy said we were done, and yet, I couldn't wait to do it again.

One night after practicing, we went to the cafeteria for dinner, where we ran into Winny, Ally, and Henry, who looked like he just won the lottery. "Hey—I'm glad I found you. Do you guys want to come over to my room tonight? I have something really cool to show you—it's a surprise."

"Be careful," Ally warned, "you heard Principal Grogan's new edict: no specials without a professor—no exceptions."

I looked quickly at Billy—wondering if this had anything to do with Uncle Dan's trip.

Henry frowned. "Is he going to go from room to room checking? He's such a jerk. God forbid we have any fun. Come on, no one will find out, and it's sooo cool."

"I'm in," Winny said, her eyes large with excitement.

"Ya, me, too—but everybody better keep their mouths shut. My parents will kill me if I get expelled." Ally stared at everyone in turn. She might look fragile, but she was clearly someone to be reckoned with.

When we reached Henry's room, I was alarmed to discover a strange blue powder swirling around the floor. "Is that dangerous?" I asked, scrunching up my nose.

"No," he answered, as if I were the crazy one.

"Okay. We're going to play hide-and-seek. You guys are going to leave the room one by one, and I'll be able to find your hiding spot right away." Henry looked as gleeful as a five-year-old at his birthday party. "Billy, you first. You have two minutes starting now, and you can't leave the building. Aaand," he said, pushing a button on his wrist watch, "go!"

Billy sighed in resignation as he left the room. After two minutes Henry picked up a flashlight, walked out the door, and within a minute returned with Billy.

"All right." He cackled. "Who's my next victim?" he said, rubbing his hands together.

Despite myself, I laughed—he did look so much like a mad scientist.

"Ah—I see a volunteer," he said, winking at me from behind his glasses. He escorted me by the arm to the door. "I'll be right behind you."

Not knowing the dorms, I was clearly at a disadvantage. I

climbed the narrow wooden stairs to the roof deck and hid behind the steep pitch of the turret. I was completely in the shadows, but as promised, he walked right over to me. "Hey, how'd you do that? There's no way you could've seen me."

He grinned at me sheepishly. "Promise you won't tell the others? Not yet?"

I nodded.

He swept his flashlight along the roof, revealing a clear trail of blue footprints leading directly to me. He removed the light, and they were invisible again.

"What—"

"It's my new invention. This isn't a regular flashlight. It utilizes only certain colors from a beam of light—blue, red, indigo, and violet. When you came in my room, you stepped on the mist, which is a substance—"

He was so excited to tell me about his discovery, but I finally put my finger to his lips. "If we don't get back, no one's going to believe you found me." I smiled. "You are amazing."

Henry removed his glasses. He looked at me very seriously, a spark in his pale blue eyes. I felt my heart beat faster as I returned his gaze.

An owl flew nearby, thinking *hungry*, startling me. I turned away. "Let's go," I said. As I walked toward the door I could feel his eyes on my back. On the stairwell I stole a sideways glance at him. He wasn't just funny and smart, he was really cute. And since I probably would never see Dylan again, it was ridiculous to keep thinking about him. Henry was right here. And I felt safe with him, which was a nice feeling.

"That wasn't as fast," Ally said suspiciously.

She didn't miss a thing. I felt myself turn crimson. "I hid pretty far—but he found me right away."

Ally continued to regard me with skepticism, but Winny was so excited for her turn she was practically jumping out of her seat. "Me next!" she said, rushing out the door. Henry returned with her minutes later.

"That just leaves you, Ally," Henry said.

She smirked. "We'll just see if you can find me." She darted nimbly out of the room, as graceful as a ballerina. Henry waited the allotted amount of time, then went after her. Five minutes passed, and they still hadn't returned. Ten minutes, and we were all getting anxious.

Finally Henry returned, alone. "There's no sign of her." The concern was apparent in his voice as he paced back and forth. "I'm following your footprints," he quickly explained, "and hers end in the middle of the hall. It's as if she disappeared."

Disappeared. The word hung heavily in the room.

Billy started to freak out. "Disappeared where? No one can just disappear!"

A terrifying thought popped into my head—what if someone took her? I ran to the window and threw it open, listening intently. I could only hear the owl, and it was the usual stuff—*thirsty, hungry*—nothing about danger or people out wandering. Suddenly, the door swung open.

I whipped around, and there in the doorway was a triumphant Ally, grinning widely, her shoes in one hand. "I told you you wouldn't find me," she taunted.

Henry shook his head. "I should have known you'd figure it out."

Relief washed over Billy's face; I knew he had been thinking the same thing as me.

I sat down on the edge of the chair, letting my pulse return to normal. Talk about overreacting; I was definitely spending too much time with my mother.

Henry perched himself on the arm next to me. I could feel his hand brush against my shoulder. It was nice being so close to him. Ally caught my eye and grinned mischievously.

We talked and listened to music until curfew. Henry offered to walk me home, but Billy mumbled an excuse about needing something at the house and ushered me out the door.

On our way out I glanced backward and smiled awkwardly at Henry, but in truth, I found myself relieved not to be alone with him again.

* * *

Soon we were outside, cutting through the quad, the earth still moist from the rain. As the moon passed through the clouds, it illuminated our way.

"Did you open the window to hear the animals?" Billy asked.

"Yeah, I was really worried something happened to Ally. I thought they might tell me."

"Did you hear anything?"

I shook my head. "Just the usual—thirsty, hungry."

"You have to practice training your mind. Try to hear more complex thoughts."

"You mean right now?"

He nodded encouragingly.

I stopped, closed my eyes, took in a deep breath, and thought *focus*. As I exhaled it felt as though my breath swirled out of my body and enveloped me, gently lifting me up as if I were in a cloud. Above me a mother owl flew by, worried about leaving her nest. Nearby in the woods a deer smelled a newly planted vegetable garden and wondered how to get over the fence. I opened my eyes and saw Principal Grogan's fat cat, Tabby, sitting outside her house. She was thinking *tired, hungry*. That's what they were always thinking. I closed my eyes again and concentrated, feeling weightless, like I was floating. And then I heard, *He's been gone all day. Where is he? When will he be home?*

I opened my eyes and looked over at Billy's expectant expression. "Well?" he said.

"I did it—I actually did it!" A fierce joy filled me. "I could hear them—*really* hear them! An owl, a deer, and Tabby—she's worried because Principal Grogan's been gone all day."

He raised his eyebrows. "See? That's good. You're already doing better."

"Will you work with me more tomorrow?" I pleaded. Opening my mind was like nothing I had ever felt before; it was completely exhilarating, and I was addicted.

"Maybe. We have qualifying tournaments, so it depends."

"On what?"

"Whether I advance to the next level. If I don't, I won't be in any mood to help you."

"Oh. Have you had any luck moving the heavy balls?"

He shrugged. "A little, but not much."

"Maybe you shouldn't try."

He looked at me like I was crazy.

"I mean, you've avoided it so far, haven't you?"

"Yeah," he admitted. "I move the smaller ones in right away, then block the other team. But someone's going to figure out I can't move the big ones, and that's the whole point of the game."

"No, the point is winning. Play to your strengths. Winny says you're really accurate and a great defensive player. She's your partner tomorrow, right?"

He nodded slowly, trying to figure out where I was going with this.

"I hear she's amazing—she can move really heavy objects."

"She can. Winny's almost as good as Chey. She'll give Maggie and Nik a run for their money, and I don't even think she practices."

I laughed. I didn't think so, either. "Let her move the big balls. You move the small ones and block the other team. Get a strategy."

Billy didn't answer, but I could tell he liked the idea.

When we reached the steps to the house, he turned and looked at me. "Since you're in the mood to give advice, how 'bout taking some?"

I didn't like where this was headed.

"Why don't you come clean?"

I bit my lip. "Let's just take it one step at a time, okay?"

He shook his head slowly. "I know better than to argue with you," he said. "But I just don't get you. Why hide it?"

How could I explain? Even if people didn't think I was a fraud, then what? Who could train me? And worse still—what if I could have learned to communicate with animals, but now it was too late? I just couldn't face it.

Billy snorted at my lack of response. "You really make things complicated, Claire," he said as he turned and started walking away.

I realized he didn't really need anything at the house; he just wanted to help me practice. "Billy?" I called after him.

"Yeah?"

"Thanks. And good luck tomorrow. Come and find me after you win!"

When I went inside, the first thing I noticed was the grandfather clock, its stern face reminding me I was twenty minutes late.

I braced myself for a lecture, probably a punishment, and walked down the hall to the family room.

"But Dan, he never perfected the machine, and either way, it was destroyed. How can this be?" my mother said into the phone.

I stopped dead in my tracks and listened from the hallway.

"Besides, we would have heard *something*, from the ghosts or clairvoyants….A large shipment was sent to Boston? Are you positive?" Her husky voice became high-pitched.

There was a long pause before she spoke again. "How many have the skill to build it?" There was a much shorter pause. "If you're right, this will forever alter the course of—of life, in every sense of the word. No one will have the courage to stand against whoever controls that machine. Keep me informed."

I stood there paralyzed with fear. What machine could alter the course of life?

I heard the sound of voices again, so I peered around the corner. My parents were sitting next to each other on the sofa muttering about something as they pored over a folder. It was the same ratty file Uncle Dan had been looking at the night of Charlotte's birthday. I tiptoed into the room, trying to read it, when my mom suddenly looked up.

"I'm home."

My parents stopped talking immediately. "Good, well, good night, honey," my father said with forced cheer, a strained smile plastered across his face.

"Is everything all right?"

"Of course," my mother answered casually, setting the file aside as if it were nothing.

"What are you reading?"

She shrugged. "Oh, just school stuff. Nothing interesting."

"Can I see it then?"

"You know school files are confidential." My mother picked up the crystal glass on the end table and swirled the amber-colored liquid around absentmindedly. That was not a good sign; she hardly ever drank. "Did Billy walk you home?"

"Yup." As if I couldn't manage the walk by myself.

She nodded again and took a long sip from her drink. "Sleep well," she said, forcing a smile.

"Yeah, good night." I walked over and gave each of them a kiss on the cheek, trying to get a peek at that folder—but my mother had concealed it under papers.

She didn't even notice that I'd blown curfew—I was pretty sure that was a first. Clearly, she had other things on her mind.

As I climbed into bed I wondered who would invent such a terrible machine. Was the answer in that file that both my mother and Uncle Dan had hidden from me? ANIP—what did that mean? Was it someone's name? I ran through everyone I knew or had heard of, but no one's name began with those letters. If it wasn't a name, what was it? I tossed and turned for a few minutes, but I was so exhausted from working on my special that I couldn't help but surrender to a deep, dreamless sleep.

# CHAPTER 8
# A Desperate Cry

The next morning when I woke, my heart leaped to see the clear blue sky. Anxious to work on my special, I barely paid attention in any of my classes. Of course, I wouldn't complain if the afternoon sun brought Dylan to me, either. I darted out of science before Winny could ask me where I was going and ran across the quad to the forest. I hurried through the woods to the stream, almost falling a few times in my haste, until I finally reached the meadow. From my perch on the rock, I scanned every direction for Dylan, but there was no sign of him. Pushing away my disappointment, I began to write. It was useless; I couldn't hear the animals at all. I guess I was too preoccupied with Dylan to focus. Then I heard a rustling behind me. I turned quickly, and there he was, in the shadow of the trees.

"Hi." I waved. My pulse quickened. I had started to think I'd imagined him, or at least how handsome he was. I hadn't. He was even more gorgeous than I remembered.

He strode across the meadow and jumped up next to me. "I thought I was going to have to build an ark it rained so much."

I nodded in agreement. "Spring in New England."

He peered over my shoulder at my notebook. "Still working on that independent study?"

I turned it over. "Yup."

He cocked his head to the side, regarding me closely. "So you only go to school for half a day? That must be nice."

"It is," I agreed.

"What do you study?"

I laughed. "Do you even remember high school? Same thing as everybody else. Math, science, history, English."

He nodded. His expression was very serious today, not at all playful like the last time. "Are you all right?"

"What do you mean?"

"You seem different today, that's all."

He grinned, but the smile didn't reach his eyes. "Just busy at work."

"What do you do?"

He shrugged. "Whatever my boss tells me to. I guess I'm sort of a jack-of-all-trades."

"Oh." Whatever that meant. I shuddered as a cold wind blew.

"You're shivering," he said, taking my hands in his large, rough ones.

I immediately felt warmer. Almost involuntarily, I leaned my body toward him.

"What happened here?" he said, tracing the long scar on the back of my hand.

"My brother shoved me off my bike." I chuckled. In truth, he had hurled a branch at me using telekinesis, which got caught in the wheel and sent me flying. My great-grandmother Barbara told Charlotte all about it, and she, of course, tattled to my mother. Billy and I refused to talk to Charlotte for days.

His fingers found my watch. He glanced down at it, and then pulled his hand away abruptly. "Where'd you get that?"

"It was a birthday gift from my Uncle Dan."

All of a sudden, he stared at me closely. "So, what's your last name, anyway?"

"Walker, Claire Crane Walker."

He looked away quickly, but before he did, a shadow crossed his face. He was silent for a moment before he spoke again. "I'm sorry I missed your birthday." He smiled.

"Oh, it's not until the end of June. But he gave it to me early because he has to go away."

"Where's he going?"

Why did he care? "He does a lot of…alumni relations."

"So, why'd you transfer from Lakeville?"

I squirmed around on the rock. When he sat this close to me, it was hard for me to think—especially to think up a lie. "I got in a bit of trouble at my old school, and since my parents work at Cambial, they wanted me to go here."

The corners of his lips turned up in a small smile. "I wouldn't have taken you for a troublemaker. So as a punishment, they sent you here. That sucks."

"Not really. I liked Lakeville, and when my parents enrolled me at Cambial, I—let's just say I didn't take it well. I was sure I wouldn't fit in with all of the…"—I searched for a way to explain it without violating the rule of secrecy—"*really talented* kids, since I'm pretty average. But they seem to accept me."

He leaned in closer to me. "There's nothing average about you."

My heart lurched. God, he was handsome. I had to take a deep breath to steady myself.

Too soon he turned away and looked out into the woods. "I have a hard time believing any high school is accepting. Mine sure wasn't."

"Where'd you go?"

"Nowhere around here. So how's the writing going? I'd really love to read your story."

"Why?"

He looked away again and shrugged.

I shook my head. "Not a chance."

"I could just take it from you," he teased, tugging playfully at my notebook. "I don't think you could stop me."

"Ha! I'm stronger than I look!"

In an instant he grabbed the notebook out of my hand, laughing. "I guess you're not that strong," he taunted.

"Give it to me." I leaned over him and snatched at it frantically, but he kept it just out of my reach. I hadn't written much today, but it had other stories in it, and there was no way I was going to let him see them.

Without thinking, I gripped his arm and roughly twisted it behind his back. "I said give it to me, in case you didn't hear!" My words were harsher than I intended.

With an impish grin he held the notebook out, and as I quickly grabbed it my sudden shift caused me to lose my balance and fall off the rock. Right before I hit the ground, he pulled me back up and held me, his face only inches from mine.

I tried to wriggle out of his embrace. How dare he!

"I'm really sorry. I shouldn't have done that," he said, his voice barely above a whisper.

I tried to hold on to my anger, but my body was betraying me. As I inched closer to him my mind shouted orders—*do not kiss this mysterious boy*—but my heart was saying something else entirely. I had kissed two boys before, though I had never felt like this.

He bent down closer to me, holding me again in his gaze. I parted my lips, waiting.

And then he gently released me, sitting up. "It's getting late. I should go."

I was so stunned, I couldn't answer at first. "Yeah, me too." I smiled, hoping my disappointment wasn't too obvious.

"Maybe I'll see you again," he said as he jumped off the rock. "Bye."

I watched him stride through the grass and disappear into the forest. And then I sat there replaying what had happened over and over again in my mind. Had I done something wrong? Said something to upset him? Maybe he was just toying with me. He was positively gorgeous and way out of my league; he probably just considered me a nice younger friend. He probably would have been just as nice to Charlotte.

I felt like a fool, trying to kiss him. And because of that, I would probably never see him again. *Maybe* I'll see you. In other words, don't count on it.

When I couldn't take the cold anymore, I headed home. I could hear the animals, but I practiced shutting out their thoughts. I didn't care what they were thinking.

I was lying on my bed wallowing in regret and self-pity when I heard Billy yell my name from the kitchen. I considered not answering. I wasn't in the mood to practice today.

"Claire—I won!"

I jumped off the bed and ran downstairs. "That's great!"

"You were right! I talked to Winny, and I sent the small balls in, she took care of the big ones while I blocked, and we finished before the other team even got half of their balls in. Next is the qualifying tournament. If we win that, we'll be in the semis!"

"And after that the championship! I knew you could do it."

"Then I'd actually be in the Exceptional Society." He shook his head as if not even daring to hope. "Last year's winners automatically make it to the last round of the qualifiers, and they can ask anyone they want to be their partner. Of course, Chey asked Winny, but she said no. She knows he'll win, and she wanted to do it on her own, so I was sure he'd ask Nik." He smiled triumphantly. "But he didn't. He chose a freshman who's the worst of all of us—he totally chokes. You should have seen the kid's face! It was like he just won the lottery."

I couldn't help but smile. Chey was as great as Winny made him out to be.

"Well, come on, let's go," Billy said.

"Nah, I'm not up to it today. Let's do it tomorrow."

"What's the matter with you?"

I shrugged. "Nothing, just tired. Let's get dinner and try again when you have time, okay?"

"Fine. I told Winny I'd meet her, anyway, so we could go over strategy."

We made our way over to the caf and sat with Winny, Henry, Maggie, and Ally. After they ate, Winny and Billy got up and sat alone so Maggie wouldn't overhear their tactics. It looked to me like Winny was sitting a little closer to Billy than the situation required.

Soon after they left, Henry moved next to me and told funny

stories about experiments gone wrong. Despite my bad mood, he made me laugh, especially when he acted a few of them out. It was nice to get my mind off things. I kept watching Henry—he was cute, smart, funny, and obviously interested in me. I should like him. And if I kept spending time with him, who knew?

Over the next couple of weeks, Billy continued to help me when he wasn't practicing, and my abilities slowly improved. I went to the stream during specials many times—every sunny day, in fact—but I never saw Dylan. Even though I knew he probably wouldn't be there, each time I was utterly disappointed.

But I didn't let that keep me from going to the stream. I felt peaceful there, and for some reason it was easier to open my mind. It was like the place itself was enchanted.

One Saturday afternoon as Billy and I walked around the quad we came across Tabby. Apparently, Principal Grogan was away for the weekend again because all she kept thinking was *Where is he? How long will he be gone? Will I be home alone again tonight?* I focused on the birds, a hawk in particular, who was worried about leaving her babies. One was small and still not ready to fly like the others. I was pretty proud of myself since hers were the most complicated thoughts I'd been able to read yet.

On Monday I was eager to go to the stream during specials and hone my new skills. Finally last period came, and I walked with Ally to Maxwell's Hole, a small pond about a mile into the woods, where we had a combined math and science class. Winny was sick, so it was just the two of us. When we arrived, both Professor Higgins and Professor Arnold were there with several sets of long rubber pants and boots, microscopes and flasks.

The two teachers could not have been more different in both appearance and personality. Professor Higgins was short and round, with a mass of wiry black hair, bearing a striking resemblance to a porcupine. Everything in nature and science excited him, and right now he looked like a kid in a candy shop. Professor Arnold was so thin and pale, he looked almost ghoulish in the sun, and he never spoke with any inflection whatsoever. It was clear he was bored, as though teaching us was a colossal waste of time.

"Claire, Ally!" Professor Higgins waved, his belly bouncing. "Come here!"

We walked down the hill toward him. "Can you put the data sheets on the clipboards for me?"

"Sure," I said, relieved he wasn't going to make me wear the rubber pants.

"Class, you're in for a real treat today!" he boomed. "Does anyone know what we're standing on?"

"A kettle pond. I live near one in Ireland. There are loads of 'em by my house in Galway," Maggie answered.

Professor Higgins spread his arms out toward the pond. "Amazing, isn't it? Today we're going to collect samples and test the acidity of the water. You see, kettle ponds can become acidic due to decomposing organic matter. We are also going to measure the perimeter, diameter, volume—and, of course, search for fossils! Claire and Ally, since you helped me, you can be the first ones to use the rubber pants," he said, holding out a pair to each of us.

I tried my best to look happy. "Thanks."

Ally cracked up when she saw me in my pants. I was starting to get annoyed, but when she put on hers and climbed into the freezing water, I saw how ridiculous I must look. The thick pants ballooned up high on her waist, her toothpick frame sticking up in the middle. We sat on the slimy rocks, testing the water and giggling; each time we moved, the friction made the rubber pants sound like whoopee cushions.

"Okay," she said, looking at the graph paper, "now we need to find the volume."

"*Blahck.* I don't care what the teachers say—I can pretty much guarantee I will never in my life need to figure out the volume of a kettle pond again."

Ally chuckled. "Oh, copy mine."

"So you're good at science *and* you're a code breaker?"

She looked away. "I'm not great at that," she admitted.

"Nobody's perfect."

She smiled. "Henry sure thinks *you* are." She looked at me slyly out of the corner of her eye.

I felt myself blush: my pale skin always gave me away. I looked over at her paper. "How many cubic feet?"

She laughed. "So? What's the story?"

I shrugged. "He's really nice, very sweet, obviously smart…" My voice trailed off.

"That bad?" she said, wincing.

"What? He's great. He's perfect."

"He absolutely is. He's a great friend, loyal, funny.…He's mister perfect, but not mister right." It was a statement, not a question.

Hearing her say it, I felt terrible. I was passing on mister perfect for what? For someone I barely knew, whom I hadn't seen in weeks, and who obviously wasn't interested in me. "You think I'm an idiot."

She laughed again. "What does Professor McAllister always say? The heart has no reason or something?"

"'The heart has reasons that reason cannot know.'" Ain't that the truth. "So how about you? How long have you been dating Nik?"

"Not long." She paused. "I don't even think I can explain it. We've been friends for years, but I never liked him like that. Sometimes he can come across as full of himself. He isn't though. He's a great guy when you get to know him. He dated Jane Morse for a long time, the snob." She shook her head. "Anyway, then—I don't know—he kinda grew on me."

Grew on her? Huh. Maybe Henry would grow on me. Maybe if I didn't see Dylan, which I probably wouldn't, I'd stop thinking about him and start thinking about Henry. That's what I'd do if I were smart.

"Is. Everybody. Done." Professor Arnold glanced hopefully at his watch.

I looked over at Ally's paper in a panic. We had been so busy talking, I had only finished one question. I started to scribble the answers down furiously.

"Relax," Ally whispered. "Professor Arnold?"

He walked over to us. "Yes."

"Claire and I did it together, so can we just hand in one sheet with both our names?"

"Fine," he answered in a tone of profound indifference. "Professor Higgins is collecting them."

We turned in our analysis to Professor Higgins and gratefully peeled off our pants.

"Great job, ladies. Perfect!" he exclaimed as he scanned our results. "Recommendations?"

I started to panic again, but once more Ally came to the rescue. "The fertilizers have run off into the stream, causing the organic growth to accelerate. Cambial banned pesticides years ago, but they should also ban fertilizers and continue to reevaluate the pond," Ally said.

"Excellent analysis; I entirely concur. I am going to propose just that to Principal Grogan. Would you both like to come with me to explain your scientific findings?"

Ally nodded enthusiastically. "Absolutely."

When professor Higgins turned to talk to other students, I rolled my eyes. "Suck-up," I muttered under my breath.

She laughed. "Hey, when I'm in Think Tank, Professor Arnold completely ignores me. At least Higgins is nice to me, and I'd like to keep it that way. Ready for lunch?"

"I'm going home today. I have a bunch of stuff to do," I lied. "But thanks for bailing me out. You're a lifesaver!"

She smiled coyly. "You have no idea."

When Ally was out of view, I climbed over the embankment and veered off toward the stream. After about a mile the forest grew thick with trees. A red fox darted in front of me thinking *hungry*.

I listened to the animals and soon saw a mole waddling by, its stomach almost skimming the ground. It was thinking *thirsty and hungry, drink and eat at the stream*. I opened my eyes and followed behind it until a strong thought startled me.

*Help me! Please help me!*

It was a desperate cry. I froze in place and looked all around. *Can you hear me? I need help, please!*

My heart skipped a beat. It was like the animal *knew* I could hear its thoughts. I had to find it! Frantically I searched the woods, looking for any sign of an animal in distress.

*Where are you?* I thought, urgently trying to communicate. Then I started yelling, "I'm trying to help you, but where are you?"

*Help me, please* was all the poor creature thought.

*You can do this, Claire,* I thought. *Concentrate.* I closed my eyes and focused. I felt a strange energy flow through me and surround me at the same time. Then I felt light, like I was floating. I couldn't hear anything at first, and then all the sounds around me became crisper. Not only could I hear the animal—a bird, I thought—I could feel it. I opened my eyes and followed the sound of the voice, letting the energy draw me to it, and found a baby hawk hiding underneath some wild blackberry bushes. The baby gazed at me with frightened, inky-black eyes, pleading, *help me.*

"I don't know if you can understand me, but I will. I promise." I looked up and spotted a nest far above. He must have fallen out of it and wasn't strong enough to fly back. If it wasn't for the bush breaking his fall, he would surely be dead.

I listened for the voice of his mother, my eyes focused on the sky. I heard cardinals, blue jays, finches, but no hawk.

Suddenly, another voice came through very strongly—the fox. It smelled the bird and was moving in to attack. I picked up several rocks and stood in front of the bush protectively, scanning the woods for the predator. Yes, I knew this was the circle of life—the fox needed to eat, too—but I didn't want to witness it. And I couldn't simply ignore the baby's desperate cries.

Finally I saw the great hawk glide above me, anxiously searching her nest. She was hysterical, thinking *Where is my baby? What happened to my baby?*

I waved my arms furiously, calling out to her. "He's here!"

Of course she couldn't understand me. She started to fly

away. I had no choice. I scooped the baby up in my hands, hoping he wasn't going to bite, and reached up toward the sky.

"He's here!" I yelled again.

It worked—she looked down at me. Unfortunately, her first thought was *that girl stole my baby!*

She circled back, regarding me with black, beady eyes, her razor-sharp talons reaching out toward my face. I had to fight the urge to drop the bird and run.

As she approached, I could see both her breadth and strength. Her wingspan was at least four feet long. She dove toward me, crying out angrily.

My whole body trembled as I watched her furious advance. I stretched my hand up toward her, hoping she would realize I meant her baby no harm. When she was only feet away, I squeezed my eyes shut, but she scooped the baby up in her claws without even touching me. I could feel the breeze in my face as she turned, placed him back in the nest, and flew above me again. She was beautiful, her chestnut-red tail spread out like a fan as she soared across the sky. I couldn't take my eyes from her.

She looked down at me. *Thank you*, she thought.

"You're welcome!" I yelled, even though I knew she didn't understand me.

*Thank you for saving me*, the baby thought. I looked up at the nest, but the bird was safely tucked away, out of view.

"You're welcome," I said again, this time softly, more to myself. I stopped and leaned against a tree to catch my breath and found I couldn't stop smiling. I'd done it! I'd used my gift to save the baby hawk's life. Maybe my special wasn't stupid after all.

I walked on, practically skipping I was so happy, until I came to the clearing. I made my way through the tall grass to the rock and climbed up, looking in every direction for Dylan. I was utterly alone, as I knew I would be. With growing resignation, I searched the thoughts of the animals surrounding me, but none were thinking about a stranger—other than me. I tried to push away my disappointment. Of course he wasn't going to be there.

After a few minutes I took out my notebook, closed my eyes in concentration, and listened.

It was amazing. I could hear far more complex thoughts. The turtle had laid her eggs and was nervous they would be discovered and eaten. The butterfly flittering lightly near me was searching for a delicious pink flower. The large doe hiding in a thicket was worried—her fawn had hurt his leg, and it was going to slow him down. And then the fox came, eyeing me angrily. *Mind your own business*, he thought. And then, *hungry*.

As he sauntered past me I noticed the outline of his ribs protruding through his mangy fur. I threw the peanut butter sandwich I had packed for lunch over to him. "There, stop trying to make me feel bad for you," I said.

He sniffed it, never taking his eyes from me, thinking, *What is she up to now?* But his hunger got the better of him and he gobbled it up. He looked at me again. *That was awful. Not nearly as good as a bird.*

"Next time I won't give you anything!" I yelled at him.

He took one last disgruntled look at me and then trotted away.

After a few minutes I began writing and soon became completely engrossed. It was like wearing glasses for the first time; everything was in sharp focus. My hand began to ache, and I realized I had been writing for hours. As I shook my fingers I heard it—the frantic jumble of many thoughts at once.

*Man, stranger, danger, run, hide, freeze.*

And then, silence.

# CHAPTER 9
# Duplicity

I whipped around and saw Dylan striding toward me, his dark curls blowing softly in the wind. I felt my stomach lurch, I was so nervous…happy…excited to see him. But then a paralyzing thought struck—would he be happy to see me? I froze, studying his face for some clue.

He broke into a broad smile. "Hey there."

Whew! I smiled back.

"I was wondering if I might run into you." He climbed up on the rock next to me in one agile movement.

Run into me? He would undoubtedly think it pathetic if he knew I came here every sunny day, longing to see him—and he'd be right.

I looked up at him, his green eyes regarding me warmly. "Hi," I said. My voice was dry. I coughed lightly to clear my throat.

"So how's the writing going?" he said, nodding toward my notebook.

I couldn't help but smile. "Good."

"And school?"

I shrugged. "Fine."

"So, you used to go to Lakeville and now you're at Cambial, but in the afternoon you do an independent study, and you're not…like the other kids." He frowned, trying to work it out.

"Yeah, I already told you all that. Why do you keep asking about Cambial? It's like you're obsessed with high school."

He laughed, leaning back against his elbows. "Sorry. It's hard for me to believe anyone likes high school. I sure didn't."

"Why?"

"After my parents died, I lived with my grandparents. But they weren't exactly thrilled to be stuck with me, so they sent me off to boarding school as soon as I was old enough. At first I loved it—for the first time I really felt like I belonged, you know?" His expression was a mixture of pain and confusion. "Then I got expelled for breaking the rules." He glanced at me quickly, trying to read my face.

"Everyone makes mistakes," I said softly. I was no hypocrite.

He shrugged. "So anyway, I'm still deciding what to do with the rest of my life."

"What are the choices?" I hoped one of them would keep him coming to the woods.

"I have a couple of options—I don't want to pick the wrong one. Until recently, I was absolutely sure, but now I have a nagging feeling. Does that make sense?"

It was like talking to myself. Do I tell my parents about my ability and get training even though it may be too late? Do I work on it with just Billy? It was hard to figure it all out. "You said before you did whatever your boss wanted you to—so what does he want you to do?"

He looked stunned by the question for some reason. "He's really brilliant. I'm learning a ton—about a lot of different things—but..." His voice trailed off.

"Is there anyone you can talk to?"

"No one objective," he sighed. "My boss—who I really admire—wants me to keep working for him, but now I don't know. I'm not sure I can trust him," he said in a small voice. "I don't know if it's the right thing to do."

He was quiet for a while, lost in his own thoughts. Eventually he turned back to me, his eyes smoldering. "I guess the person I can talk to is you."

The way he said it felt intimate, illicit even. I felt the heat rise to my cheeks.

The corners of his mouth turned up in a small smile. "I don't know what to do with my life, so I wander around the woods—and lo and behold, I meet a beautiful girl sitting by a stream, as if I fell into a dream, and I pour my heart out to her."

It sure felt like I was dreaming. I knew he was trying to make light of the subject, but my pulse still quickened at *beautiful girl.* "Do you live close by?"

He looked away. "I'm just passing through."

Passing through from where? To where? "Where are you from?"

"All over, really." His expression was veiled when he turned back to me. "I told you, I'm a wanderer. So tell me why you write about animals."

Other than the obvious reason, which I couldn't tell him? "I love animals. I always have. They seem simpler than people, but they're not really. They're just truer. They care about the important things—their children, their friends, staying safe." I thought of the magnificent hawk soaring above me, her baby in her talons. I realized for the first time that I didn't write about animals simply because I could hear them. "They know who their enemies are and who their friends are. There's no duplicity in the animal world."

"That must be a nice world," he said wistfully. "Of course, except for the getting eaten or hunted part," he chuckled.

I nodded in agreement.

"Duplicity," he continued pensively. "Sometimes it's hard to tell the good guys from the bad."

"Which are you?" I teased.

He looked back at me, stunned.

"I didn't mean—" I began.

"Shh, no need to apologize. That's a fair question." He leaned forward, his glorious face just inches from mine. "I guess I'm a little bit of both."

"So am I," I breathed, and leaned forward, too.

But then he moved his face away.

I slowly exhaled. What was he playing at? If he liked me, why wouldn't he just kiss me already?

"I feel like a good guy when I'm here with you"—

Maybe a little too good.

—"like I could talk to you about anything...."

"You can," I urged.

I saw a flicker of desperation in his eyes. He opened his mouth as if to say something but then thought better of it. He turned away again.

"Look, I think you should listen to your instincts. If you're not sure you can trust this guy, you probably can't." I thought about my own mistakes—and there were plenty. "I don't know the right thing to do a lot of the time, but I usually know the wrong thing. I guess you should just try to avoid that."

He looked at me, surprised. "How will I know if it's wrong? It seems like you only know in retrospect."

"Deep down inside, you'll know."

After that, we talked and laughed for a long time, about nothing in particular, until it suddenly got very cold. Dylan pulled me close, warming my bare arms. I could have stayed like that for hours, but I glanced at my watch. "Wow, it's getting late."

"I don't want you walking home alone in the dark. I'll go with you."

As much as I would have loved that, it was definitely not a good idea. No one was supposed to bring outsiders on campus without permission. Technically, he wasn't even supposed to be on the grounds. I jumped down. "No thanks! It's fine—I can take care of myself. I like to walk in the woods."

"I'm glad you do, otherwise I never would have met you," he said with a wink.

My heart lurched at his words. I felt the color rise to my face, again, and quickly turned away, unable to wipe the smile from my face. "Bye!" I called over my shoulder.

"Hey, wait! Don't forget this. Wouldn't want you to fail that independent study of yours."

I whirled around to find him glancing down at my notebook. I rushed over to the rock and grabbed it from him. He quickly climbed down after me.

Suddenly, Dylan looked very serious. "I only read a few lines, but you're a wonderful writer." He paused. "It's as if you can hear the birds talking to each other."

If only he knew how true that was. "I'm a regular A. A. Milne."

He continued to stare at me, looking puzzled.

"You know, Winnie the Pooh?"

He shrugged. "No one ever read me bedtime stories." He watched me for a long minute before turning away, as if trying to figure me out. "Be careful walking home." Just before he disappeared into the forest, he looked back at me and waved, knowing I'd still be watching him.

The sun was low on the horizon, sinking quickly behind the trees. I had to hurry to make it home before dark. I rushed down the path trying to outrun the sunset, hoping tomorrow would be sunny, and longing to see him again.

# CHAPTER 10
# A Disturbing Dream

When I reached the house, I was surprised to find Jane Morse coming out the front door. Instead of her usual perfectly composed self, she was pale and drawn.

"What are you doing here?" I asked.

For an instant I thought I saw fear flicker in her eyes, but her expression quickly changed to contempt. "I needed to see your mother about something important," she smirked, taking a step toward me and lowering her voice. "You wouldn't understand, since you aren't *special*." She paused, letting the weight of her words sting me. "But you see, I have a powerful gift, one that is vital to the school."

"Well, by all means, don't let me keep you from your *important work*," I snapped.

"I'd love to stay and chat, but I wouldn't want to be late for my meeting with the Exceptional Society."

"I'm sure they would never start without *you*," I said, my voice dripping with sarcasm. I stormed past her into the house, only to come face to face with my very irate mother.

"Claire, where were you? Do you have any idea what time it is? If you think for one minute—"

"I was writing!" I yelled back, holding the notebook to her face. "In case you want to scrutinize it."

She held my gaze, reading my thoughts. I concentrated with all of my might on the truth of my story. *I was writing, I was writing*, I repeated over and over in my head like a mantra. I hated it when she did this. Supposedly I couldn't feel it, but it always made my head hurt. My mother dismissed this as ridiculous.

"I see. Where were you writing? Were you doing anything else?" she asked, frantic.

She was even worse than usual today. "Do you need to know my every move? I'm almost sixteen, and it isn't even dark out yet! Do you even know where Billy is? How about Charlotte, who last I checked just turned eleven! I don't see you freaking out about them!"

She let out a deep breath. "Perhaps I overreacted."

That was the closest thing to an apology I was ever going to get from her.

"But—" she continued.

Here we go. "No, I don't want to hear your buts. You are such a hypocrite! You have a million secrets about everything, like what was Jane Morse doing here?"

She looked away. "I see Jane every few weeks, privately."

"Why?"

"I interview her regarding her visions, but that's school business, which is—"

"I know, *confidential*, and since I don't really belong here, it doesn't even concern me. Blah, blah, blah—"

"You do belong here!"

"I don't, and everyone knows it! But let me tell *you* something: there are some parts of *my* life that are confidential, so leave me alone!" I bolted upstairs, slammed my door, and hurled my notebook against it.

My father came up a few hours later with two big bowls of Almond Joy ice cream. "I thought you might be hungry," he said, sitting beside me on my window seat.

I gave him a halfhearted grin and took the bowl. "My favorite dinner."

"Mine, too," he chuckled.

After a few minutes of comfortable quiet, he put his bowl down on the cushion. "Honey, listen, I know how your mother can be."

"Dad, she's so much harder on me than Billy or Charlotte."

He paused before answering. "I know. Probably because she

knows when you're home and when you're not. She worries—we both do."

I snorted. That was an understatement.

He put his big arm around me, and I rested my head on his shoulder. "You do belong here; you belong with your family. Your mother has a lot on her mind."

I sat up and looked at him. "Is this about Jay Burke? Has anyone heard from him yet?"

He shook his head slowly. "No. For now, your mother and I would prefer that you not leave school grounds, okay?"

Hmmm. I knew he meant the buildings and the quad, but Cambial owned hundreds of acres. Technically, I hadn't left school grounds. I nodded, and leaned back against his chest, unable to meet his eye. We finished off the rest of our ice cream in silence.

That night I had a disturbing dream. Nana Marie was sitting on the edge of my bed. She didn't look like a ghost, though (not that I had ever seen one), more like a hologram. She was thin and haggard, and obviously very worried about something. "Claire, listen to me. This is very important. Don't tell anyone else about your special—not even your parents. Promise me," she urged.

Her appearance was becoming hazy. "I promise, Nana."

"And Claire—" she began, but then she disappeared like a puff of smoke.

I awoke with a start, my heart pounding. I sat up and quickly turned the light on, half expecting to see her sitting there, but I was alone. I picked up the tarnished silver frame on my nightstand. It was a photograph of my entire family, taken on the porch right before my grandparents died. I looked into my grandmother Marie's face, so much like my own. Was that just a dream? Or had I seen her ghost? I'd have to ask Charlotte about it tomorrow.

I didn't know what to believe—but for now, at least, I was going to listen to my grandmother.

I awoke the next morning to another glorious spring day, as if the cosmos approved of me and Dylan. I threw open my window and breathed in deeply. The air was sweet and heavy with the scent of lilacs from the bushes below my window. I dressed quickly—eager to start the day, as if rushing could somehow bring the afternoon, and hopefully Dylan, to me sooner.

"Claire! Let's go!" My dad yelled from the back door.

I ran down the stairs and took my juice and granola bar from him before we headed out together.

"You're in a good mood today," he remarked, sounding relieved.

I couldn't keep from smiling. "It's so nice out."

"So how's your special going?"

I was stunned. How did he know? Did Billy tell him? Was Charlotte passing information from Great-Grandma Barbara again? "What do you mean?" I said more sharply than I intended.

"Well, I know your mother told you to choose what you like, so I was wondering…" His voice trailed off.

Oh. He only meant what I was doing during specials. "It's going really well. If the weather holds, I'll have something to show Mom this weekend."

His eyebrows rose in mild surprise. "Why does the weather matter?"

Shoot, I had slipped up—but it was an easy fix. "I'm more creative outside."

"So you're writing?"

"As if you didn't know!"

He chuckled and looked away, but not before I saw his Cheshire cat grin.

"What?"

"Nothing. It's just, you seem happy—perhaps it wasn't the worst decision to send you here." He sounded like he was trying very hard not to say I told you so.

I shrugged, but he knew I was happy. If I was going to be honest with myself, I was a lot happier than I'd been in a long time. I liked Lakeville High when I was there; but socially, so much of it was nonsense. Trying to fit in, but not stand out, making sure I had the right clothes, boots, backpack…the list went on. Things like that didn't matter at all here. Everyone loved Winny—who would be at the bottom of the social strata at Lakeville. I liked myself better at Cambial, too; I was less judgmental. And I loved learning about my abilities, even if only with Billy.

And then there was Dylan.

"Does a boy have anything to do with your good mood?" my dad asked as if reading my mind.

I scowled at him. "Dad!" I certainly wasn't going to talk to him about Dylan—Dylan what? I realized then I didn't even know his last name, although I told him mine. Now that I thought about it, I hardly knew anything at all about him.

I hurried into English, late as usual, but class hadn't started yet. Winny and Ally were talking softly, leaning in toward each other when I slipped into my seat.

"So what are we whispering about?"

Winny turned to me, her eyes red and swollen.

"What happened?" I asked.

"It's Chey. He's disappeared."

# CHAPTER 11
# Disappeared

I must have heard her wrong. "What do you mean?"

"No one's heard from him since he went camping on Friday." She paused and inhaled deeply, her breathing ragged. "He stopped by my room and said the weather was so nice, he was heading off for the weekend. But today's Tuesday, and he still hasn't come back."

"Does he normally do that?"

She nodded. "He's not like me—he's a free spirit."

I couldn't imagine anyone more free-spirited than Winny. "Maybe he's still camping," I said, trying to reassure her.

"He isn't. I know it. I can feel it. Something's happened to him!"

I put my arm around her, wanting desperately to tell her he was fine—but Billy's words echoed through my mind. Maybe someone was recruiting the most talented students, or worse, kidnapping them. "Winny, is Chey as amazing as everyone says?"

She nodded, wiping her eyes. "He's best in his year—best in the school. He's an Exceptional." She paused, lowering her voice to barely a whisper. "At home—never here—he can move *me*. But don't ever tell anyone—no one can know: it's forbidden."

Unfortunately, I had a feeling someone already knew. "You need to tell Principal Grogan right away."

"No," Uncle Dan said from behind me. I turned, surprised to see him. I didn't even know he was back from his mysterious trip.

"We'll go right now and see Maura Walker. She'll know what to do." His voice was full of authority.

That was strange. Why didn't Uncle Dan want Principal Grogan to know?

"Great to see everyone—but I'm sorry, class is canceled for

today. Go outside and read. Enjoy the day—carpe diem," he announced to the students. "Claire, you come with us."

We followed him as he strode purposely across the quad toward my mother's office in Crane Hall. Uncle Dan went in first—we stood outside in anxious silence. Anything I thought to say to comfort Winny sounded stupid and trite.

Finally my mother opened the door and called me in alone. She sat behind her enormous mahogany desk, her face even paler than usual. "Dan, please go and get more information from Winona, but try to be as reassuring as possible."

He nodded solemnly and left, closing the door behind him.

"Claire, tell me everything Winona told you—every word."

I sat down on the stiff wooden chair across from her and repeated what she had said as best I could remember.

My mother shook her head, grimacing. "You should *never* have asked her if her brother was talented," she scolded. "Now she will suspect it has something to do with the school."

"It does!" I shouted. "She's my friend—and her brother is missing! She has a right to know."

My mother's lips formed a thin, straight line as she glared at me over her glasses. "No, she doesn't. First of all, it is not unusual for Chetan to disappear for a few days. He often wanders into the woods to meditate—it helps him with his special. You have to understand, the first school Winona and Chetan ever attended was Cambial. Their mother raised them here and there, finally settling in that commune in Vermont where they roamed free," she said with disdain.

"Has he ever disappeared for this long?"

She didn't answer me.

"He's been in the Exceptional Society for years. He always wins the TT. Everyone knows how talented he is. You think something's happened to him, just like Jay Burke."

She sighed. "Honestly, I'm not sure. But I need to find out. Remember when you saw Jane at the house? Well, she had a vision of Jay Burke in a dark, dismal place. I'm sure now he's been kidnapped. If something has happened to Chetan, too, then I need to get to the bottom of these…disappearances, and I need the element of surprise on my side. Once people's minds are guarded, it's much harder for me to determine if they're lying."

I could tell she was keeping something from me, and I hated it. Suddenly, I realized what she was going to do. "You're leaving to investigate this, aren't you?"

She nodded. "I just contacted your father—we're leaving today. Time is of the essence." She got up and sat down on the chair next to me, placing her hands on my shoulders. "Don't worry—everyone in our community knows you don't have a special. But just to be on the safe side, don't tell anyone, and I do mean *anyone*, that you thought you could hear animals, okay?"

Thought I could? Now she didn't even believe that I could before?

She leaned forward and hugged me tightly. "I love you so much," she whispered in my ear.

I looked into my mother's dark eyes and saw something there I had never seen before—fear. A dreadful sense of foreboding washed over me, the same feeling I'd had when my grandparents left for their investigation. "Mom, please don't leave. Uncle Dan's already looked into this—why can't he go again?"

She stroked my hair gently, like she did when I was a little girl. "He was looking into some…science issues. I need to try to locate Jay and Chetan, and I can investigate that more effectively—I'll be able to get to the truth easier than Dan."

"What about Dad, then?"

My mother smiled sadly. "I'm sorry, but we both need to do this. If Jay and Chetan were kidnapped, wherever they're being held undoubtedly has high security. I may need your father's help."

My eyes began to water. I shut them tightly; my mother didn't need to see me like this. When I opened them, she was examining me closely. "While I'm away, trust no one besides William and Dan. You must be on constant guard, and whatever you do, don't leave the school grounds. I've asked Dan to keep an eye on the three of you, but I want you to look after Charlotte—she needs you. Which reminds me, you'll be staying in the dorms for the time being, with Charlotte. I'll reassign Lana."

This situation was getting worse by the second. No way was I rooming with Charlotte—she'd drive me mad. Besides, Charlotte and her equally bratty roommate, Lana, were a perfect pair. But I knew complaining to my mother would get me nowhere. "Mom, Charlotte doesn't have a lot of friends, and she loves Lana. Don't you think it would be better if I roomed with Winny? That way I could get information about Chey and give it to you."

She paused, considering this. "That could prove very useful. All right, but you must promise me you'll check on Charlotte every day."

"Of course."

"Winona's in a single. If I assign you to a double, do you think you can get her to move in? I don't want to arouse her suspicion by reassigning her. If she tells you anything about Chetan, anything at all, you are to call me at once. I'll have phone lines installed in all three of your rooms in case you need to reach us."

"Why aren't you telling Principal Grogan?"

She sighed. "I tried to talk to him about Jay this weekend, but he had the flu and was too sick to see me. That, and well, someone at the school may be involved. I don't suspect George, but I don't trust him to do the right thing, either. Information is power, and in the wrong hands..." She shook her head slowly. "Although he can be a stubborn buffoon, he's not evil. But for now, at least, I'm not taking any chances."

"Mom, Principal Grogan wasn't sick with the flu this weekend. He was away."

She froze. "How do you know that?" she said, her dark eyes narrowing suspiciously.

I immediately looked down at the floor, away from her penetrating gaze. I felt panic grab hold of me. *Do I tell her the truth?* Yes, I decided, she deserves the truth, and besides, she would know if I was lying. I looked up and saw the photograph of my family, the same one I had in my room, on the desk behind her. My grandmother Marie seemed to be staring out at me reproachfully. I focused on Marie's face and tried to close my mind. "I saw

Tabby outside all weekend, even at night. Mom, I know Grogan was away."

For a long minute she held my gaze, her face blank. I focused on the truth—*Grogan was away*—while I tried to stay calm.

Finally her expression softened, and I could tell she believed me because she looked both furious and worried at the same time. "He hardly ever leaves campus, and he never goes without telling me." She rubbed her forehead as if trying to make her brain piece it all together. "Claire, stick with Winona, find out everything you can, and don't go anywhere alone. I need to talk to Winona now. Please find William and Charlotte—they're both in class at Grove Hall—and meet us at home."

As I ran across the grass I noticed that the clear blue sky of this morning had disappeared. Ominous, dark clouds had gathered over the forest. A storm was headed this way.

The three of us rushed home to find my dad packing the car. Billy and Charlotte helped him while I went inside to discover my mother, already home, studying a thick folder in her office. "Have you been in this file?" she said sternly.

It was the same stained folder she and my dad were poring over a few nights ago. "No," I said, trying to read the name scribbled in blue on the tab: Ani—

She put it down, turning it over so I couldn't see it, and peered at me over her glasses, penetrating my thoughts again. "Are you sure? There's a page out of order."

"Do you really think I'd lie right now?" I said, rubbing my temples.

"No, of course not." I had never seen her so frazzled. "Since no one will be home, Dan's going to take care of Darwin at his house. I expect you to walk him every day, though. And do not forget about Charlotte. It will be hard for her with us gone."

Then I remembered Charlotte's party, when I had seen Uncle Dan with the same worn folder hidden in a newspaper. "Mom, I'm pretty sure that's the file I saw Uncle Dan reading the night of Charlotte's birthday. When I got home, he was sitting on that chair with it. Maybe he moved the page."

She shook her head curtly. "That's impossible."

Was it? Could he have been looking in her secret files? But why? And that was the day he told me about forbidden talents, and specifically asked me not to tell my mother. Was that file about a forbidden talent?

I looked at my mother staring out the window, her face drawn. "Mom, don't worry. We'll be fine. Just be careful." I hoped I sounded strong because it was the opposite of how I really felt.

She turned to me and touched my cheek with the back of her hand. "I know you will. I'll be out in a minute; go and say good-bye to your father."

I ran outside and into his arms, nestling my head under his chin.

"I love you, Claire. Be careful, promise me."

"I will, Dad."

My mother came out a minute later. "Claire, I want you to have this," she said, giving me my Nana Marie's ring. It was a gold star with a small diamond in the center. My mother hardly ever wore it; she said it made her too sad. "Nana would want you to have it."

I slipped the ring on my finger. I knew if I opened my mouth to speak, I'd cry; so I hugged her as tightly as I could to let her know how much it meant to me. When I finally let go, she hurried into the car, but I could see her shoulders shaking.

As they drove off, the heavy air exploded in a burst of thunder, followed by a single bolt of lightning zigzagging across the dark sky. It felt like a bad omen.

The bell rang soon after, and Charlotte ran off to lunch, blessedly unaware of the danger my parents were in. I filled Billy in on what happened as we sat on the steps watching the storm unfold, petting Darwin. He normally went crazy during thunderstorms, but all he was thinking was *What's wrong? Where are they going? How long will they be gone? The suitcase means a long time.* Sometimes I hated knowing what he was thinking.

We walked slowly to lunch, not caring that the rain soaked us. When we met up with Winny and Henry in the caf, Winny was ecstatic. Her mom had heard from Chey, and he was fine. He was going to camp out awhile longer. "That's wonderful," I said, smiling, but I had a bad feeling that wasn't the case. I fought to keep my emotions in check as I casually told everyone my parents went to help their friend in the government and I'd have to stay in a large double alone. Then I hinted that I wished I had a roommate.

"I know," Winny exclaimed, taking the bait, "I'll room with you! It'll be fun."

While Winny was at specials I went to our new room, happy to have some time alone. The room had a double window overlooking the woods I loved. Otherwise, it was a typical dorm room—two twin beds, two dressers, two desks. All of the furniture was dark and slightly beat-up—just like home.

I called my mother to tell her about Chey, but as I suspected, she didn't sound reassured. "Do you think he's still camping?" I asked.

"I don't know," she said flatly. "It could mean the kidnapper knows we're on to him."

I hung up the phone feeling even worse. After I finished unpacking, I sat on my bed and looked out the window, watching the storm recede. The sky had lightened to a pearl-gray. My thoughts kept turning to my parents; I didn't even know where they were going.

But then something occurred to me. Maybe there was a clue in that file—it sure seemed important to my mother. I knew I shouldn't, but I couldn't help myself; I had to know what was in there. I ran home and into my mother's office. Her desk was locked, of course, but I knew where she kept the key. I retrieved it from inside a resealable bag of frozen peas (yes, I was actually that desperately hungry one night when my mother had forgotten—again—to go grocery shopping) and opened each drawer in turn. There were plenty of folders, but they were all crisp and clean. I double-checked each drawer—nothing. It was infuriating; she'd had it right before she left. She must have taken it with her. I locked everything back up carefully, returned the key to its hiding spot, and slammed the front door shut.

## CHAPTER 12
# Dylan's Departure

Billy and I got to dinner right before the cafeteria closed, so we sat alone. I was grateful our friends weren't there—I just couldn't pretend everything was fine.

"Did you tell Mom and Dad that you can still hear animals?" Billy whispered.

"Almost, right before they left, but I didn't," I admitted, feeling more than a twinge of guilt.

"Why not?" His tone wasn't accusatory, as I had feared, but it was disapproving.

I sighed. "I had a dream. I meant to ask Charlotte about it, but with everything going on…" I shuddered. "Anyway, in this dream Nana Marie told me not to tell anyone that I could hear animals, not even Mom and Dad. I promised her I wouldn't tell them." I paused, knowing how ridiculous it sounded. "It was a very real dream."

I could almost hear Billy thinking. "Do you think it could have been her ghost?"

"I don't know. I've never been able to see ghosts—not even Charlotte has seen her, but it seemed important," I said softly. "All of this is so strange—the disappearances, Mom and Dad leaving, my dream. I feel like they're all connected somehow."

"Maybe Nana Marie thinks you could be powerful and she doesn't want anyone to know what you can do yet."

"That's ridiculous," I scoffed.

"No, hear me out. What if you could learn to do more than just hear their thoughts? What if you could communicate with them? Claire, you could ask a squirrel to tell you who'd visited someone—think about it. The possibilities are endless."

I shook my head. "I've never been able to—I've tried."

"Maybe it's time to try harder," he said urgently. "I practice telekinesis all the time and I hardly improve. I see sixth graders better than me. But I keep at it. I keep working." He paused. "Just tell me, do you want to get better or not? Because I don't mind helping you—but I'm getting sick of being your cheerleader."

I was stunned. And I was furious with him. I opened my mouth to argue, but I couldn't think of anything to say, because I realized he was right. "All right...I'll keep trying."

"I'll come every day after specials."

"Won't you and Winny be practicing then?"

"No, after dinner. 'Absolutely no telekinesis without a professor present, no exceptions,'" he said in a nasally voice—a fair imitation of Principal Grogan. "So now there's a sign-up sheet. Maggie already signed up for almost all the time slots," he added, rolling his eyes.

"Who's her partner?"

"Nik," he sneered.

When we returned to my dorm room, I opened the door and was surprised to find that the it had been transformed into a seventies movie set—complete with beads, incense, dream catchers, a lava lamp, and vintage orange-and-yellow quilts on the beds. "Whoa, time warp!" I said.

Winny was beaming. "I just finished decorating. What do you think?"

"It reeks!" Billy answered, holding his nose.

"Not you!" Winny said, throwing a tie-dye pillow at him. "Claire!"

I bit my lip. "Well, it's different." It certainly was not my taste, but I couldn't help but laugh—something I would have thought impossible a few minutes ago.

"My mom was clairvoyant. Her family thought she was weird, so she ran away when she was seventeen, even changed her name to Stargazer. She lived on a couple of reservations— she met my dad on one of them—but they had too much structure for her. That's why we ended up in the commune. So this is how I grew up," she said, holding out her arms. "Do you mind?"

"The incense is giving me a headache, but other than that, not at all."

"Well, I'm outta here," Billy said, still pinching his nose as he shut the door.

I sat down on my bed. "I'm surprised you're not clairvoyant. That usually runs in families, doesn't it?"

Winny blew out the incense, the purple smoke swirling around her amber skin. Smiling sheepishly, she looked up at me with her big eyes. "Actually, I am. I'm sure you know that some people have more than one gift. I love telekinesis, so that's what I chose to be trained in, but I'm also clairvoyant. I practice that, too, sometimes with your mother. But once you can open your mind, it's not that different, no matter what the special is."

I looked at her, completely awestruck. Two gifts! I felt another familiar pang of regret hearing about my mother's encouragement. If only I had gone to her, maybe…but no. I'd made my decision; there was no point looking back.

As we lay in bed that night Winny told me all about growing up in Vermont with no rules at all—no school, no bedtime— and I told her what it was like to grow up here with *lots* of rules. Winny was the first friend I could share that part of my life with. It felt nice. I realized then that maybe I'd chosen to hang out with superficial friends at Lakeville—friends who dumped me as soon as I transferred here—because I knew they would never ask about my family or my childhood. It was a wonderful feeling, having a real friend.

I awoke the next day earlier than usual courtesy of Winny, who was much too chipper in the morning, and for once made it to English on time. The sunny skies made me happier than I should have been. When everyone else went to specials, I hurried into the woods. The forest was teeming with wildlife today; the birds made nests, telling each other where to find the best materials, and a rabbit was bringing her children to the meadow to eat. I saw the majestic hawk again, dancing across the sky as if she flew for the sheer pleasure of it. She dipped down toward me. *The girl who saved Talrin*, she thought. So the baby's name was Talrin. That was the first time I heard the name of an animal.

When I reached the field, I caught my breath. He was already there, sitting on the rock, lost in thought. As I stepped out into the tall grass he turned quickly, and his face relaxed in an easy smile. I beamed in return.

He stared at me, his brilliant green eyes soft and warm. "I was worried you weren't coming."

He was worried *I* wasn't coming? I smiled shyly at him, feeling the familiar current between us. "It took me a little longer than usual—the ground was slippery. Which way do you come?"

He nodded with his head to the left. "Through the conservation land."

"That must be a long hike." The nearest road was miles and miles away.

"I love the woods," he said wistfully, and then added with a wink, "you never know what you'll find."

I giggled, sounding like a silly schoolgirl. Ugh. And then I noticed that his hand was bandaged. "What happened?"

He shrugged. "I burned it, no big deal."

It certainly looked like a big deal from the size of the bandage. "On what? Does it hurt?"

He brushed it off. "I'm fine. So anyway, where's your notebook?"

In my haste to see him, I had forgotten it. "I guess I don't feel like writing today."

"Is something wrong?" he asked, regarding me closely.

"My parents went away, and I'm just worried about them."

"Where'd they go?"

I shrugged. "I don't know."

"How long will they be gone?"

I shrugged again.

"Do they do that often? That's strange," he said.

"They sometimes work for the government, top-secret stuff. But this time feels different. I have no reason to worry, but I can't help it." I tried to hide the strain in my voice.

"Wow, top-secret stuff—that's pretty cool."

"Pretty dangerous." I looked away, not wanting him to see me blinking back the tears. He did, of course. He put his arm around my shoulders, and we sat there together for several minutes. I felt safe resting against his strong chest.

"Do you know what they're doing?"

I shook my head.

"Then why does it feel different?"

"Because a couple of the more gifted kids from Cambial are missing." I said the words without even thinking.

His body stiffened. "Missing? Like kidnapped?"

I immediately regretted saying it. I don't know what came over me, except that I felt like I could trust him with anything. "They're probably fine. Just off having a good time or trying to figure out their lives, like you. My parents want to make certain that's all there is to it."

His expression was unreadable. "I'm sure you're right." He stroked the back of my hair. "You're very close to your parents, aren't you?"

I nodded again.

"So since you don't board at Cambial, you'll have to leave, right?"

What? Did I hear him right? He sounded happy, almost relieved to be rid of me.

He looked at my face, and then his voice softened. "I mean until your parents come home. If kids are being kidnapped and your parents are gone, it just makes sense for you to leave; it would be safer. Isn't there family you could stay with for a few weeks?"

"I don't want to stay with family. And how do you know it will only be for a few weeks? Why are you so eager to get rid of me? It's not like I force you to meet me here. If you don't want to hang out with me, don't come."

"That's not what I said. I only thought it sounded safer if you left."

I cleared my throat. "I have my reasons for wanting to stay." *Number one reason—you, you idiot!*

Like a fool, I was waiting for him to tell me that he really wanted me to stay; he was just worried about me, and if I left, he'd miss me terribly.

He didn't. Instead, he looked away. "Well, I think you should go. Nothing here is that important."

I recoiled, my eyes stinging. *Not important?* So that's how he felt. Well, I wasn't going to let him see me upset. "You're right about that."

His expression turned dark. "I better go," he said abruptly, jumping down from the rock.

I watched him storm away—wanting desperately to call after him—but I kept quiet. He turned back and looked at me, and then disappeared into the shadows.

He was gone.

Gradually the thoughts of the animals around me filled my head. The fox darted out from behind a tree, looking up at me expectantly. I hurled the extra sandwiches I'd packed at him and headed home, replaying the conversation all the way back to campus. I was *nothing important* to him, just a minor distraction. I felt like such an idiot; yet—I couldn't help it—I still cared about Dylan far more than I should.

# CHAPTER 13
# CROSSROADS

The next day I barely paid attention in class. I wolfed down a peanut butter and banana sandwich at lunch, begrudgingly made a turkey sandwich for the fox to take with me (just touching the slimy meat grossed me out), grabbed my notebook, and then ran to the woods. Maybe he was waiting for me—just as upset. Maybe he didn't sleep at all last night, either. I'd still be mad at first, but eventually I'd forgive him. Then he'd take me in his arms and *finally* kiss me.

When I arrived at the field, I was utterly alone. I looked around in every direction, but there was no sign of him. Anger quickly eclipsed my disappointment. How dare he flirt with me and then act like it was nothing? I climbed up on the rock, hoping he would come, just so I could tell him—casually of course—that maybe I'd go away, maybe even for the whole summer.

I saw the fox watching me warily from the other side of the stream. I tossed the sandwich toward him. "It's turkey—so we're even," I yelled.

He sniffed it, and then gobbled it up. *Better. Next time bring two,* he thought, and trotted away.

"Ingrate!" I yelled after him.

It was an unseasonably warm day. I lay down on the cool rock, feeling the sun warm my face and arms. The animals were quieter than usual; they seemed sluggish in the heat. I listened to them halfheartedly and, giving in to my despair, soon fell asleep.

I awoke much later when someone lightly brushed my cheek. I sat up quickly, completely disoriented.

"I'm sorry, I didn't mean to startle you," Dylan said tenderly.

"I have to go soon, and I didn't want to leave you here asleep." He held my notebook out to me. "I know you didn't want me to—but I read your stories. They're really great. Please don't be mad at me," he added quickly, reading my expression. "I could have just put your notebook down and not told you I read it, but I didn't want to lie to you."

I sighed. It was hard to be angry at him. And I was so relieved that he had come. I *was* mad—at myself—for sleeping through our time together.

"I can see why you don't show anyone. They're…unique." He stared at me intently. "You're a very special person, Claire Walker."

"Thanks," I said, blushing as he continued to stare at me. His eyes were filled with regret.

"Is something wrong?" I asked.

The corners of his lips turned up in a sad smile. "I wanted to say good-bye. I have to go away for a while. I didn't want you coming here, waiting for me and thinking I didn't want to see you, especially after yesterday. I really just want you to be safe."

How well he already knew me. "Will you be gone long?"

"It depends. I don't know. For a year at least, maybe longer."

My stomach twisted; a year seemed like an eternity. I bit my lip, trying to hide my disappointment.

"Do you think you know me, Claire?" he asked, startlingly serious.

I had only seen him four other times. But in some ways I felt I had talked to him more honestly than I had to anyone. "I hardly know anything about you," I answered, "but yes, I think I know you."

He smiled, exposing his dimple, suddenly looking much younger. "I think you do, too, and I think I know you. You've been quite a surprise to me," he said, touching my face gently with his uninjured hand. "If I don't see you again, I want you to know how much I enjoyed…knowing you."

*If I don't see you again?* I had to see him again!

We sat in silence for several minutes while I fought back

tears. I focused on the stream, the wildflowers swaying in the breeze—a blurry haze of yellowish purple. The wind caught my hair, twirling it around my face. He gently put a wayward strand behind my ear, his fingers lightly caressing my neck. I breathed in deeply, trying to steady myself.

He leaned toward me, then suddenly turned away and leaped off the rock. "I really do have to go," he said, his voice heavy. "Take care of yourself, Claire." He studied my face for a moment, then disappeared into the forest.

I sat there dumbstruck, my eyes fixated on the spot he last stood, as if my wishing it could make him reappear. I prayed he'd run back to me, like in a bad made-for-TV movie, declaring his undying love and saying something like "I can't live without you." I just couldn't believe he was gone.

And then reality set in. I was a fool. He had never given me any reason to believe he thought of me as anything more than a friend—acquaintance, actually. He said good-bye without even asking for my phone number or email address. He was at a crossroad in his life, deciding which path to take, and either choice was away from here, away from me.

I told myself all of these things. But it didn't matter; as I sat there on the cold, hard rock sadness enveloped me like a fist around my heart.

As the animals left the stream, no longer safe as night approached, I realized I had better get going, too. I stepped into the dark woods, the long shadows chasing me as I made my way through the trees. Suddenly, I had an eerie feeling that I wasn't alone. I searched the thoughts of the animals, but I was so nervous I couldn't focus. Quickening my pace, I turned to look over my shoulder every few minutes, but it was too dark to see far. Just as I glimpsed the lights of Crane Hall shining in the distance, I saw something—or someone—whirl past me out of the corner of my eye. I broke into a run.

# CHAPTER 14
# Expelled

I sprinted as fast as I could down the path and out onto the lawn behind Crane Hall. I was running toward the door when I saw Billy up ahead, under the lampposts. "Billy!" I hollered.

He whipped around. Even from a distance I could see the relief on his face. "Where have you been?"

I leaned against a cold iron post to catch my breath. "I went to work on my writing, and I fell asleep."

He stared at me angrily. "We were supposed to meet after specials. I've been going crazy looking for you! You shouldn't be in the woods alone right now, not with everything that's going on."

I frowned. There really was no reason to go anymore. Then I remembered why I had gone to the stream in the first place—to listen to the animals. I wasn't about to stop just because Dylan wouldn't be there. "It's a good place to practice. Besides, who'd want to target me? I'm the safest student on this campus. Mom even said so."

And yet, this wasn't the first time I had the feeling I was being followed.

"I don't care—just don't, okay? There're plenty of animals in the quad." His voice was firm.

I folded my arms in defiance. But as much as I resented being treated like a child, maybe staying out of the woods wasn't such a bad idea. I went to my room, waiting for my parents to call, unable to stop thinking of Dylan. I was alone, since Winny and Billy were practicing. Again. I think he was driving her a little bit crazy getting ready for the big playoff match tomorrow. The four best teams were competing for two spots. I suspected if it were up to her, they wouldn't practice at all.

I knew she was must be anxious about Chey, too. No one had heard from him since the one call to his mother, and it wasn't like him to miss the playoffs.

I read several chapters of *Jane Eyre*, finally putting it down when I realized I couldn't recall anything I'd read. I opened the window and listened to the leaves rustling, the cool night breeze on my face carrying the scent of peonies from several stories below. As I watched the stars glow in the darkness I wondered where Dylan was—if he was far away by now, and if I would ever see him again.

My eyes swept to the quad, bathed in cold white moonlight. In the distance Principal Grogan left his house and drove away. My mom said he never left campus, and now he was gone all the time. Where was he going?

Suddenly, the phone rang loudly, startling me.

"Claire?" It was my mother's soft voice on the other end.

I exhaled in relief. "Are you okay?"

"We're fine. We've discovered some startling things. I don't want to say anything over the phone, but we're getting closer to finding the missing children and unearthing the truth. William didn't answer—are he and Charlotte all right?"

I felt a twinge of guilt at the mention of Charlotte—I hadn't checked on her today at all, or yesterday for that matter. "They're fine. Don't worry. You and Dad be careful."

"Of course we will. Tell William good luck tomorrow; we're very proud of him. And Claire, be vigilant—stay on school grounds and don't go anywhere alone. We love you." Click.

I swallowed hard, the dial tone humming in my ear.

I realized I had broken two promises to my parents. I was glad that I had already decided my solitary ramblings in the woods were a thing of the past. Now I needed to go check on my sister.

I was surprised to find her lying on her bed, crying. "Charlotte, what's wrong?" I said, sitting down next to her.

"As if you care!"

"Of course I do. Tell me what's going on."

She looked up at me, her teary brown eyes angry. "You and Billy are always off together. You have each other. I saw Mom and Dad all the time, and they always visited me in my room. Now they're gone, and I don't have anyone!" She burst into tears again.

I put my arm around her shoulders, but she shrugged me off. "That's not true. You have me. You can come talk to me anytime."

"Ha!" she snorted. "I go by your room all the time and you're never there. Besides, you hate me."

"No, I don't."

"Well, you always say I'm annoying."

"That doesn't mean I hate you."

She burst into tears again.

"It's just, well, you brag a lot. And you're a big tattletale sometimes."

"At home I talk to the ghosts because you and Billy always ignore me," she sobbed. "Then I get mad at you, and it sort of just comes out. But I'll try not to tell on you guys."

"And I'll come and see you more, I promise." In truth, I'd paid more attention to Darwin than to her. Of course, Darwin was a lot less irritating. "I know you must miss Mom and Dad a lot. I miss them, too."

She sat up and wiped her eyes on her sleeve. "Can I go with you sometime to walk Darwin?"

"Sure."

"But in the quad," she sniffled. "Grandma Barbara says you should stop meeting that boy in the woods. He's trouble."

My stomach lurched at the mention of Dylan. "He's gone. But I don't want you to tell anyone about him, and I don't want to talk about it, either."

She stopped and blew her nose. "And she said to stay out of the woods altogether."

Here we go again. She just couldn't help herself. "Listen, Charlotte, grandmothers worry, okay? I have no plans to go to the woods. So anything else Grandma Barbara wants you to pass on that sounds like nagging, just skip it."

"But she says it's really important. She says—"

"Charlotte!" I scolded.

"Okay!" Her lower lip starting to tremble again. "I'm worried I'm getting worse at my special, Claire—I hardly ever see ghosts anymore! Just Great-Grandma Barbara once in a while. That's it. I'm afraid if I don't do what she tells me, she won't visit me anymore, either."

I put my arm around her narrow shoulders. Charlotte's talent was the most important thing to her. I could imagine how awful she'd feel if she thought it was slipping away. "I'm sure it's because you're worried about Mom and Dad, that's all. You're the great Charlotte Walker! Don't ever forget it," I said, pulling up her pointy chin with my finger.

She sniffled, and then nodded, grinning. "You're right. And I did see Nana Marie in a dream, but it seemed so real."

I caught my breath. "When?"

"Right before Mom and Dad left."

"I did, too. Did you see her ghost?"

She shook her head. "No, it was more like a…" She paused, searching for the right word.

"Like a hologram?"

"Yeah," she nodded.

"That's what I saw, too."

She stared up at me, her eyes wide. "What did she say to you?"

I hated all these promises I'd made to keep secrets, I really did. I looked down at my hands. "She told me to be careful who I trust." In a way, that was true. "What did she tell you?"

"She told me to be careful, too, and that our family was in danger. Then Mom and Dad left. What she said is true, isn't it?"

"I don't know, but listen to her and be careful. Don't go anywhere alone, okay?"

"I'm usually with Lana."

"Good, stay with someone *all* the time, though. After breakfast we'll walk Darwin together."

She broke into a huge smile, throwing her arms around me. "Thanks, Claire."

As soon as I left, I went to Billy's room to tell him about Charlotte's dream and to wish him luck at the playoffs. I knocked quickly and threw open the door. He was standing in the middle of the room with Henry, a large ball in midair. It promptly fell to the floor with a loud thud.

"Jeez, Claire, don't just barge in!"

Henry leaned back on Billy's desk. "Whew—what a relief it was you."

"What's the big deal?"

"'No practicing anywhere except the gymnasium, and a professor must be present,'" Henry said, mimicking Principal Grogan.

"Yeah, I know; but I mean, what's the worst that can happen? He's not going to expel you for moving a ball."

Henry looked at me, his forehead creased. "Oh yes he will. He already expelled Ed, a kid I know from the labs. He was working on an experiment in his room, Grogan caught him, and he's gone."

"What?" I couldn't believe Grogan would be so harsh.

Billy sighed. "Now that Mom's gone there's no one here to argue with him."

"Well, don't worry. I just saw him drive off."

"I wonder where he's going," Billy said, giving me a knowing look. Immediately I knew what he wanted me to do—visit Tabby for information.

"Well, anyway, I just wanted to let you know I heard from Mom and they're fine. I'm gonna go check on something."

"I'll go with you. Later, Henry."

"Be careful, you guys," Henry said, looking disappointed we didn't include him. "And Billy, you did great, man."

I followed Billy to the turret staircase and out onto the lawn. Once we were sure no one was around, I filled him in on Charlotte's dream, which he didn't think was a coincidence. It couldn't be. What were the odds we both would have a dream about Nana Marie? But what could it mean?

We reached Principal Grogan's dark house just as Tabby pranced out of the woods with a mouse dangling from her mouth. She trotted lightly toward home, finally dropping the poor thing's lifeless body on the front step and licking her paws luxuriously.

I concentrated on her, trying to shut my mind to everything else.

*He'll be so pleased. It's such a big mouse. I am the best hunter,* she thought. None of her thoughts were about where Principal Grogan went.

"Nothing," I said, shaking my head.

"Try to ask her."

I sighed. "I told you"—*time and time again,* I thought—"I can't."

"You'll never be able to with that attitude. That's why we're *here.* That's what we learn in specials. To open our minds. And now something bad's going down, and Mom and Dad are right in the middle of it"—

I flinched, but he kept talking.

—"and you might be the *only one* with the power to do something about it. But hey, maybe you *have* waited too long, and you'll never get any better. *I* don't think so. But our talents come from our minds; so as long as you believe you can't communicate with animals, you can't."

I was taken aback by the accusation in his tone—and the bitter truth of his words.

But maybe, just maybe, it wasn't too late.

*Who's that?* Tabby thought suspiciously.

"We're not alone," I whispered before I whirled around. There, not ten feet from us, was Henry, his eyes huge as he took in the situation. I gulped. I opened my mouth to say something, but I couldn't think of anything that might explain what he obviously overheard.

"How much did you hear?" Billy said evenly.

"Everything," he admitted.

"Were you following us?" Billy asked.

Henry looked down at the ground. "Yes, but it's not what you think! I saw you walking across the quad toward Principal Gro-gan's house. I panicked—he could come home any minute and it's after curfew. If he saw you, with the mood he's in...I was wor-ried you'd get expelled. I came to warn you, and then I heard..." his voice trailed off.

"Look," Billy said firmly, "Claire can read the minds of ani-mals. No one else can know—you have to swear."

Henry nodded. "But why's it a secret?"

I sighed, and reluctantly explained my dream and why I had lied in the first place.

"I won't tell anyone, but I can help you, too. One more thing," he said sheepishly. "Why were you trying to read the mind of Principal Grogan's cat?"

"Just practicing," Billy said a little too strongly.

Henry nodded, but I could see the doubt in his eyes.

# CHAPTER 15
# Missing

As promised, the next morning after breakfast Charlotte and I walked Darwin during Billy's playoff game, since spectators were only allowed at the TT. We anxiously waited for Billy to come up from the field. Finally we saw him, Winny, Nik, and Maggie coming toward us with huge smiles plastered across their faces.

Charlotte ran across the quad to Billy. "Did you win?" she hollered.

Billy waved his fist in the air. "Whoo-hoo!" he answered, picking Charlotte up and swinging her around while Darwin jumped on him, barking.

I was thrilled for Billy; it meant so much to him. Winny, I knew, probably didn't really care. There wasn't a competitive bone in her body, and she hated the fact that if someone won, it meant someone else lost. I suspected the only reason she tried so hard was for Billy, who had no idea she had a crush on him.

I gave each of them a hug. "Congratulations! I'm so glad you guys made it!"

Maggie's smile faded. "For now. Next week only two of us can win, and two will lose."

"Sorry, but I'm rooting for Billy," Charlotte said.

Everyone laughed.

"One team's lucky to be here at all," Nik said, looking at Billy longer than necessary. "Lucky Chey's gone, because no one can beat him."

Winny closed her eyes, her face crestfallen, trying to regain her composure. But it was too late. She burst into tears and ran across the grass into the woods.

I gave Nik an exasperated look before chasing after her. Billy called him a stupid idiot, then followed us. At first we couldn't find her, but I clearly heard *danger, girl, run* coming from an area off the path. I finally saw a jumble of crazy curls peeking out from a thick tree trunk.

I sat down and put my arm around her. Billy looked at us awkwardly, and then sat on her other side rubbing her back. We sat like that for a while, letting her cry. Finally, she wiped the tears away with her dirty hands, leaving black streaks across her cheeks. "I know something's happened to him. I've known for a while."

Her certainty caught me by surprise. "Have you had a vision?"

She shook her head slowly. "No, but I can feel it. He's in trouble."

I wished there was something I could say to make her feel better, but there wasn't. She was right.

As I sat on the hard forest floor listening to the heartbreaking sobs of my best friend, I decided something. No, *decided* is too weak a word. I *resolved* that I would do everything within my power to find her brother. I *would* learn to communicate with animals. "Winny, listen to me. I don't know where Chey is, but I swear I'll do everything I can to find him. I'll talk to my parents tonight, and we'll get to the bottom of this. I promise."

I don't know if it was my tone or the determination she saw in my eyes, but Winny stopped crying and nodded. "I believe you, Claire."

That night I talked to my mother, and she was now certain Chey had been kidnapped when he left Cambial to go camping. She told me to talk to Uncle Dan and make sure no students left the grounds. I called him right away, and he promised he would talk to Principal Grogan about making it a school rule. I kept checking on Principal Grogan's house from the window, but it was pitch-black. I hadn't seen him in days.

The next morning Billy and I met up after Sunday brunch to try, once again, to get information from Tabby. On our way across the quad, we saw Nik swaggering toward us. Billy turned abruptly, pretending he didn't see him, but it was too late. Nik stretched importantly and waved.

I tried to see what Ally saw in him, other than the obvious—and I had to say, I didn't even find him that cute anymore, now that I knew him better.

"Hey." I smiled feebly.

"So, did you guys hear about Jane?" he whispered, although no one was nearby.

"No, what?" Billy asked.

"She's gone."

"Gone? Wh-what do you mean?" I stammered.

He shook his head slowly. "No one's seen her for days. Poor kid, I think seeing me with Ally was just too much for her."

Neither Billy or I could speak at first. A hundred thoughts jumbled through my head at the same time. To say I didn't like Jane was an understatement, but I certainly didn't want her to be kidnapped. "What do you mean, Nik? Did she go home?"

He shrugged. "I guess so. Her roommate asked me if I knew where she went—no one's seen her, and she hasn't been at specials. She must've taken off."

"Do the teachers know?" Billy asked, panicked.

"Her roommate told Professor McAllister, and he said not to worry about it—she went home sick," Nik said skeptically. "But she didn't look sick when I saw her a few days ago."

"It's probably that stomach bug everyone's getting," I said quickly. "We better go walk Darwin. See you later, Nik!"

I grabbed Billy and we ran to Uncle Dan's house. We burst through the door to find him sitting at the kitchen table poring over a sea of folders. As soon as he saw us, he quickly shuffled everything into a pile.

"Do you know what happened to Jane Morse?" Billy spat out.

"She's missing," he sighed. "How do you know?" There was a note of disapproval in his voice.

"Nik. Why didn't you tell me last night when I called you?" I asked.

"I wasn't sure last night, and I didn't want to worry you. Her parents are traveling in Europe, so they didn't know if she'd gone home. I checked it out myself—she's not there."

Billy frowned. "When was she last seen?"

He paused. "Thursday."

I leaned against the wall to steady myself. Three days—she had been missing for three days! She could be anywhere by now, even out of the country.

"Did you tell Mom and Dad?" Billy asked.

Uncle Dan shook his head. "I've tried—no answer. When they call you tonight, tell them to call me immediately."

"We will. Come on, Billy, let's go."

Before I shut the door, I turned back to find Uncle Dan deep in concentration, a thick folder in front of him. Could it be the one my mother had? I quietly took a step forward, but he covered it before I could get a good look.

"What is it, Claire?" He sounded irritated, which wasn't like him at all.

"Oh, nothing. Just let us know if you hear anything."

He nodded, a forced smile on his face.

Uncle Dan didn't take his eyes from me as I shut the door. I could have been mistaken, but he seemed relieved when I left.

# CHAPTER 16
# The Telekinesis Tournament

I was determined to learn how to communicate with animals if it was the last thing I did. But despite a week of intense lessons with Henry—Billy had to practice for the TT—by Friday I hadn't improved much at all. Henry kept telling me to imagine I was floating in the air like a feather; but after hours and hours of practice, I felt more like I was anchored at the bottom of the ocean. Something I wanted more than anything was within my reach, but I couldn't find a way to grasp it. It was so frustrating.

But I wasn't giving up. I promised Winny I would find Chey, and it was a promise I intended to keep. I know it didn't make any sense, but I couldn't shake the feeling that if I didn't find him, no one would.

On Saturday I awoke early for the TT. I was looking forward to seeing Billy play, but my excitement was overshadowed by an impending sense of doom. First Jay, then Chey, now Jane. Who would be next?

I picked up Charlotte and we walked through the drizzle to the stadium. It was a strange day, warm and damp at the same time. A blanket of fog swirled around our feet.

"Do you think the weather will hurt or help Billy and Winny?" Charlotte asked.

I shook my head. "No idea."

"I think it will help them."

I tried to smile. Charlotte, ever the optimist.

"There you are," Ally said, coming up behind us. "It's so crowded, I thought I'd never find you!" The campus was crawling with students, teachers, alums, and family members. The only time I'd ever seen it more packed was graduation.

We met up with Henry as we waited in line to enter the stadium. Uncle Dan was in charge of security, and he told me there would be three checkpoints this year (usually there was only one). The first one was manned by my mother's truth seekers, who asked us our names and intentions. I was happy to see that Pete from my English class was going to examine me. "Hi, Pete."

"Hey, Clay-er," he drawled. "I rilly hope Billy wins. I don't thank I could stand listenin' to Nik brag on for the next year."

Ally whipped around. "Hey!"

"Shoot—sorry, Ally."

He turned his attention back to me, an abrupt change in his tone. "What is yer purpose here?"

"I'm gonna watch my brother play in the TT." As he glared into my eyes it felt like there were bugs crawling inside my head; it was quite unnerving. After a few more questions he released me, my head pounding.

At the second checkpoint we had to put our hand on a screen to verify our identity. This was manned by the Think Tank kids. Finally, we had to pass by a professor who questioned us and verified who we were with three tests: voice recognition, fingerprint analysis, and an eye scan (as if they didn't know each and every student already).

Once we were through, we sat down in the middle of the second row of seats. I looked across the field for Uncle Dan, who was guarding the players' tents behind the stadium, but I could barely see the trees through the mist, let alone a person.

Henry bought us each a huge bag of caramel popcorn, and we ate and joked around while we waited for the tournament to begin. Finally, the horn sounded, and the players walked onto the field, Winny and Billy on one side, Maggie and Nik on the other. They all shook hands and returned to their positions under each goalpost.

Henry wore an odd expression, as if he was hiding something. "All right, what is it? What do you know?" I asked.

He shrugged.

Ally laughed. "Oh, just tell her. She'll find out soon enough."

"Billy just asked for my help with something," he answered mysteriously just as the whistle blew to signal the start of the game. The tournament consisted of a series of fifteen-minute periods, each one followed by a five-minute break. But once a team sank all their balls in the other team's board, the game was over. The game could last minutes or hours.

"Go, Billy!" Charlotte screamed.

Each team was told to summon their equipment. Bats and rackets whizzed onto the field. But something strange flew into Billy's outstretched hand—it was like a huge lacrosse stick but with an extra-wide head on either end of the shaft.

"Cool, huh?" Henry said, obviously quite pleased with himself. "See the net? I designed it so it can snugly fit any size ball. Once the ball's inside, it won't come out."

Principal Grogan gave a short speech about fair play, and then the tournament began. Unfortunately, so did the rain. To my surprise the teams were pretty evenly matched. Billy quickly dunked the smaller balls, and Winny moved in two of the heavy ones. The players darted across the wet field, moving their hands in a flurry, trying to control their balls and block at the same time.

Billy was amazingly accurate, able to sink all of the small balls while keeping Maggie from scoring for quite a while with his new stick. Henry, in fact, was beginning to look nervous. If the stick cost Maggie the game, she was going to kill him.

Pretty soon, Winny and Billy had a big lead. Charlotte was beside herself she was so happy, boasting to everyone in the stands that Billy was her brother, including a few ghosts who came to watch. When the horn blew signaling the start of the second period, the rain began to really pick up and the fog swirled up like spirits around us. Maggie fell several times, and each time she got up, she was a little muddier. On the other hand, Winny danced around the field as if she were in a ballet instead of hurling two-hundred-pound balls through the air.

At the end of the period, Winny and Billy only had two balls left, and Maggie and Nik had five. Maggie stormed off the misty field to their team tent, with Nik trailing after her.

I sat on the edge of my seat as they returned amidst a sea of applause for the start of the third period. Once again they summoned their equipment. This time when Maggie waved her hands, an enormous log zoomed toward her. For a minute I wondered how it was going to help her block the balls any better than a bat. And then I realized it wasn't for blocking at all; with its jagged edges the log could only be for one purpose— smashing Billy's net. The rules were clear: players could use anything they could move with their minds. The log was definitely heavier than two hundred pounds, but if she could move it, she could use it.

As soon as the whistle blew, Maggie doggedly sent the log after the net. Billy was ready, but he was having trouble dodging the log while trying to catch Maggie's balls. Soon the two teams were tied—each had one ball remaining.

Winny's largest ball whizzed toward the goalpost, but Maggie blocked it at the last second. Then Nik hurled their one remaining ball at the hole. As Billy positioned his net Maggie's log zoomed straight at it. I thought Billy was going to get the net out of the way in plenty of time as he swooped it down, but then something strange happened: it was as if he changed course and aimed the net directly at the log. In an instant the log crashed into the net, and as it fell to pieces on the ground Nik's ball sailed through the opening.

Maggie and Nik won.

The crowd erupted in cheers. Everyone said it was the most exciting TT ever.

Principal Grogan led all four players off the field and back to the two team tents. A few minutes later he returned to the podium and announced Winny's and Billy's names. I cheered as loud as I could as they received their second-place medals. I was proud they had made it so far and done so well.

Principal Grogan left the field with Winny and Billy,

disappearing into the fog near the woods with Tabby at his heels. I knew how disappointed Billy must have been, and I had no desire to see Nik strut out to the podium, so I decided to go and comfort Billy and Winny.

"I'll be right back, Charlotte. Stay here," I said, rushing down the stairs two at a time toward the exit. I ran through the rain to the back gate, guarded by Professor Higgins, as Professor Vlaspin, head of telekinesis, gave a long and boring speech about the tradition of the TT and why my great-grandfather invented it.

"I'm sorry, Claire, but only teachers can use this gate," Professor Higgins said.

"Please, Professor Higgins? I just want to see Billy and Winny—they'll be so upset. They're my brother and my best friend. What harm could *I* do?"

"Well," he started to waiver. He knew as well as anyone that I didn't have a special.

"And with our parents gone..." I took a page out of Charlotte's book and looked up at him with big, sad eyes.

"Oh, all right, go. But don't tell anyone I let you through."

As I approached the players' area the mist thinned and I saw someone near Maggie and Nik's tent. But before I could tell who it was, the fog formed a curtain. The only thing I knew for certain was that it was a man. Something about him unsettled me, but when I got to the tent, the man was gone. Although I looked everywhere, I couldn't see anyone—not even Uncle Dan, who was supposed to be guarding the tents. Where was he?

I pulled open the curtain to quickly congratulate Nik and Maggie, but the tent was empty save Tabby, sitting up on a table strewn with water bottles, towels, and granola bars. Where were Maggie and Nik? Had they already been announced and I missed it?

I went back outside and walked through the mist until I could see the podium, but only Professor Vlaspin was there, still droning on. I turned back. "Maggie! Nik!" I called.

There was no response.

With a sinking feeling in the pit of my stomach, I ran into Billy and Winny's tent and found them talking to a reporter for the school paper. "Have you guys seen Maggie and Nik?"

Both of them looked at me like I was crazy. "Yeah—a few minutes ago, going into their tent and celebrating," Billy said, annoyed.

Where were they? This time it was Principal Grogan's nasally voice I could hear as I went back outside: "Thank you, Professor Vlaspin, for that fascinating history of the Telekinesis Tournament. I want to thank all of you for coming here today, especially in this dismal weather. And now, without further ado, I would like you all to join me in giving a big round of applause for our winners, the talented and resourceful Nik Patel and Maggie Cullinane!"

My eyes were riveted to the podium, hoping against hope they would run up and receive their medals.

They didn't.

They were gone.

# CHAPTER 17
# The Healer

I rushed back to Maggie and Nik's tent. If I could communicate with Tabby somehow, she might be able to tell me what happened to them.

I stared at the cat sitting before me licking her wet fur. "Tabby, where are Nik and Maggie?" She stopped grooming herself and looked up at me, her tawny eyes meeting mine. I had a feeling she knew exactly what I was saying.

In the distance I could hear the crowd erupt in cheers and applause. "Our newest Exceptionals, Mr. Nik Patel and Miss Maggie Cullinane!" Grogan yelled again.

"Who took them?" I asked, walking slowly toward Tabby.

*I don't like you very much*, she thought, and then darted past me. I thundered after her, following her into the woods as several people—I couldn't tell who in the fog—burst into the tent I had just left.

I pushed through the thick underbrush, wiping the rain off my face as I went, but I couldn't find her. "Tabby!" I called in desperation, but even if she heard me, I knew she wouldn't come. "Maggie! Nik!" I yelled futilely.

I leaned against a tree to catch my breath. Just then an unnatural stillness descended upon the forest; even the rain had slowed to a drizzle. Behind me the once-roaring stadium was now completely quiet as Grogan was no doubt explaining what had happened and the horror of the truth was settling in— Maggie and Nik were gone.

I focused as hard as I could, straining to hear the animals. Nothing. I couldn't even hear the usual *hungry, thirsty*. It was maddening. I picked a direction at random and began to walk, searching for any sign of Maggie and Nik. I couldn't see five feet in front of me, nor could I see the ground through the mist swirling around my legs.

But all at once I knew I wasn't alone. I scanned the woods, but I couldn't see anyone. Then up ahead on an embankment, something blurred past. With a sudden rush of adrenaline I charged up the hill. I could just barely make out the figure of a man standing behind a tree. As I ran toward him a branch snapped back, slashing my forehead. I yelped in pain, stumbling backward. By the time I looked up, he was gone.

I could feel the warm blood trickle down my cheek. I wiped it away with my sleeve, cursing my clumsiness, and continued to the spot where I had seen him. I searched everywhere, looking for a clue—anything that could lead me to my friends or whoever had them. Before long I found a set of footprints in the mud, but only one set—and they didn't lead anywhere. It was as if someone had stood here and then vanished into thin air.

Undaunted, I concentrated with all of my might. Finally, I could hear the animals. *"Hungry, wet, cold…."* Nothing interesting. Nothing about a man, Nik, or Maggie. A squirrel darted in front of me. "Wait! Have you seen people in the woods? Please," I urged, "tell me."

The squirrel continued on, running away from me, thinking *cold* and *wet*. I was so frustrated, I almost screamed. The animals must have seen *something*! If only they could understand me.

Finally, with a heavy heart, I turned back toward the stadium. With each step I felt like I was giving up on my friends. When I reached the players' area, dozens of people were searching for Maggie and Nik. I slipped into Billy and Winny's tent to find them sitting alone, Winny sobbing into Billy's chest. They both looked up at me.

I slowly shook my head, feeling like a failure. "If you guys had won…"

"I know." Billy swallowed hard. "You'd be looking for us. The funny thing is, I was sure we were going to. The net was moving right where I wanted it to, and then…never mind."

"No, what?"

"It sounds like I'm making excuses."

"I know you better than that. Tell me," I demanded.

"I don't know how to explain it.…" He paused. "But it felt like someone else was controlling the net."

"Maybe someone else was."

"But why? Why would someone want us to lose and Maggie and Nik to win?"

"I just wish I knew if Chey was okay. I can't stand this!" Winnie cried.

I crouched down next to her. "Listen, he's fine. I'm sure of it. The students who were taken were the Exceptionals, *that's* why it was them. Someone wants them for their abilities. I'm certain Chey isn't hurt."

"You don't understand," she said, tears streaming down her face. "Chey won't do what they tell him to."

"Winny, hang in there—we'll find him."

In the distance we could hear the teachers still yelling Maggie's and Nik's names, as if they had taken a walk in the woods and lost track of time.

"What happened to your head?" Billy asked.

I absentmindedly touched the gash on my forehead. "It's nothing."

"It doesn't look like nothing. You might need stitches," Uncle Dan said from behind me. I hadn't heard him come in. "You need to see the nurse."

I had no intention of going to the nurse, but I nodded, anyway. "Uncle Dan, what happened?"

"I don't know. When Maggie and Nik came off the field, I heard something in the woods, like a motorcycle. The fog was so thick, I couldn't see anything; so I went to investigate. I was only gone a couple of minutes, but when I came back, Maggie and Nik were gone." He paused. "You three go back to your dorms, and I mean straight back, no detours. I need to keep looking for them," he said grimly.

We left the tent and started walking toward the quad. "Oh no!" Winny cried, "I lost the good-luck bracelet Chey made me!"

She held up her wrist, and the intricately beaded bracelet that she always wore was gone.

"I'll go check the tent," I said. I dashed back, and sure enough, it was in the middle of the floor. As I picked it up, I heard raised voices coming from outside.

"You were not supposed to leave your post!" Professor Higgins said angrily.

"I told you, I heard something strange in the woods, and I went to check it out," Uncle Dan answered defensively.

"You should have had another teacher do it. That was the agreed protocol. *You* were responsible for guarding the tents!" Higgins accused.

"I was only gone for a few minutes."

"A few minutes too long." Higgins paused. "I saw you in the woods before the game, too, McAllister. Why were you there?"

"Grogan asked me to patrol them. Not that I have to explain myself to *you*."

I heard someone storm off, then a minute later, Principal Grogan's voice. "Any sign of them?"

"No," Professor Higgins answered. "Why did you ask McAllister to patrol the woods before the game? Were you worried something like this would happen?"

"I never told him to patrol the woods. What gave you that idea?"

"He did."

There was a long pause. I held my breath, listening.

"Excuse me, I need to speak with him," Grogan said.

I heard the sound of receding footsteps. After a minute I peeked out the flap, and finding no one in sight, I ran back to Billy and Winny.

"Oh, you found it," Winny said, gripping the bracelet tightly, as if she were holding on to a piece of her brother.

"Come on, Claire, we better call Mom and Dad right away."

As we walked through the desolate field I kept replaying the conversation I had overheard. If Uncle Dan was supposed to guard the tents, why'd he leave? Why risk it? He was the head of security, after all. And why was he in the woods *before* the game? More troubling still, why did he lie about it? I couldn't help but notice that there had been more than a note of accusation in Professor Higgins's voice.

I was still lost in thought when we reached the dorms. Before I could talk to Billy alone, we needed to check on Charlotte. We found her in her room with Henry and Ally.

"What happened to your head?" Charlotte asked. "Are you okay?"

"Oh, no big deal—I got scratched by a branch."

Henry peered at the gash. "You need stitches."

"I'm not going to the infirmary, not with Maggie and Nik missing."

Henry opened his mouth like he was about to argue, and then a huge smile spread across his face. For some reason, this made me nervous. "Come to my room. My healing cream will help."

Oh no, the fluorescent green goop. Something about him applying it so near my brain didn't sit well with me.

"First we need to go to my room to tell my parents what happened," Billy said.

"I'm going to run and change," Winny said, pointing to her muddy clothes. "I'll meet you guys there."

The rest of us went to Billy's room and called, but there was no answer, so we left a vague message.

"I'll go get the cell accelerator," Henry said.

"I don't know, Henry, thanks and all, but the cut's on my face and—"

"It's fine! I doubt it will leave a scar—maybe just a small indentation—and besides, it's composed of all-natural ingredients....Just wait here. I'll be right back."

"Why don't you both go with him," Ally said to Billy and Charlotte. "I could really use a few minutes alone with Claire."

Billy raised his eyebrows in annoyance but got up anyway. "Come on, Charlotte. It seems I'm being kicked out of my own room."

Charlotte stood up, her hands on her hips. "You never even would have gotten that cut if you had listened to me and stayed out of the woods!"

"Charlotte—go!"

"Hmff," she snorted, trailing behind Billy.

After they left, Ally came and sat next to me on the bed.

"I'm so sorry about Nik. How're you holding up?" I asked.

She shrugged. "Nik is…" She paused, searching for the right words. "He's amazingly talented, don't get me wrong, but I'm really worried. He can be a little clueless sometimes. Wherever he is, I'm kinda glad Maggie's with him."

I put my arm around her. "I really don't think whoever has them is going to hurt them."

"I hope you're right."

We sat in silence for a few minutes. "Is there anything I can do to help?"

"No, but I think I can." She paused, pushing a long, blond strand of hair behind her ear. "I think I've told you—I'm not a very good code breaker," she said in a small voice.

"Everyone has different abilities," I said reassuringly.

She frowned slightly. "No, that's not it. I'm a…a healer."

I was confused. I had never heard of that special. "So you can heal people?"

She shrugged her narrow shoulders. "Not all of the time. If I touch someone, I can usually tell if they're sick, and sometimes I can heal them." She paused. "When I was little, my mother had breast cancer. The doctors gave her six months to live. No one told me, but she smelled different. I told her she smelled sick, and she told me she was—she had a lump that was growing. I asked her to show me where, and I ran my fingers over her skin. I concentrated really hard, and I felt heat come from my fingers. When I pulled my hand away, her skin looked sunburned. She told me that I had healed her, she could feel it. When she went back to see her doctor, the cancer was gone."

"Wow," I said in awe, "that's incredible. I can't believe I've lived at this school my whole life and no one ever told me about healers."

She looked at me from under her long, pale eyelashes. "I'm the only one at Cambial. And it's sort of a secret—only Nik and your mother know."

I smiled sadly, thinking of my mother, wishing she would call. "My mother does love secrets."

"No, it wasn't like that. She just told me to be careful who I told. She warned me that I could have people constantly asking me to heal everything wrong with them, and to heal their friends and family—and how would I say no? And then I might not have the time or energy to develop my gift. But she told me it was ultimately my decision."

"Are there other healers?"

She shook her head. "Not that we know of, but my mother said her grandmother was a healer, and people came from all over the county to see her. It's been hard without your mother here. She usually works with me privately once a week after specials."

I didn't know this about my mother. I felt another twinge of regret. She would have worked with me, too, if only I had trusted her—or if she'd had faith in me.

"Anyway, I think I can heal you."

I smiled. "I'd definitely prefer that to the green goop."

"I thought you might."

She placed her hands over my forehead. My skin felt hot and wet as Ally closed her eyes and rubbed her fingers in circles, spreading warmth inside me, like a cup of hot chocolate on a cold day. After a few minutes she pulled her hands away and opened her eyes.

"Well?" I asked, touching my forehead with my finger.

She examined my face, looking utterly exhausted. "Perfect."

"Are you all right?"

"The energy drains from me to you, so I'm tired now."

"And I feel great. That doesn't seem fair."

She smiled halfheartedly. "Well, I guess I have to come clean now."

"Why?"

"Like I said, you look perfect—no trace of the cut." She paused, her eyes filled with guilt. "I don't want to lie, but I'm just not ready to tell them."

"I completely understand." I hoped she'd understand if she ever discovered my secret. I felt terrible that she had to pay such a high price for helping me. "Hey—wait a sec," I said, opening Billy's closet door and pulling out a first aid kit. "My mother put one in all of our rooms." I quickly ripped open a Band-Aid and slapped it over my perfectly fine forehead, just in the nick of time.

A moment later Winny returned, followed closely by Billy, Charlotte, and Henry, who was clutching a vial. His face was crestfallen when he saw my forehead. "It really wasn't that bad after all," Ally said.

"Darn it!" Charlotte pouted. "I really wanted to see it work."

"So sorry I'm not more badly injured."

"Is anyone else?" she asked, hopeful.

"Charlotte!" Billy chastised.

Just then the phone rang, startling us. Billy grabbed it. "Hello? Hi, Dad." Billy filled him in on Jane and the events of the afternoon, culminating in Maggie and Nik's disappearance. "I don't know where Grogan was during Professor Vlaspin's speech—I didn't see him. Uncle Dan was patrolling the woods. Yeah, okay." He handed me the phone.

"Claire, we can't talk," my father said. "But we're getting closer."

"Closer to finding Chey, Jane, Nik, and Maggie? Who's behind this?"

"We're doing all we can to get to the bottom of this, honey, I promise you. We'll call your room tomorrow night. We love you. Be careful."

I shut my eyes tightly. I was not going to cry.

After we got Charlotte settled back in with Lana, Winny and I returned to our room exhausted. Sleep found me more easily than I expected, and I soon drifted into a dream. I was walking in the forest following a hawk—just like the day I found the stream. But then the hawk turned into Dylan. He was soaring above me. I was running as fast as I could to keep up, but he kept getting farther and farther away until he disappeared.

I woke up twisted inside my sheets and quilt, sweating. I took several deep breaths, and then I decided that hard as it was, I was going to let my obsession with Dylan go. He'd made it painfully obvious he didn't want me waiting for him. Besides, I had to get information that could help my parents before it was too late. Time was precious, and I wasn't going to squander it on him.

I lay back down and slept a deep, dreamless sleep.

When I awoke the next morning, I felt like a weight was pressing down on me. I *had* to learn to communicate with animals and help find my friends. On my way to practice, I stopped by the cafeteria to grab a muffin and saw Henry, Winny, and Ally whispering together at a table. All at once I realized that the entire cafeteria was unusually quiet.

"What's going on?" I asked, sliding into a seat next to Ally.

Henry shook his head angrily. "Three kids were expelled last night."

"Were the kids talented?" I asked.

Ally nodded. "Yeah—really talented. In fact, come to think of it, they were all in the Exceptional Society. Why?"

I shrugged.

Ally shook her head. "It's like Grogan's having a breakdown. He's canceled all the end-of-year specials competitions—no science expo, no code breaking and unsolvable math contests, nothing. Everything we've trained for all year long, gone. He's acting really weird, too. He came to talk to Professor McAllister after class, and I heard him ask where your parents were. When Professor McAllister said he didn't know, he told him he didn't believe him."

Why was he trying to find out where my parents were? My mother said she didn't believe he was involved, but what if she was wrong? He was expelling the most talented kids and disappearing all the time. He had lied to my mother about having the flu, and he was one of the last people to see Maggie and Nik before they disappeared. Was he the man I saw near the tent?

Another thought kept popping into my mind no matter how hard I tried to push it out. Why did Uncle Dan leave his post, and why did he lie about his reason for patrolling the woods before the game? I kept trying to convince myself there had to be an explanation, but I couldn't think of one. I almost told Billy, but even saying my doubts out loud seemed like a betrayal.

I just didn't want to believe Uncle Dan was involved, so I turned my focus back to Grogan. I was determined to find out what he was up to, *today*. I'd get Darwin, who had an uncanny ability to sniff out Tabby, and then I'd find out what Tabby knew, even if I had to kidnap *her*.

I mumbled something about having to walk Darwin and raced out of the caf before anyone could join me. I was almost at Uncle Dan's house when I saw him and Principal Grogan walking out his back door, both looking around furtively. I hid behind a large tree and watched them from a distance. Uncle Dan was holding something in his hand—a thick folder that looked suspiciously like the one I'd seen my mother studying. But I was too far away to be certain it was the same one, so I crept a little closer, ducking behind a huge rhododendron bush.

"I appreciate you showing me that file, Dan."

"I took it from Maura's desk right after she left," Uncle Dan said.

Tabby spotted me through the leaves. "*MEOW!*" she screeched indignantly.

Both of them looked nervously in my direction, and then lowered their voices. I couldn't hear anything else. *That damn cat!*

I watched as Uncle Dan went back inside with the file and Grogan crossed the lawn to his house. A few minutes later Uncle Dan came back out—empty-handed—and left in his car. It didn't make sense. Just a few minutes ago I was certain Uncle Dan would never betray us, and yet I couldn't deny what I had just witnessed.

There was only one thing to do. I was going to search Uncle Dan's house.

# CHAPTER 18

# Lost

I let myself in the back door and was immediately greeted by a very excited Darwin. *Walk, walk, walk, walk,* he thought.

"We'll go in a minute." I scanned the kitchen, but nothing was out of place. Uncle Dan was a neat freak, so a ratty file would be easy to spot. I ran into his office and looked in his desk. There were a ton of files in a rainbow of colors—all clean, with printed labels. Not one manila folder.

I searched the entire house, hoping Uncle Dan wouldn't come home and catch me. Nothing. I closed my eyes and focused. "Darwin, where's the folder Uncle Dan had?"

*Walk, walk, walk, walk, walk.*

It was maddening! If only he could understand me! "Oh, come on," I said, grabbing his leash and slamming the door behind me. If he couldn't help me, maybe Tabby could. I was approaching Principal Grogan's house just as he came outside. I quickened my stride. The last thing I wanted was for him to question me.

"Claire," he called, "can I see you for a minute?"

This just wasn't my day. I stopped and slowly walked up the wooden steps. Darwin pulled at his leash to get to Tabby, who yawned and stretched lazily on the doormat as if she didn't see him. I had an irresistible urge to kick her.

"H-Have you heard from your parents yet?" he stammered. He looked worse than usual, like he hadn't slept in days.

"Yes, I have. They're fine," I answered with forced cheer.

"Where are they?"

"I don't know. They didn't tell me."

He cleared his throat. "When your mother contacts you, tell her to call me."

"Sure."

He nodded, shifting his weight uncomfortably. "And I assume you've received the list of rules I handed out *again* to everyone?"

"Yes, but most don't apply to me, since I don't have a special."

"Th-that's right," he stammered again, clearly embarrassed. "But make sure you follow curfew, and do not leave the grounds under any circumstances. And Claire," he said in a kinder tone, "if you need anything in your parents' absence, please don't hesitate to come to me."

"Thanks." As if. I retreated toward my house as he waddled across the quad. When he was out of view, I turned around abruptly and marched up the porch steps.

"Tabby," I called, holding out a treat I had stuffed in my pocket.

She eyed me suspiciously. *What does that nosy girl want?*

I threw the cookie in front of her. Darwin ran toward it, but the leash snapped his neck backward. He looked at me and thought, *traitor.* I had an extra one in my pocket, so I broke off a piece and threw it to him. He gobbled it up, then continued to yank at the leash toward the other treat.

Tabby languidly walked over and sniffed it, and then sat down and licked her paws without touching it. Finally, she swatted it toward Darwin, just barely out of his reach. *See if you can get it,* she thought, taunting him.

I closed my eyes and tried to let myself relax. (Not easy when I felt like strangling her.) *I am as light as a feather, floating in the clouds,* I thought. When I felt as calm as I thought I ever could without being asleep, I opened my eyes and said, "Tabby, where are Maggie and Nik? Where are the missing students?"

She stopped licking her paws and looked up at me, regarding me curiously.

"Where is Principal Grogan going at night?"

She narrowed her golden eyes.

I was getting angry. "Where are the missing students?" I demanded.

She sniffed the treat again, and then swatted it away. *I'd rather have a mouse.*

I dropped Darwin's leash and lunged for her, but she was too quick. In a flash she jumped up on the porch railing and leaped onto the lawn. With her head in the air, she threw a superior look back at me and trotted into the woods.

She was infuriating. As ridiculous as it sounds, sometimes I thought she knew I could read her mind and purposefully thwarted my attempts.

I sighed, defeated. I leaned over to grab Darwin's leash, but he immediately thought, *Who's that?*

I looked up and saw a man standing in the shadow of the trees, watching me. My heart sped up. It was Dylan.

I blinked, hardly believing my eyes, and he was gone. I scanned the woods frantically, a panic growing in the pit of my stomach. I *had* to find him. I grabbed Darwin's leash and ran into the forest. *Find him, Darwin,* I pleaded with all of my might. Darwin caught Tabby's scent and began pulling me toward her. "Not Tabby, Dylan!" I yelled at him.

"Dylan!" I called again and again as we wandered aimlessly through the woods. There was no answer. With dwindling hope I checked the stream, but he wasn't there, either. Finally I gave up.

As we walked home Darwin sniffed along the decaying leaves and then thought *rabbit.* Before I could react, he bolted and the leash slipped through my fingers. I sprinted after him, screaming his name, but he was gone.

That stupid dog! I ran through the forest calling him, listening to the animals for some clue as to his whereabouts, but I couldn't hear anything. Where was he? I decided to get Billy to help me look, then I realized I had no idea where I was or how to get back to the school. I searched in vain for a familiar landmark, but I was exhausted and completely lost. I sat down on a fallen tree and began to cry.

Soon a shadow passed overhead. When I looked up, I saw the mother hawk. She was thinking, *What is she doing? She seems lost.*

I sighed with relief. She could fly to the school, and I could follow her. I stood up and yelled, "Show me the way to the school!" But, of course, she couldn't understand me. She just kept circling, keeping a watchful eye.

I closed my eyes again, tried to relax, and concentrated on the other animals around me. None were thinking about a dog, or the school, or a man. Then I had a terrifying thought—what if the man wasn't Dylan? What if it was the person who followed me before? What if it was the kidnapper? The woods seemed to darken suddenly before my eyes.

I couldn't sit still for another moment. I walked quickly, randomly picking a direction, all the while listening to the animals for clues or signs of danger. The hawk continued to glide overhead; I felt a little better knowing she was watching after me. But as the sun sank lower in the sky, an icy wind rustled the trees, chilling me to the bone. I rubbed my hands against my arms, trying to warm them. I had to find my way home, and soon.

As dusk descended, the forest I had always loved seemed sinister. The trees were so dense, I could barely see. To make matters worse, a low moan of thunder reverberated around me in the unfamiliar woods. All at once I heard a noise behind me, and then the hawk swooped lower as her frightened thoughts cried, *The girl is in danger!*

I sprinted as fast as I could in what I prayed was the right direction. Suddenly, my toe caught the gnarled root of a fir tree, sending me sprawling sideways, then down with a thud.

I blacked out—I don't know for how long—but I had the nicest dream. Dylan had found me, and he held me in his arms. He stroked my face softly and told me I was beautiful. Then in a muffled voice, as if from very far away, I heard yelling. I opened my eyes, but it was Henry's anxious face staring back at me. As I sat up, a pain radiated from my head to my tailbone.

"BILLY! I'VE GOT HER!" he screamed. He turned back to me. "What happened? Are you okay?"

I tried to nod, but the pain was like a jackhammer against my skull. "Yeah, I fell."

He laughed lightly. "I know you fell. But what are you doing out here?"

At first I didn't know, and then I remembered seeing Dylan—or imagining I saw him—and being followed. I wondered if the hawk was still watching over me. I looked up, and although the moon and stars now filled the sky, very little light filtered through the lush tree canopy. And then a beam of moonlight illuminated her, perched high above me on a tree limb. Our eyes locked.

*She's safe now.*

I nodded in response. "Thank you," I whispered, wishing she understood me.

She cocked her head to one side, and my heart skipped a beat.

"Are you okay?" Billy said, completely out of breath.

Reluctantly, I looked away from her. "Yeah. I took Darwin into the woods to practice, but he got away. I got lost chasing him." My thoughts immediately turned to Darwin. "You have to find him—there are coyotes, foxes, even bears in the woods!"

"Relax, he's fine. He came home with his leash still attached to his collar—that's how Uncle Dan knew you were gone. We've all been looking for you for hours." Billy sat down next to me, his nervous face relaxing. He ran his hand through his thick hair. "I even called Mom—they're freaking out."

I sighed. I was sure that was a huge understatement. "Help me up," I said, reaching my hand toward Billy. Then I noticed that my wrist was bare. "Oh no, my watch is gone. Can you guys help me find it?" I said, scanning the forest floor.

Billy swept his flashlight in a circle around me. "We'll never find it in the dark. We have to go now, Claire. Mom and Dad are really worried."

As I nodded, I winced from the pain. I felt the side of my head—the source of the throbbing—and found I had a huge lump.

"Henry—can you help Claire back? I want to run ahead and call my parents and Uncle Dan."

"Sure, we'll meet you back in my room."

Henry put his arm around my waist, gently guiding me up. He held me firmly with one hand, his flashlight with the other. I leaned against him, feeling safe. "Thank you for rescuing me," I said in a small voice.

He didn't respond at first. Then he said softly, "Claire, when Billy told me you were missing, I was so worried. I really care about you, a lot."

I didn't know what to say. I liked him so much, and he was someone I could count on, I knew that. And Dylan was gone. But when I closed my eyes at night, it was Dylan's face I saw. I liked Henry too much to lie to him.

I stopped walking and looked up at his kind face. "I'm confused about a lot of things right now. I want to put all my energy into developing my special, no distractions." I paused, then said the words everyone who exposed his heart feared: "Can we just be friends?"

His expression was unreadable. He held my eyes with his stare. "For now," he finally answered. We continued on in an uncomfortable silence.

Although I couldn't see the hawk in the darkness, I could feel her presence.

"I hope Billy reached my parents. I'm sure they're worried I was kidnapped."

It was his turn to stop walking. "Your parents aren't helping the government. They went to investigate, didn't they?"

I frantically tried to think of something to say, but my head hurt too much to focus. Besides, I trusted Henry. "Yes," I admitted.

His eyebrows furrowed together. "But they left before Chey and Jane disappeared." He paused again, working it out. "Because something's happened to Jay Burke, too."

"That's right. I forgot that you were the one who told my parents he was missing. Were you guys friends?"

"Sort of, I didn't really know him that well. Actually, I was surprised when he called. He's amazing at science—probably one of the best the school has ever seen. So someone's kidnapping the most talented kids in each special," he said, putting it all together.

I didn't answer; there was no need.

"Who do they think is behind it?"

"They don't know," I answered.

"I've never told anyone this before," he began, his voice trembling slightly, "but my father was a follower of Timothy Wilder. My mother would have no part of it; she told my father he had to choose, her or Wilder." He paused, the weight of the confession wearing on him. "He chose Wilder, and then she found out she was pregnant. I never even met him," he said angrily.

"I'm so sorry."

"Your mother knows, of course, and Principal Grogan, but my mother asked them not to tell anyone else. I took my mother's name—I was too ashamed to be known as Henry Grainer."

I shuddered at the name. Clayton Grainer was a brilliant scientist who had joined Wilder early on. He developed all sorts of terrible inventions—bombs, lethal gases, the list went on. He and Wilder sold them to unstable governments to fund their projects. I couldn't believe Henry was related to such a monster.

"Do you know that they never found Wilder's body? The explosion was tremendous, so he's probably dead, but..." He wasn't able to finish his thought. "So what I'm saying is, I want to help. I need to."

I caught my breath. It couldn't possibly be Wilder behind the kidnappings. He was killed—or had disappeared—years ago. If he was alive, what was he waiting for? Why strike now? And surely the clairvoyants would have seen him.

"Claire—tell me what you know. Please."

My heart ached for him. I tried to live up to my family's reputation; he lived in the shadow of his. I knew I was breaking a promise to my parents, but so be it. I told him everything we suspected and everything we knew, which was hardly anything at all.

As we crossed the lawn to the dorms the hawk called out to me. I looked up, and our eyes met again. I still felt strangely connected to her. *Be careful in the woods*, she warned.

*I will*, I thought, nodding. She swept across the sky in a perfect arc, her body silhouetted against the moon. With a graceful flap of her wings, she sailed back over the trees, disappearing into the night.

"Claire? Hello?"

"What?"

Henry shook his head. "You just stopped and completely zoned out. Are you sure you're all right?"

I did? Huh. "I'm fine," I mumbled.

He guided me up the stairs to his room, the concern apparent on his face. "I'm worried you really hit your head hard. I want to make sure you don't have a concussion." He opened the red first aid box and removed an ice pack, which he gently placed on my head, his fingers delicate.

"Did my mother ever say anything to you about your father?"

"Just once," he said with a small smile. "When I applied to Cambial, she took me aside after the interview. She could tell I was nervous. She told me once I came to Cambial, I was responsible for myself, and only myself." His eyes grew soft at the memory. "And then she said I was very gifted, and she knew I would do great things."

I smiled, too. I couldn't believe it, but I really missed my mother.

Just then Billy burst into the room, looking worse than he had in the woods.

"What's wrong?" I asked.

"It's Mom and Dad," he spat out. "They're not answering their cell phones. They said they would check them every second until we found you—that they were coming home, they were so worried. Something must have happened to them."

As his words sank in, I was filled with a consuming dread. I knew, deep down, he was right.

# CHAPTER 19
# The Prophecy

The waiting was unbearable. We tried unsuccessfully to reach Uncle Dan, who was still out looking for me. With each minute that ticked away, I was more certain that something terrible had happened to my parents. They hadn't known I'd been found—nothing would keep them from calling or answering their phones. I closed my eyes. My head was throbbing, and it had little to do with the lump.

Henry put his hand on my back, rubbing it gently.

Billy paced around the room. "All right. We have to work together to find Mom and Dad, Maggie, Nik, Chey, Jane, Jay—and whoever else has disappeared that we don't know about. I'm going to make a chart."

If I wasn't so sick with worry, I would have laughed. That was just like Billy.

He grabbed a red marker and made a column in the middle of Henry's massive whiteboard:

MISSING
Jay Burke—science
Chey Stargazer—telekinesis
Jane Morse—clairvoyant
Maggie Cullinane—telekinesis
Nik Patel—telekinesis
Maura Crane—truth seeker
Charles Walker—math/code breaker

I inhaled sharply when I saw my parents' names there, in ink, along with the others. It somehow became more real.

I kept staring at the list.... There was something strange about it. And then it hit me. "Hey—isn't it odd no mediums were taken?"

"Yeah," Billy agreed. "But looking at it—there's something they all have in common. Since the winners of the TT are automatically in the Exceptional Society, every student, including Jay, is an Exceptional."

He made another list, writing:

*Possible suspects—Wilder? Dead or alive?*
*motive—exploit powers?*
*next target—?*
*school connection—George Grogan?*

Seeing it on the board made it clear we hardly knew anything.

"Any ideas?" Billy asked.

I sighed. Unfortunately, I had a few. I knew more than they did about the mysterious file from Mom's office and Uncle Dan's highly suspicious behavior. I was about to tell them when Winny threw open the door. She looked at the whiteboard, her face anguished.

"Don't worry—we'll find him. We'll find all of them," I said. In a strange way, comforting her helped me to focus. And then it suddenly came to me. "We're going about this all wrong! We have something that the kidnapper doesn't—at least not yet: the talent of the people at this school. *That*'s what he's after, and we already have it! We need to mobilize. We need code breakers, mediums, clairvoyants, truth seekers. In short, let's make a list of who we can trust."

"You're right!" Henry jumped up and began furiously writing on the other side of the board. "Okay, Billy and Winny—telekinesis; me—science, and I'm pretty good at math."

I was sure that was an understatement.

"Let's see, Ally," he scribbled, "code breaker."

"Who's the best medium?"

Billy frowned. "Charlotte."

"Well, we're certainly not involving her in this," I said. "Who else?"

Henry answered. "Sam's great, and so is Lilly. They're both Exceptionals."

Winny shook her head. "They were both expelled for breaking Crane's Commandments."

"I know them really well—they would never do that!" Henry frowned, his eyebrows drawn together in a long, straight line. "Let me think about it."

"Who for clairvoyance?" I asked.

Billy answered immediately. "Jane's the best, but after her it has to be Mike."

Henry nodded. "Yeah, Mike's great, and we can trust him. And Pete will be our truth seeker."

"Didn't you hear?" Winny asked.

We all looked at her, startled, afraid of what we might learn next.

"Mike and Pete were expelled this afternoon. No one knows why."

Henry answered the question. "I do. They were both Exceptionals, too. Grogan's expelling the most talented students so they'll be easier to get to."

The words hung heavily in the room.

The door swung open, and there stood a very disheveled Ally, looking frantic. "Henry, Grogan's looking for you! I'm sure it's to expel you! He's on some sort of a crazy rampage."

Winny's face was filled with rage. "No! They're not going to get you, too, Henry."

"We'll have to hide you," I said, racking my brain for a spot. "I know—my house! There's a bomb shelter in the basement. My great-grandfather designed the house to withstand almost anything he could dream up—and he had quite an imagination. There's even a tunnel from the bomb shelter to an old shed in the woods."

Ally, Winny, and Henry stared at me in disbelief.

Billy nodded. "The clairvoyants have predicted pretty scary stuff over the years—terrorist plots, nuclear bombs. Of course, the problem with clairvoyance is no one knows when in the future the vision will take place—a month or a century, if at all."

Another thought occurred to me. "Are the visions recorded?"

"Yes—by your mother," Winny said. "She's really strict about recording the visions herself. I've had a few, and she always wrote them down."

I remembered Jane meeting with my mother about her visions, too. And then it hit me. "Wait a minute—the visions! That's it! One of the clairvoyants might have seen Wilder—or whoever's behind this—and maybe even where my parents are! We have to get those files!"

"Do you know where they are?" Winny asked. "When I had visions, she always came to my room to record them."

That was strange. She met with Jane and other clairvoyants at the house. "She keeps them locked in her desk at home, but I know where the key is. Come on, let's go!"

"Just a minute, I have to get some stuff together." Henry grabbed his backpack and started throwing a hodgepodge of things inside; soon it was jam-packed with everything but clothes.

"Ready," Henry said as he reached out for my hand. I pretended not to notice and walked out the door ahead of him with Winny. Luckily, the sky was overcast, enveloping us in utter darkness. Neither of us had to see the other's expression.

When we finally reached my house, I unlocked the door and stood there, frozen. My home had been ransacked. Broken dishes were all over the floor, paintings had been tossed off the walls, and even the chair cushions had been ripped open.

"Claire, move," Billy said, snapping me out of my trance and locking the door behind us. We stood in the dark, feathers floating around us each time we took a step. I ran into my mother's study. Her desk, the same one that had been my great-grandfather's, was now in a hundred pieces. Every file, every piece of paper—gone.

Billy put his arm around my shoulder. "Come on, let's get Henry to the shelter."

I swallowed hard and followed Billy down the basement stairs. The bomb shelter was a long, small, windowless room with four sets of metal bunk beds pushed against the walls. "Let's see," I said, trying to keep the emotion out of my voice. "Henry, there's food over there and a bathroom behind the shelves." I pointed. "And I hope you don't need it, but if you have to get out of here, the shower connects to a tunnel that leads to the shed behind my house. Turn the shower nozzle twice counterclockwise and once clockwise to open it."

Henry nodded, looking about glumly.

Winny put her arm around me. "I'm so sorry."

I shook my head dismissively and looked away. "It's just things—nothing that can't be replaced." In truth, I was devastated. It wasn't just that all her files, along with the clairvoyant predictions, were gone. Whoever broke in had wanted something, something from my mother's desk. And if that's what they would do to her desk, what would they do to her?

"We have to warn all the Exceptionals," Henry said. "None of them are safe."

I looked around at my friends, relieved only Henry was an Exceptional. "How are we going to do that? What would we say?"

"I'll figure something out," Billy answered. "Let's go—I want to do it now before more are expelled."

I nodded. "And I guess I should check on Charlotte."

"Hey—wait a minute, I almost forgot," Henry said, rummaging around his backpack and handing each of us a bag of an opaque, pearly substance. "This may come in handy; it'll open any lock. It oxidizes immediately, so you won't have long. Push it in the keyhole and wait until it solidifies. Use as little as possible. And I just wanted to say…" He paused, casting his eyes down at the cement floor. "Thanks."

Winny threw her arms around him. "You don't have to thank us—we love you! We'll see you tomorrow."

Following a very awkward good-bye, we all left and had a short visit with Charlotte, who kept relaying useless advice from ghosts (particularly Great-Grandma Barbara, who was even kookier in death than in life). I tried to be patient and listen attentively, which wasn't easy. I kept telling myself that Charlotte was only eleven and must be worried and frightened with our parents gone. I didn't even roll my eyes when she conveyed Great-Grandma Barbara's dire warning, *again*, to stay out of the woods.

Finally, Lana returned, so we left Charlotte and quickly headed back to my room. At five of eleven Billy and Ally said their good-byes. Ally looked so fragile, I couldn't bear the thought of leaving her alone. "Ally, you should stay with us tonight."

I thought she might argue, but she smiled weakly and nodded. "Is that okay with you, Winny?"

Winny was looking off in the distance, still as a statue.

"Winny? Are you all right?" I asked.

She didn't respond.

Ally waved her hand in front of her face.

"What is it? What's wrong with her?" I felt the panic rise inside of me.

Ally shook her head. "Nothing. I think she's having a vision."

After a few moments she came out of it. She plopped down on her bed, rubbing her temples. I sat down next to her. "What just happened?"

She smiled feebly. "I keep having the same vision," she said softly, "and I'm having it more often. There's a girl standing in a meadow. I can't see her face. She holds her hand out, and a hawk flies down and lands on her finger. She tells it something, and the bird nods as if it can understand her, and then it flies off." She paused. "Pretty weird, huh?"

I had to grip the side of the bed to steady myself. I could feel Billy's eyes boring into me.

"When have you had it before?" Billy asked with forced calm.

"A bunch of times—the first was a few weeks ago, right before your parents left."

"What did my mother say?" Billy asked carefully.

"It was really weird. You know how your mother's so...in control all of the time? She sort of freaked out. She kept asking me if I was sure, and if I could see a face, but I couldn't. She told me if I ever had the vision again, or saw the face, to come and tell her—even if it was in the middle of the night."

My mother knew the girl was me! Why didn't she press me more to work on my special? It didn't make sense.

Winny yawned, stretching her arms. "I'm sorry, but that really tired me out. I'm going to bed."

As exhausted as I was, I knew I wasn't going to get much sleep. I couldn't wait to find the hawk again.

The next morning Billy woke me early. I quietly threw on my dirty sweatshirt, not wanting to wake Winny and Ally, and followed him across the quad to the bomb shelter. After we checked in on Henry, who was sleeping so soundly he didn't even stir when we opened the door, we went upstairs. The house looked even worse in the stark morning sunlight; torn pieces of our lives were scattered everywhere.

When (and I refused to think *if*) my parents returned home, I knew they would be devastated, so I took a deep breath and started picking up, but Billy stopped me. "They could be back," he warned. "We don't want them to know that we know."

As much as I hated to admit it, he was right. We stood in the kitchen, surveying the mess. "Billy, I don't get it. If mom knew I'd be able to communicate with animals, why didn't she tell me?"

He shrugged. "Winny said she had the vision right before they left—maybe she never got a chance. She had a lot on her mind."

That was certainly true; she had been distracted for weeks before she left.

"What do you think they were after?" Billy finally said.

"I don't know, but Mom's desk certainly bore the brunt of it."

"Do you think they got what they wanted?"

It was my turn to shrug. I was about to leave for class when I looked out the window and noticed Darwin's leash hanging on a peg. "Billy—Darwin!" We'd forgotten all about him. "If Uncle Dan still isn't back, he's been alone since yesterday afternoon!"

We sprinted across the yard to Uncle Dan's house. As soon as we had the door open, Darwin jumped on us, licking our faces, he was so relieved to see us. I looked around in dismay—Uncle Dan's immaculate house was anything but. Darwin had *not* been a good dog. Apparently lack of food brought out his hunting instincts. The neat glass containers of cereal and pasta lay shattered on the floor.

"Whoa," Billy said, surveying the mess. "I'll take him outside—you pick up."

"Hey!" I was about to argue, but Billy had already shot out the door.

I walked over to an expensive-looking shoe that had been chewed to pieces and cringed. Uncle Dan wasn't a big animal lover to begin with; he was not going to be happy. I went into the paneled mudroom to get the dog food from the closet and saw that Darwin had knocked over all the recycling, which had tipped into the huge memo board filled with photos of me, Charlotte, and Billy.

As I straightened it, something caught my eye—a tiny keyhole in the paneling behind the memo board. That was strange. It was in a groove, almost impossible to see. Obviously, Uncle Dan had gone to great lengths to keep something hidden. I pushed and pulled, but the panel wouldn't budge.

Suddenly, I remembered Henry's goop, still in my pocket from the night before. I took out a small amount and pushed it inside the hole. It hardened immediately, forming a miniature key. I turned it gently until I heard a soft click, and a one-foot section sprang open.

I found myself staring inside a small safe. All that was in it was a thick file: a worn, ratty folder with a coffee stain. *The file.*

My heart racing, I removed it gently, as if it were crystal instead of paper, and read the word scribbled across it in blue: ANIPATHY.

"What's that?" Billy said from behind my shoulder, making me jump.

Quickly I filled him in on the history of the folder: that Uncle Dan had hidden it from me, that I had seen Mom with it, that she accused me of going through it, that just yesterday I had seen Uncle Dan holding it and talking to Principal Grogan. "Have you ever heard of someone named Anipathy? Or do you know what that means?"

He shook his head. "No clue."

I plopped down on the mudroom floor and began to scan the papers. "I don't believe it," I said in disbelief. "Anipathy is telepathy with animals!" Wow, my special even had a name!

I read on, hardly believing my eyes. "And anipathy seems really important!"

"Of course it is! Come on, what does it say?"

"These visions are all about anipathy, and they're all related... almost like a prophecy. The first one is from 1937: 'anipath will be crucial to school; 1949, girl will befriend hawk, uncover plot.'" *Hawk!* These visions *were* about me! "And in 1960, 'powerful anipathic girl will save students.' It goes on," I said, shuffling through the papers. "I think these are all about the same person!"

"The same *anipath*—you! I told you your special was powerful!"

I looked up at him, overcome with joy. "I'm going to learn to communicate with the hawk—and that's how I'm going to save everyone! I'm the girl in the prophecy—I'm anipathic!"

"Read Winny's."

I flipped through the papers, feeling euphoric. "Ahhh...here it is—it's the last one. 'Anipathic girl in field communicating with hawk—no face seen.'...And the one right before it is Jane's. 'Anipath stops plot to destroy school.' And listen to this! Jane had a vision of an evil man lurking around her, and it terrified her. She must have had a vision of Wilder, or whoever's behind this!" I remembered that day I saw her on the porch after she'd met with my mother. No wonder she'd looked so strange.

I stared at my mother's handwriting, and then my happiness

quickly gave way to anger. "If Mom knew I'd be able to communicate with animals this whole time—that I was an anipath, maybe even *the* anipath from the prophecy—why didn't she tell me? I could have gone to school here! I could have been trained!"

Billy shook his head slowly. "I don't know. It doesn't make sense."

I looked through her file again for some clue. Then I saw it, right there in black and white. I read the words, but I couldn't bring myself to say them.

"What is it?"

I opened my mouth, but nothing came out.

"Claire, you're white as a ghost. What does it say?" He snatched the folder out of my hand and read. "'Anipathic girl saves school,'"—he paused, and looked up at me, his face ashen—"'dies in process.'"

# CHAPTER 20

# Ferana

"Claire, this doesn't mean..." He couldn't even say the words.

No wonder my parents accepted that I could no longer hear animals, no questions asked. They didn't want it to be me.

I took the folder from him and read the previous entries. There had been two more predictions about the hawk girl—both that she would die.

My mother had made a notation after the last one (before Winny's and Jane's), a little over five years ago. Beneath the big, angry X, I could just make out the words: "last prediction made." I could almost see the relief in her flowing handwriting, so different from the sharp, slanted words above. So many things now made sense.

Gently Billy took the folder from me. "Come on, this doesn't mean anything. You weren't trained. Maybe if you were, you'd be more powerful, and then you would die—or maybe everyone would know you could talk to animals and that would put you in danger. Hey—that's probably why Nana Marie told you not to tell anyone. We changed the prophecy; I'm sure of it."

I looked up at him, hoping it was true. It could be. I tried to smile. "You're right. Nothing to worry about." But in the pit of my stomach, I knew different.

"It's good we know about it, though. No more trying to communicate with animals; it's not worth the risk," he said, as if it were obvious.

I didn't respond. My special was even more important now—my parents' lives were in my hands, and I was the only one who could save them.

I read prediction after prediction, but it was hard to focus. There were even a few about Timothy Wilder—that he was still alive and would attack the school again. My mother had written in the margins of most. On the top of one page she had scribbled, "Josephine holds the key."

Josephine—where did I know that name? "Have you heard of someone named Josephine?"

Billy scrunched up his face. "No. Sounds sort of familiar, though. Let's meet and try to figure it out later—we should get to class. Now is not a good time to play hooky, not with Grogan on the warpath."

"Fine, but I'm taking the folder with me."

"Uncle Dan will flip if it's gone."

I sighed. "Billy, aren't you wondering how Uncle Dan ended up with Mom's folder in the first place? He told Grogan he took it from her office *after* she left."

He looked at me, surprised.

"And right before Mom left, she had it—and she was freaking out because someone had gone through it."

"Well, she must have told him to come and take it because she was worried someone else would get their hands on it." He paused, rubbing his temples. "Claire, this is Uncle Dan you're talking about."

"Then how do you explain him showing this to Grogan when he knows Mom doesn't trust him?"

Billy was quiet. "There has to be a reason."

I hoped there was. But neither of us could think of one.

"We'll ask him when he comes back. He's still not answering his phone—I hope nothing's happened to him, too," Billy said, his eyebrows knitting together.

"So do I." And I really hoped he could explain all of this.

We quickly fed Darwin, picked up, and ran to campus.

Billy stopped before we reached Crane Hall. "You're okay, right?"

I nodded vigorously. "Of course," I lied. "Remember, no one else can know."

"Claire—"

"I'm not arguing with you about this. I already told you, I'm listening to Nana."

Later that afternoon Billy and I went back home, and after I hid the anipathy file in a pizza box in the freezer, we went downstairs to check on Henry. Soon we were joined by Ally and Winny.

The bomb shelter was stuffy with all of us in it. I tossed my sweatshirt in the corner and asked, "Do any of you know someone named Josephine?"

Ally, Winny, and Henry shook their heads.

"Why?" Winny asked.

"Ummm...I remember my mom saying something about her, that she was the key or something. I thought she might be able to help us find everyone or lead us to whoever took them. Hey—I bet she was a student here!"

Henry rubbed his chin. "Hmm. You two know more about the school than almost anyone. Where would we find out about a former student? Is there a computer file or something?"

Billy shook his head. "No—too easily hacked."

"They must keep track somehow. An encrypted program?"

I shrugged.

"Your parents never said anything about protected files?" Ally asked.

"Not that I remember," Billy answered.

I thought back to all of the conversations about the school that I had tuned out. Then something flashed in my mind. "Wait! I do remember my parents talking about confidential files a couple of years ago—student records, clairvoyant predictions, discoveries, and stuff. They wanted to look at them, but Grogan claimed he couldn't find them in Grandpa Paul's office. Mom and Dad offered to help him search it—but he refused. They were furious. I vividly remember Mom saying that if they weren't secure and someone got their hands on them, it could be disastrous."

"Yeah...I remember that too." Billy paused. "That was right after Grandpa Paul died."

I sighed. "We need those files."

Winny's face lit up. "Then that's where we'll start."

Billy looked at her. "What do you mean? Where?"

"Your Grandpa Paul's office, which is Grogan's now, of course. I think we should do it tonight," she said cheerfully, as if she'd just announced we were having ice-cream sundaes.

Billy looked at her as if she were crazy.

"She's right. He'll have the old records," Henry said as he paced back and forth in the tiny bomb shelter, "and maybe even current ones."

I could almost see Billy's mind working, considering all of the dangers and risks. Right now I just didn't have the patience. "Look, Billy, our choices are to figure this thing out or wait around and do nothing while more students get expelled and kidnapped."

He sighed, defeated. "We don't even know where to look. Grogan may have even been telling the truth—he may not know where they are. How the hell are we supposed to find them?"

"Just because Grogan couldn't find them, doesn't mean we won't be able to. There are five of us. We can do it," Ally said softly.

Billy snorted. "There's no way Claire's going."

Winny stared at him. "Why not?"

"I *am* going! I have nothing to worry about, remember?" I said adamantly.

"Claire—"

"I'm going."

Looking both angry and worried, Billy opened his mouth to say something, and then shut it. "Fine, we'll meet outside the shed tonight. Eleven o'clock."

Soon they left for an early dinner, and I offered to stay with Henry. I had an ulterior motive, though; if I was going to learn how to communicate with that hawk, I'd better start practicing. I made up an excuse to Henry about needing to walk Darwin, then, not wanting to risk being spotted, I decided to go through the tunnel. I hadn't been in it in years. I climbed into the small shower stall and turned the nozzle twice counterclockwise, once clockwise. When I heard a small pop, I pushed the hot/cold lever in, pulled it down, and then pushed again. The door swung open.

I stepped inside the narrow passageway, as I had countless times when I was younger. My grandfather had made us practice emergency drills at least once a month. We were never allowed to tell anyone about the tunnel or play in it. He was strangely compulsive about that. As I walked across the hard dirt floor a dim light shone on either side of the tunnel—motion-operated fluorescents added by Grandpa Paul. I hesitated to look up or down—I didn't want to see what creepy-crawly things lurked around me.

After a few minutes the tunnel gradually began to rise, and then it abruptly ended. I pulled the string hidden among the many dangling spiderwebs, and the ceiling groaned as a two-by-four-foot trapdoor fell down toward me. I hoisted myself up into what used to be a workshop but was now filled with assorted junk—old bikes, skates, tools, and half-finished projects.

I crouched under the grimy window and peered out, searching the woods until I was certain no one was there. I slipped out the door and hurried toward the hawk's nest, glancing over my shoulder several times to make sure I wasn't being followed. As I walked, I scanned the sky for Talrin and his mother. I wasn't sure which was the hawk from the prophecy. I'd almost asked Winny how big the hawk was, but I thought that was too unusual a question.

As I approached the nest I closed my eyes and tried to open my mind. It was useless. All I could think about was *"girl saves school, dies in process."* If I stopped trying to communicate with the hawk, I would live. But what about my parents? And everyone else?

It seemed I had a choice to make, and it was an easy one. I couldn't live with myself knowing that I could have saved them but didn't.

With renewed determination I stood under the nest, the same spot where I had found Talrin. The late afternoon sun cast a golden glow on the trees, making them appear as if they were statues cast in bronze. The air was so still, not even a whisper of a breeze rustled the branches to break the illusion.

Again I looked to the sky and tried to imagine myself floating on the wispy cloud above me. I felt the last fingers of sunlight warm my face, and then the heat radiated through me. It was the strangest feeling—I was completely relaxed and yet hyperaware at the same time. Everything became crisp: the smells of the forest intensified, as did the sounds. And the animals! I could hear their thoughts clearly.

I closed my eyes and listened for the hawk.

I don't know how long I stood there—it could have been five minutes; it could have been hours—I wasn't bound by time anymore. Behind my closed eyes I saw a veil fall away, and I was engulfed by a pure white light. A sense of peace washed over me, a calm stronger than I had ever before experienced. And then I heard her clearly.

*Why is she here?*

I opened my eyes and looked up. She was watching me from a branch several feet above my head, her snowy chest glimmering against the magenta sky.

I took a deep breath and answered. "I'm looking for you. My name is Claire."

*I am Ferana. How is it you can speak to me?*

I felt a surge of energy between us. I couldn't hear any other animals now, just Ferana. It was as if she and I were in a separate place together, still in the forest and yet apart from it.

"I've been able to hear animals my whole life. I heard Talrin call for help—that's how I was able to save him. But animals have never been able to hear me."

Ferana swooped down and landed cautiously on a branch right in front of me. She was magnificent. Her belly was white and fluffy, but in the center was a round golden circle of feathers, darker in the middle, almost like a bull's-eye. Her face was level with mine, her intelligent, velvety eyes regarding me closely.

*You have a strange gift, Claire. I have been watching over you since you saved my son. I am forever in your debt.* She paused. *Why did you risk yourself to save him? Surely you knew I could have harmed you.*

"When Talrin cried for help, it was the strongest voice I had ever heard." I shuddered, remembering his desperate cry. "I knew he was calling you, but it felt like he knew I heard him and was calling me, too. I couldn't just leave him there to be eaten."

*You have a good heart, Claire.*

"Thank you for helping me in the woods. I felt better knowing you were there, and I could hear you tell me to run." I took a step toward her and tentatively put my hand out. She gently glided from the branch to my finger, careful not to hurt me. She was heavier than I expected.

*I see a sadness in your eyes. What is troubling you?*

"There is a bad man who's taken my parents, and I don't know where they are. I can't explain it, but I feel like he has them someplace close."

*Trust your instincts—they will guide you well. There is something strange happening on the other side of the lake. Many animals have moved to our forest from there. They say there is an evil lurking in the shadow of the mountain. I can fly there and tell you what I see.*

"Thank you, Ferana."

*Be careful in the woods, Claire.*

She opened her wings like an enormous fan, and with one great flap soared above me. I watched her climb higher and higher until she was just a black speck against the violet sky.

I took a deep breath, and everything went back to normal. I could hear all the animals again, and the sounds of the forest. Any uncertainty I had before was gone. I knew I was on the right path—no matter where it led me. This is what I was meant to do.

I turned and walked back toward the shed. I sensed something strange, though; an eerie quiet had descended in the forest. I leaped over a large tree trunk, almost falling, and grabbed a branch to steady myself. Suddenly, I heard footsteps behind me. I snapped my head around, and there he was. Dylan.

He didn't look good. His handsome face was drawn, a

shadow of a beard on his chin. But it was his eyes that startled me most; his eyes were wild.

"What's wrong?"

He took my hand. "Claire, if I asked you to do something, would you—no questions asked?" His voice was rough and urgent.

"I'd try."

"Come away with me, right now."

"What? Where?"

He shook his head impatiently. "The *where* doesn't matter. I'm in over my head, and I need to go—but I can't go without you. I'll explain everything later."

Oh, how I longed to say yes, but I couldn't. "A different time I would have, but I can't now. There's something I need to do, and I'm afraid I may…" I paused, searching for the words to tell him I would probably be dead soon. "I may need to go away, and I'm not sure I'll be able to come back."

My breath caught in my throat as he suddenly pulled me in to him, holding my waist tightly. I could feel his heart pounding against my thin tank top. "Please, come with me." He leaned forward, his face barely an inch from mine, and then, for the first time, he kissed me. I had dreamed of it a thousand times, but it was so much better than I had imagined. He kissed me like I was all that mattered, and I melted into his arms.

He pulled away, his face still so close I could feel his warm breath on my lips. His eyes were desperately searching mine, but I didn't know what he hoped to find there. "You have to come with me right now," he pleaded.

My heart was beating so fast, it took me a few seconds to breathe normally enough to talk. "I can't—my parents are missing. I can't go."

"What? Your parents?" He closed his eyes. "Oh no," he said, shaking his head. "For how long?"

"Since yesterday. I can't go anywhere until I find them."

He stared at me, his eyes full of regret. "I'm sorry," he said as he caressed the side of my face with the back of his fingers.

His skin felt strange, all wrinkly. I put my hand on his, and he quickly pulled away, but not before I grabbed it. I turned it over and gasped. His hand was black in parts, pink in others, and the palm was flat and smooth, with no lines whatsoever.

"What happened?"

He frowned. "I told you, I burned it."

I stared at his deformed hand. I could only imagine the pain he must have felt. "On what?"

He pulled it away without answering.

"Claire? Is that you?"

Dylan's eyes darted in Billy's direction. "Who's that?"

"That's my brother. Come meet him."

He shook his head furiously. "Quick—take my hand! Come with me—just for a few weeks," he pleaded.

"I wish I could, I do, but I can't."

He closed his eyes, as if he were in pain.

"Claire!"

I looked in Billy's direction. "Over here!"

I turned back, but Dylan was gone.

It was as if he had vanished into thin air.

# CHAPTER 21
# Uncle Christopher

A moment later I could see Billy. "Were you talking to someone?"

I continued to scan the woods, but there was no trace of Dylan.

"Claire?"

"No, I wasn't talking to anyone," I said distractedly, looking over Billy's shoulder. Where did he go?

"You look funny. Are you feeling okay? You're face is all red."

"I'm fine," I said a little too forcefully. "What are you doing out here?"

"I think it's safer to use the shed entrance."

I nodded. "Me too."

He gave me a rueful look. "Listen, I don't want you in the woods—period. I'm afraid that somehow it's suddenly just gonna come to you, and you'll be able to communicate with animals. We can't let that happen. So promise me, okay?"

I looked away from him. Another person I cared about pleading with me, and again I couldn't do what he asked. But I wasn't going to lie to him—at least about this. "I was practicing, and it worked," I admitted. "I communicated with the hawk."

"Claire, what are you doing?" He rubbed his temples as if trying to keep his head from exploding.

"Don't, Billy, all right? It's not like I *want* to die."

"Then stop it! Go away from here!"

I shook my head vehemently. "Put yourself in my place. You know you can save all of them, but you run away to save yourself, and then they all die. How would that feel? Do you think a day would go by when you didn't think of them and regret your decision?"

He looked away. "It's not what Mom and Dad would want."

"Well, I have news for you: we don't know what they'd want, because they're not here." I could feel my eyes start to water. I shut them tightly and took a deep breath. "I have to try. It's my destiny."

At ten to eleven Henry grabbed his backpack and told Billy and me it was time. We left the bomb shelter through the tunnel and waited in the woods near the shed. After a few minutes I saw a doe watching us cautiously from behind a row of pine trees. She was leery of us, but neither she nor the other animals were aware of anyone else in the woods. Then suddenly, all of the animals buzzed with the same thought—*strangers*. "Ally and Winny are coming—let's go," I said.

"Are you sure?" Billy asked. "I don't see—"

"There," I pointed. I could just make out their shapes in the darkness. They were walking through the trees toward us, wearing dark, hooded clothes.

"You both look like assassins or something," Henry said, laughing lightly.

I laughed, too. It felt funny in my throat; it was the first time I had laughed in a long time.

We crept through the forest in single file; I was last. The night was moonless, which was certainly to our advantage. I listened for Ferana, but I couldn't sense her.

Billy waited for me to catch up to him. "Do you hear anything?" he whispered.

"It's hard to tell—the animals keep thinking *stranger* and *danger*, but it's probably only us."

Henry took a step into the quad, peering across the lawn. "Let's go."

I kept glancing at Principal Grogan's house—one light was on in an upstairs corner room. I prayed he stayed at home as we sprinted across the grass.

Soon we reached the French doors at the side of the dining hall, but they were locked. Henry quickly opened them with his insta-key, and we all slipped into the cafeteria, our footsteps echoing in the massive hall. Then we climbed the stairs and darted to Grogan's office, which was adjacent to my mother's.

There were several locks on the door, but Henry opened them quickly. Once inside, Billy shut the blinds and swept his flashlight across the room. Grogan had a suite, with a reception area, an office, and a bathroom. "Let's split up," Billy said.

"What are we looking for?" Ally whispered.

Henry stroked his chin in concentration. "Probably an electronic storage chip—something that he could access but wouldn't leave a trace."

Ally shook her head. "A chip? How are we going to find something that small?"

"I have something that'll help." Henry opened his backpack and, grinning from ear to ear, removed a small cell phone.

"How's a cell phone gonna work when Cambial's a dead zone?" Winny asked skeptically.

"I modified it. It will detect any electronic device."

"What if the device isn't on?" Billy asked.

Henry sighed at our collective ignorance. "High-powered electronics emit a pulse and monitor for a response. Do you want me to explain exactly how it works?"

"No—definitely not," Ally answered.

"Then let's get going already. Look everywhere you can think of. A chip could be under a cup or taped to a doorframe."

"Come on," Winny said to me, walking over to the far wall where the yearly school photographs were hung. "Maybe there's a safe behind one of them." But she didn't pick up any of the pictures; she just stood there, staring at one.

"Winny? What is it?"

She pointed at Chey, her bottom lip quivering. I put my arm around her shoulder. For the first time I could see the resemblance between Winny and Chey, not so much in features, but in expression—Chey was wide-eyed and happy, as if eager to see what life had in store for him.

"We'll find him—don't worry. We're going to find all of them."

She nodded and helped me remove all the photographs, but there was nothing behind them.

"Hey! Come here!" Henry called from the bathroom.

We all crowded into the bathroom as Henry held his contraption in front of him. "I'm getting a very weak reading from in here."

"The bathroom?" Ally sounded skeptical. "Who hides things in the bathroom?"

Winny whipped around. "Claire—your family does!"

Of course! Billy's eyes met mine. There was no shower, but I'd bet anything there was a secret room behind one of the walls.

But which one? And how were we going to access it?

It was a typical bathroom—just a toilet, a pearly marble vanity, and white paneled walls. "It has to be behind the vanity," I said.

And then I heard a noise: the soft tread of footsteps in the next room. I put my hand up to signal everyone to stop talking. How loud had we been? Had someone heard us?

As if answering my unspoken question, the crystal doorknob slowly turned. I looked from one terrified face to the other—we were trapped; there was no way out. Henry took the flashlight from his pocket and stood behind the door, ready to pounce.

The door crept open. There, on the other side, was Charlotte.

"Charlotte! What are you doing?" I was relieved and furious at the same time. "You should be in your room!"

"So should you," she snapped. "I saw you guys running across the quad—that sweatshirt's not a good disguise, Billy, and I could see the silver strip on your backpack, Henry. Anyway, I want to help with whatever you're doing."

Billy frowned. "You shouldn't be here—it isn't safe!"

"Whatever! No one's told me anything! What's going on?"

"I'm sorry, Charlotte," I said. "We'll explain everything later, but right now we're trying to find student records on a chip or something, and we think it's behind that wall."

Billy disconnected the sink pipe. "That should do it. Now, let's try to move it." He and Henry each took an end.

"On my count," Billy said. "One, two, *three*." They strained against the marble, but it didn't budge.

"Billy, it's no use; this thing is solid," Henry said, his breath labored.

Billy continued to pull, groaning, his face tomato red. Finally he let go. "Wait, William Crane built this, right? So maybe there's some science or math thing you have to do."

I had a flash of intuition. "No—but you're right. It was Grandfather Paul who turned this into a bathroom, remember? And he was telekinetic…that's how you move it."

Billy shook his head. "It's too heavy. Nobody can move this!"

"Yes you can!" Winny exclaimed. "Once you can move one thing, you can move almost anything. The only difference is in your mind."

"Well, it's all yours," Billy scoffed. "Go ahead, give it a try."

"Can everyone wait outside? If it goes too far"—

Billy snorted.

—"I don't want anyone to get hurt. And please be quiet."

We all waited outside, riveted.

Winny closed her eyes for a minute. The most serene look spread across her face. She slowly lifted her hands, palms up, fingers spread out. The vanity trembled. She raised her hands higher, and it floated several feet in the air. With a gentle wave of her fingers, the vanity glided through the air to the adjacent wall and landed softly on the floor.

"You are amazing, Winny," Henry said.

Ally laughed lightly. "A goddess!"

"You can do it, too, Billy. I'll teach you."

Billy nodded, then quickly looked away.

Henry rubbed his gadget across the exposed wall. "This is it! The reading is increasing."

"How are we going to get behind the wall?" Ally said.

"It's just like our bomb shelter!" I crouched on the ground, feeling the pipe. It was stuck. "Billy, help me turn it."

Together we got it to move, two revolutions counterclockwise, one clockwise.

Click.

I pushed a panel back, revealing a small, dark room.

I peered inside and sighed. "It's empty."

Charlotte shook her head, staring over my head at something. "No it isn't." She moved forward, toward the opening. "Hello, my name is Charlotte. Yes, I'm a Crane. I'm Charlotte Crane Walker, and this," she said, pointing to me, "is my sister, Claire, and this is my brother, Billy. These are our friends Henry, Ally, and Winny."

She was talking to a ghost, and it was right in front of me.

Charlotte nodded her head, smiling. "I remember you!" She looked back at me. "This is our great-uncle Christopher—Nana Marie's brother. He used to visit me when I was little, before Nana died."

I knew the story well. Christopher had died in a car accident when he was a teenager. Although Nana Marie couldn't see ghosts, she was able to communicate with him through my dad's parents, Jillian and Edmund, and also through Charlotte.

There was a long pause. "I'm so sorry, but she's dead. Yes. He's dead, too. They were all killed in a plane crash a few years ago." She nodded her head, crying. "I don't know why. They don't visit me, either, and I miss them."

Charlotte listened for several minutes, and then turned back to us. "He says that something is very wrong. When Christopher died, he came to the school to be near his sister. Grandpa Paul was principal then. Whenever he went away, he would ask Christopher to guard this room. When they left four years ago, Christopher came, but Grandpa never returned."

"He's been in there for four years?" Billy said incredulously.

Charlotte nodded again. "Time passes differently for ghosts."

Grandpa Paul, Nana Marie, Grandma Jillian, and Grandpa Edmund were on a mysterious assignment when their plane crashed four years ago. I now had a terrible feeling that the mission involved Wilder. "Where did Grandpa go?" I asked.

Charlotte looked into the empty chamber, and then back at

us, her face pale. "To find Timothy Wilder. The clairvoyants saw that he was still alive and had built an evil machine."

I took in a sharp breath. We had worried that Wilder was alive, but to hear that he was most likely behind all of this—my grandparents' deaths, the missing students, my parents' disappearance—terrified me.

Henry hung his head low. "I knew it was him. I just knew it."

"Christopher wanted to go and help them, and stay near Marie," Charlotte continued, "but Grandpa said no, it would be too dangerous."

That didn't make any sense. What could be dangerous for a ghost?

"Well…," Billy said, his voice strong and resounding in the small room, "it's what we feared. He's behind it. We need to work together and figure out what he's up to, before it's…"

His voice got raspy and trailed off, so I continued. "While we still can. If he's able, he will eventually take over this school, like he tried to before. He doesn't just want the powerful graduates, he wants the students—because our minds are still forming and growing. But we can use those powers against him. We can do it." It felt strange to include myself, but I knew now that I belonged at Cambial. This was my school, and I would protect it.

Henry nodded. "You're right. We just need to stick together."

I looked again into the darkness. This time I could see something there—not a person, but a shadowy, glowing substance, like a puff of iridescent smoke. "Uncle Christopher, I want you to know that Nana Marie talked about you all the time." I didn't know if he could hear me, but I needed to say it. "My parents are gone, too. They've been kidnapped." My voice trembled. "Please help us. Is there a file somewhere? Something with information on it? We're trying to find out about someone named Josephine."

An unnatural silence descended on the room. All of our eyes were fixed on Charlotte. She nodded, looking very somber and then surprised. "Are you sure?" she said. Finally, she translated. "Christopher knows Josephine—she's Uncle Dan's wife."

My head was reeling. "Wife? No, he never married."

154

There was another long pause before Charlotte spoke again. "Christopher often visited Josephine. She was an Exceptional and had a few specials: she was a truth seeker, a medium, and a clairvoyant. She was doing something dangerous—if anyone found out, it could have cost her her life. Josephine and Uncle Dan married in secret, right before she left Cambial, about twenty years ago. Christopher was at the wedding."

Charlotte turned back to face Christopher, and then said, "The storage device is under a loose floorboard."

The loose board wasn't hard to find in the tiny room. I lifted it up and pulled out a small chip and several long canisters. I handed Henry the chip. "What are these for?" I asked, holding up the canisters.

"That's how Grandpa Paul contacted Christopher in an emergency," Charlotte answered. "Christopher is very upset. He's going to try to find out what happened to Nana Marie. He doesn't understand why she hasn't come to find him. Remember, if we need his help, we should shoot up a flare and he'll come right away."

"I'm so sorry," I said softly. I watched as the shimmering mist came toward me. I felt a cold gust of air swirl around me in an embrace and then fly from the room.

"He's gone."

"Could you see him?" Charlotte asked.

"No. Well, not really, just sort of a mist."

She stared at me. "Really? That's what I used to see when I was really little. Have you ever seen that before?"

I shook my head.

"It may just be because he's our uncle and you're sensitive, but you never know. You should try to work on it."

I nodded, but I felt a flash of bitterness. I would never be able to. I was just getting a taste of...well, of life, really, of developing my powers, discovering new ones, forming friendships, and feeling like I did when I was with Dylan, whatever that was, but I had to push all of it out of my mind. If I was going to save my family, that was the only thing I could focus on.

"We better get out of here," Billy said.

"Hey—wait a second," Henry said, staring at his thingamajig. "It's still going off."

"You're still holding the chip," Billy pointed out.

Henry shook his head impatiently. "It's pointing at you, Billy." He walked toward him, scanning him like a security guard at the airport. The beeping noise got louder. He pointed it toward Billy's wrist. "It's your watch—give it to me."

Billy handed it to Henry, who removed the back. "Here it is—a tracker."

I couldn't believe my ears. "What? He's being tracked? No way, Uncle Dan…" My voice trailed off. First the folder, now this!

"It can't be—Dan McAllister gave it to me," Billy said firmly. "Why would he want to track me?"

"I don't know, but someone put a tracker in this watch," Henry said gravely.

"He gave one to all of us," Billy said slowly, "Claire, me, and Charlotte."

Henry scanned Charlotte's watch. As he removed another tracker my heart sank even lower.

"Claire?"

"I lost mine in the woods, remember? Someone else must have done this," I said, desperately trying to convince myself.

"We'll figure it out later. Right now we've got to get out of here," Billy said, smashing the tracking device. "We've been here too long."

Winny and I went into the sitting area. She put files back in the credenza while I sorted the school pictures we'd taken down. I looked at an old photograph of Chey; he had to have been thirteen or fourteen. He looked so happy, it broke my heart. I prayed we would find him alive, along with my parents. As I hung it on the wall something caught my eye. Actually, not some*thing*, some*one*. I did a double take. There was no denying it. Standing two rows diagonally behind Chey was Dylan.

The bottom dropped out of my stomach.

"Winny, do you know who that is?" I said, pointing at Dylan, my hand trembling.

She moved closer to the photo, squinting at his face. "No. He sure is cute, though."

Billy stood at the door. "Come on, we *really* have to get out of here."

I felt Henry peering over my shoulder. "I know who that is—Dylan Bartow. He was a couple of years ahead of me."

"Guys, come *on*," Billy urged.

Was? "What happened to him?" I tried to sound nonchalant.

"He was expelled in tenth grade. After that, I don't know. He was bad news."

I felt like I was going to vomit. Bad news? Dylan? *Why was he expelled?*

Billy whirled around again, this time wearing a look of complete and utter panic. Footsteps were thundering down the hall, and they were growing louder.

# CHAPTER 22
# The Anipath

We all scanned the room frantically for someplace to hide. I was sure Billy was calculating how long it would take Winny to move the vanity again so we could hide in the secret room, but I knew there wasn't enough time.

Winny nodded at Billy, pointing to the awards that lined Grogan's bookcase. He nodded back. Silently the heavy metal statues flew into their outstretched hands as they both inched behind the door. I pulled Charlotte and Ally behind me.

They were right outside.

"Do you have the key?" a deep voice said.

"Got it," a muffled voice responded.

We waited, holding our breaths. A door opened and shut. But not the door to Grogan's office, the door to my mother's. Thank God she didn't keep any of her important files in there.

Billy peered out into the hall. He motioned to us and we quietly rushed away, out through the cafeteria and toward the woods. As I looked back at Crane Hall I thought I saw someone standing in the window of my mother's office, watching us. But my mind must have been playing tricks on me because the figure vanished before my eyes.

I ran behind everyone, last again, and I was thankful for the solitude. My brain couldn't seem to process what I had just learned. How could I have been so stupid? I knew nothing about Dylan, nothing at all. Except, of course, the one true thing he ever told me—he got kicked out of school for breaking the rules. That should have been a warning to me! But no, I went ahead and told him all about my life, my family—everything except specials. I'd even told him my parents were investigating the disappearance of the students! He must have run and told Wilder, who abducted my parents before they got too close. They were gone, and it was all my fault.

Soon my anger turned to rage. All the lies he told me about how he felt he knew me! It was all just a trick. He'd go out to the rock whenever he needed some information, knowing I'd be sitting there like an idiot, waiting for him.

And then it hit me; did he actually *know* I'd be there? Was he involved with the trackers? He could have slipped one in my watch easily the afternoon I fell asleep on the rock, but how could he have put trackers in Charlotte's and Billy's watches without them noticing? Either way, the sad truth was that if he needed information, all he had to do was bat his gorgeous eyes at me and I'd tell him anything he wanted to know. As furious as I was with him, I was even madder at myself. I had to set this right.

I was so lost in my thoughts, I was surprised when we reached our backyard. Yet as I waited for my turn to dash into the shed my skin began to crawl. I searched the thoughts of the animals, but they were quiet, as they often were at night. Was someone out there lurking in the shadows? Could the men who broke into my mom's office have seen us and followed? I shuddered and ran into the shed before I was supposed to.

I slid down the trapdoor, almost landing on top of Billy, who went right before me. "Claire, you're supposed to wait."

"Well, hurry up next time."

As we headed down the tunnel, Billy turned his annoyed expression from me to Charlotte. "Do you see why we didn't bring you along with us?"

"What would you have done if I wasn't there?" she retorted, her hands on her hips. "I don't think any of you can talk to ghosts."

She was right about that. But my mind wasn't on our close call—it was still on Dylan. Billy opened the door, ushering us all into the bomb shelter. "So Henry, why did that Dylan kid get expelled?" I asked softly.

"He was amazing—really talented—but he was always breaking the rules. He won the TT every year, even when he was in sixth grade, and he started Cambial a year early, like Charlotte. Story goes your mother gave him warning after warning, but he kept experimenting, you know, in what was forbidden. Finally, he got kicked out."

"Why?" I said offhandedly.

"I heard he got mad at some kid and sent him sailing into a wall. He had real anger issues."

How could I have been so wrong? "Was the kid he threw all right?"

"Yeah, but his parents had a fit, demanded Bartow go. No one was surprised, though, considering both his parents were big supporters of Wilder."

I stepped back, as if Dylan himself had pushed me. I didn't want to believe any of this. But deep down, I knew it was true.

"What's up with the questions?" Billy asked, regarding me carefully. "Do you know him?"

I looked away quickly. "No, just curious," I lied.

"Do you think he could be involved?" Winny asked, her eyes huge.

"I was just thinking the same thing," Henry said.

I wished more than anything that I were alone. I felt like punching something and crying at the same time, and I wasn't sure how long I could keep acting as if nothing was wrong. I wasn't that good an actress.

Henry downloaded the files onto his laptop. They were encrypted, of course, but it didn't take long for him and Ally to hack in. There were hundreds of files—on every student, on every significant event, and on every prediction—up until my grandfather's death.

"Should we start with that Dylan kid?" Winny asked.

"No," I said a little too forcefully. I wanted to know more about Dylan, but I needed time to compose myself. If there was more bad stuff in those files…Well, I wasn't sure how much I could take before I snapped. "We need to start with Josephine."

I looked over at Charlotte, who had fallen asleep. I envied her, wishing I could tune everything out and escape into a dream. I gently put my sweatshirt under her head.

"So," Billy began, "the first entry is written by Paul Crane." He read parts out loud as he skimmed the file. "'Josephine Morrow is one of the most gifted students in Cambial's history.' Um, let's see....Oh, get this, she was very well liked and was friends with Wilder, and when he got caught breaking Crane's Commandments—the first time—she interceded on his behalf. Wilder was given a warning and kept on staff.

"Next entry: Maura Crane. Wow, listen to this: 'After Josephine graduated, Wilder mistook her kindness for something more and fell in love with her. He was caught breaking Crane's Commandments again, with a group of Exceptionals, and fired. Wilder brought Josephine to his lab, blindfolded, on the pretense that he was making amazing discoveries to better mankind. Those who joined him expanded their powers dramatically. She reported that Wilder and Grainer had built weapons that could destroy a city, and his followers were practicing telekinesis on people. Wilder told her he was going to start his own school. He asked her to join them; she refused. He let her go and shortly thereafter attacked the school.'"

Billy paused. The air was heavy with silence. "Next entry: Paul Crane. 'Clairvoyants' predictions pertaining to Wilder's weapons become more vivid and frequent. Josephine Morrow to infiltrate Wilder's inner circle and learn plans.'

"And Paul Crane again: 'Morrow reports lab in northern Maine near Canadian border. Plans to blow up Cambial. Morrow discovered the machine he was building could alter the course of humanity, able to destroy all life forms without leaving a trace.'" He looked up at us, terror in his eyes.

I felt a chill run through me. Wilder really was a monster.

"And the last entry, still Paul Crane: 'All contact with Josephine lost. Lab eventually located. A team was deployed—myself, Marie, Maura Crane, Charles Walker, Jillian and Edmund Walker, Dan McAllister. The Premises were infiltrated, a fight ensued, the lab blew up. No bodies were found. All presumed dead, including Josephine Morrow.'"

I thought about Uncle Dan; no wonder he was so sad and lonely. And poor Josephine.

"Let's see what we can find out about Wilder," Billy continued. "While he was a student here he was almost expelled....He performed an unauthorized science experiment that went terribly wrong, exposing himself to a very high level of radiation. And here, Mom chronicled strange incidents that happened when he was a professor—things she suspected him of, but could never prove. She wrote that he was a master manipulator who could lie to anyone, including her, and that he craved power and would stop at nothing to get what he wanted. According to mom, he was obsessed with Josephine."

Ally sat next to Billy, peering over his shoulder. "Hey—look at this. There's a long list of clairvoyant predictions that he's still alive. And a bunch about an anipath. What's an anipath?"

Billy quickly moved the file away. "Let's focus on Wilder," he said, turning the page.

Ally frowned and grabbed it out of his hand. "No, I saw something about Cambial, too."

Billy shot me a helpless look as Ally continued to skim the folder. "Cool—an anipath is someone who can perform telepathy with animals. I've never even heard of it! Oh, that's so sad...." She paused. "Cambial is saved by an anipathic girl, but she dies."

Henry looked horrified. "Dies? Are you sure?"

Ally nodded. "That's what it says."

"That must be the girl in my visions!" Winny exclaimed. "And I had another vision of her last night," she said, a far-off look in her eyes. "She was standing by a stream with the hawk, and then she was alone in a dark room, her hands over her ears as if there was a terrible noise. She pulled a big black tube, and then she was lying on the ground, dead."

So that was how it was going to happen. Somehow, I'd have to find that dark room.

"Did you see her face?" Billy asked anxiously.

She shook her head.

"This vision you have—it won't necessarily come true, will it?" Henry's voice was shaking as he said it.

Ally, always perceptive, looked from me to Billy to Henry. "What's wrong? Why are you so worried about this girl?"

"I'm sure we're all worried about this girl," I answered quickly. "I mean, if that vision is connected to Wilder, some girl at the school is going to die. If we can find out who it is, maybe we can help her and it won't happen. My Nana Marie," I said, staring directly at Billy, "told me that visions could change. They were just a shadowy version of the future that may or may not happen."

Winny looked doubtful. "That's true—in theory—but your mother told me the more times someone has a vision, the more likely it is to happen. I'm positive there's a girl—an anipath— who can communicate with a hawk. She may be the one who saves the school, but she could die first, for example, and then it wouldn't come true."

How cheery to think that in either scenario I'm dead.

"Or she could have people there to protect her!" Billy said angrily.

Ally and Winny both stared at him, obviously surprised by his outburst.

"Billy, why—" Ally began.

"If only we knew who she was!" I interrupted. "But since we don't, we can't waste time on it. Let's work on a plan. We can't just hope this girl swoops in and saves the day for us." I forced myself to push aside any thoughts of my own fate; I had to stay focused. "So let's get back to the files."

"Claire's right," Winny said. "Hey—look up that Dylan kid. He sounded like he could be involved, too."

Not the distraction I was looking for. I could feel Henry's eyes fixated on me, gauging my reaction.

Billy searched through the files. "There's one little blurb in the section on Wilder. It's one of the last ones—Grandpa must have written it right before he died. 'Dylan Bartow.

Parents—John and Catherine, fierce followers of Wilder, killed in explosion with Wilder when Dylan was a baby. Raised by grandparents. Sent to Cambial at age ten, youngest student ever admitted. Loner. Extremely talented at telekinesis. Anger issues. Caught using forbidden talents. Broke Crane's Commandments three times—last time injured fellow student Sam Hutchins. Maura Crane argued to give him one last chance but was overruled. Expelled.'"

Henry shook his head in disgust. "I told you he was bad news. I remember him. But hearing that—his file sounds just like Wilder's. They're two of a kind."

He was right. I felt my heart sink. I was hoping against hope that there would be something in his file that would explain everything. Far from it. One thing did surprise me, though; my hard-ass mother argued against him being expelled. I couldn't imagine why.

Ally yawned. "We should go try to get some sleep before classes."

"We can all stay here, no need to risk getting caught," I answered. "There are enough bunks for everyone."

Henry looked relieved to have company.

We had to be up in a few hours, but I barely slept. I had screwed up royally. But maybe, just maybe, I could find a way to fix it.

I woke up early and read over the files again while everyone was still sleeping. After raiding the freezer for bagels, I announced I was going to take Darwin for a walk and asked Winny to tell my teachers I was sick. When everyone left for campus, I said a hurried good-bye to Henry, took care of Darwin at record speed, and ran to the woods in search of Ferana. There was no sign of her. Finally I saw Talrin, who by now was much bigger. I waved my arms in the air. "Hello!" I called out.

Talrin circled overhead, flying lower and lower, and then turned and dove right toward me. Normally, I would have been frightened, but I could hear him clearly.

*Thank you for saving me!*

"You're welcome." Talrin landed roughly on my outstretched arm, staring at me with his curious black eyes. I gently stroked his velvety back, all the way down to his dark gray tail. I felt an energy flow between us and envelop us, shutting out everything else in the forest.

*Mother says your name is Claire and you can understand me.*

"I can. Why is your tail gray, but your mother's is red?"

*Mine will turn red when I get bigger,* he said, fanning it out proudly behind him. It was charcoal gray, with several darker bands. *Can you hear all of the animals?*

"Yes, but some not as clearly as others. I can hear you and your mother very well."

*Why?*

"I don't know why. Maybe it's because we have a connection now."

*What's that?*

"We both care about you. Let me try something. You can understand me when I speak, but I can hear your thoughts. I wonder if you can hear mine, too. I'm going to think of something, and tell me if you can understand me." I closed my eyes and concentrated. *Move to my other arm,* I thought.

I felt something heavier than Talrin land on my other arm. I opened my eyes, and there was Ferana, staring at me.

*Surprised?* she asked.

Talrin looked like he was smiling. *I could hear you!*

*As could I,* Ferana thought.

*I'm going to the stream now. Good-bye, Claire!* He swiftly lifted off, poking me with his sharp talon. A drop of blood quickly collected on my wrist.

*Talrin, you've cut Claire. Be more careful.*

*Sorry!*

She turned her head back to me. *Are you hurt?*

*I'm fine.* I grinned. *He flies well now,* I thought, watching him rocket above the trees, and then sharply swoop down.

*He wouldn't have survived without you.*

I smiled. At least I had done one thing right.

*Claire, I have flown from here to Shadow Mountain, but I have seen nothing. The animals left because they could feel a current and sense a grave danger.*

That was it. The tube must be there, even if she couldn't see it. *Thank you.*

*Claire, do not cross the lake. I could feel the danger when I flew over it. There is a darkness surrounding the mountain, and it is growing.*

*Thank you for warning me, but he has my family there. I have to try to save them.*

*I understand. You saved my family—if I can help you save yours, I will. But be very careful.*

*I will.*

She lifted straight up, beat her wings gracefully, and then soared above me, disappearing from sight.

To my surprise I found myself at the field. With a sudden flash of bitterness, I realized that I desperately needed to see Dylan. I was sure he knew where my parents were. I climbed up on the rock, surveying the woods around me. At the edge of the water, I saw the turtle. I tried to clear my mind and ask her a question, but she couldn't hear me. For hours I listened to the animals that visited the stream, but none of them were thinking about a danger lurking across the lake.

Reluctantly, I headed for the shed as the afternoon slipped away. I hurried, knowing everyone would be concerned; I'd stayed longer than I should have. As I walked past a grove of pine trees I thought I saw something move out of the corner of my eye. I turned, and then someone grabbed me from behind.

I struggled with all my might, but I couldn't get away.

Strong arms pulled me inside the thicket.

# CHAPTER 23
# Through the Tunnel

I almost screamed for help—then I saw his face. It was Dylan.

"Let go of me!" I snarled, slapping his arm off of my waist.

"Shhh!" He put his finger to his lips.

"I know everything. I know you were expelled from Cambial."

"Listen to me—"

"So you can tell me more lies?" I spat. "Trick me into telling you something else? The only thing I want to hear from you is where my parents are."

"Wilder has them."

I was stunned that he admitted it so easily. "Where?"

He swallowed. "I can't tell you. But I'll do everything I can to save them, I promise I will."

"Oh, okay, sure. The big liar promises. I feel so much better now."

"Claire, you have to believe me."

"Then tell me exactly where they are!"

"Look, after I was expelled, Wilder found me. He was going by a different name. He didn't look the same—he was scarred pretty badly. He had a lab, and he showed me all of these amazing inventions. He was so powerful, so—I don't know how to describe it—so compelling. He taught me ways to control my special, and things I could do—it blew my mind.

"And then I met this guy Clay who worked for him. Clay said he knew my parents, and they were so talented, but they were killed by your parents and grandparents, and McAllister. You have no idea what it's like to grow up without parents! Anyway, eventually I found out I was really working for Timothy Wilder. I confronted him, and he told me how your family disfigured him, and ruined him, and murdered my parents—and what I had heard about him was lies, like the lies they told about me!" he exploded. "I never threw that kid across the room. I would have liked to, but I didn't."

"My family tried to stop Wilder because he's evil! His plan to destroy the school is nothing compared to the destruction he'll cause with his weapons!"

"I know that now," he said softly.

"And if you didn't hurt that kid, what happened?"

"Oh—I hurt him. I just didn't use telekinesis to do it—I used my fist. All he cared about was the stupid TT. I beat him every year, and he knew I'd beat him again. This way he got rid of me and didn't have to admit I beat the crap out of him."

"I don't believe anything you say!" I shouted. "You lied to me! You never cared—you just used me!"

"That's not true—and keep your voice down," he said, looking around furtively. "You weren't exactly honest when I first met you, either. You said you went to Lakeville. And then you said you didn't go to afternoon classes, so I knew you didn't have a special. I just…liked you. Liked talking to you. I figured your dad was the security guard or something. I didn't think being friends with you had anything to do with what I was doing for Wilder. And then when I saw you again and you told me your last name, I was shocked. I tried to stay away."

I snorted. "But you needed to see me—to get information."

"No, that's not why."

"Why were you in the woods to begin with? Some secret mission for Wilder? Get information on my family? Break into my house, trash it, and steal my mother's files?"

He looked away. "Yes. To all three. I didn't steal your mother's files, but I did scan them. But I swear, I didn't know why. He said he wanted to know what your parents had on him. We could use the information to start our own school, free of rules and limitations. I hated Cambial and your whole family. I blamed them for my parents' deaths, for being expelled, for ruining my life!" He paused and took a deep breath, calming down. "I let it consume me."

I crossed my arms angrily. "Don't you dare try to justify yourself to me. People are missing, don't you get it? My friends, my family!"

He shook his head. "I didn't know anyone had been kidnapped until you told me. He denied it—even you weren't positive they were really taken—but something didn't seem right. So I decided to bail. I didn't want to make the same mistakes my parents did."

"Then why didn't you leave for good?"

A shadow crossed over his face. "Something happened to change my mind. But Wilder trusts me, and I know where he's holding them. *I'll* free everyone, so you don't need to do anything." He leaned toward me and stroked my cheek. "Promise me."

I couldn't believe his nerve. "I'm not going to promise you anything!" I said, swatting away his hand.

"Claire, I swear I'm trying to help you." He ran his fingers through his dark waves. "Look—I can prove it. I'm the one who took your watch—it had a tracker in it."

I thought back to that day I got lost. "That was really you in the woods?"

He nodded. "I couldn't just leave you out there lost, so I followed you. When you tripped and fell, I stayed with you. I took your watch, and when I heard people searching, I threw rocks so you'd be found."

He grabbed my arm, pulling me back to him. "I once asked you if you thought you knew me. You said you did. Do you really think I would hurt you?"

I looked at his face, so handsome it took my breath away. Could he be telling me the truth? I wanted to believe him, but he had fooled me before.

His arms encircled my waist, and he drew me in closer. I could have pulled away, but I didn't. My brain kept telling me to leave, but I stayed there, inches from him. It felt like my heart would burst through my chest.

"Claire, come with me," he implored.

"No," I whispered, not very convincingly.

"Please trust me." He brushed my cheek with the back of

his hand, then leaned forward to kiss me. Despite everything, I wanted nothing more than to kiss him back. I truly was a fool. I summoned all my self-control and pushed him away.

"I don't trust you—I never will!" I turned and bolted toward the shed, trying to get the image of his stunned face out of my mind. I ran as fast as I could, away from him, away from the jumble of thoughts and feelings that were breaking my heart.

"I think I know where they're being held," I panted, throwing open the door to the bomb shelter. "On the other side of the lake."

Henry was alone. He stared at me, stunned. "Why do you think that?"

"I was in the woods and I heard the animals—some came from there because there's danger near Shadow Mountain. I'm sure it has something to do with Wilder." I couldn't bear to tell Henry about Ferana—I knew he'd freak out.

"I doubt he's that close."

"He is."

Just then the shower door creaked open. My nerves were on edge, but it was only Billy, Winny, and Ally.

"Claire," Billy sighed, "you're all right." His expression quickly changed from joy to anger. "You've been gone since morning, and it's seven o'clock. Where the hell have you been?"

Winny and Ally stared at me reproachfully. They were all upset with me, and I couldn't blame them. Unfortunately, it was about to get a lot worse. It was time I told the truth.

"Um...I haven't been entirely honest with you guys," I said, biting my lip. "I do know Dylan—I met him in the woods. He's working for Wilder—or was—I'm not sure now. I just saw him, and he claims he didn't know what Wilder was really up to."

"Jesus, Claire. What did you tell him?" Billy demanded.

Oh, how I wanted to lie. "I told him that Mom and Dad were looking for missing kids from Cambial."

"You WHAT?" Billy screamed.

"Go ahead and yell at me. I deserve it. Wilder knew they were on to him because of me—I'm the reason they were kidnapped. I believed Dylan when he said he was a hiker, and I…blurted it out." I felt like I was being twisted inside out. I thought I'd feel better admitting the truth, but I only felt worse.

Henry glared at me. "And now I suppose you trust him?"

"No." I shook my head. "I don't."

I told them everything except, of course, how I felt about Dylan. Although I was sure Winny and Ally could guess.

"If he's telling the truth, he could help us," Winny pointed out.

"And if he's not?" Henry snapped.

I looked down at my hands on my lap, at my grandmother's ring. I shrugged. I obviously wasn't good at judging people.

Ally took my hand. "What do you think? Could he be telling the truth?"

I wanted to believe him more than anything, but how could you trust a liar?

Just then heavy footsteps from above us echoed through the room. My eyes flashed to Billy's. He opened the door an inch and peered into the basement. Suddenly, a man yelled, "Spread out—she has to be here somewhere!"

I would know that voice anywhere.

It was Dylan.

I stood there, frozen in disbelief, until Henry grabbed my hand and pulled me into the shower. I tried to open the door, fumbling with the dial. As I tried again, an army of thunderous footsteps trampled down the stairs.

"Move over, I'll do it," Billy said, shoving me out of the way. He spun the dial at record speed—*click*—and pushed me into the passageway. "Go!"

I dashed through the tunnel and up into the shed, everyone else behind me. We ran outside and through the darkening woods until we were deep within the forest. When we reached a stream, Winny plopped down on its bank, panting in the warm, sticky air. "I'm taking a break," she announced, cupping her hands and splashing her face with the cool mountain water.

I sat on a rock, rubbing my aching calves. My head was spinning, a sensation I was, unfortunately, getting used to.

Henry sat down next to me. "Let me guess—that was Dylan."

"Yup."

"Well, I guess we know we can't trust him."

"I told you I didn't!" I snapped.

When he spoke again, his voice was much gentler. "He said, 'She's not down here,' Claire. They were searching for you."

"I know." I sighed. "I can't go back."

Ally sat down at the foot of the rock, her elbow on my knee. "What about the rest of us? Should we go back?"

"I have to—for Charlotte," Billy answered. "If they want Claire, maybe they want all of us. I'd better bring Charlotte here—she's a sitting duck at school."

"Who's they?" Ally said.

"Someone at the school's involved with Wilder—Grogan, and who knows who else," Billy answered grimly.

There was a very long pause. No one wanted to say Uncle Dan's name out loud, even though everyone was thinking it.

"Grogan's expelling the kids that Wilder wants," Winny reasoned, "but that's all we know. So many things don't make sense. Like why they're after you, Claire—you don't even have a special—or why Dylan didn't just grab you in the woods. I mean, he had you right there."

My thoughts exactly. Could there possibly be an explanation?

Henry snorted. "He thought Claire would come willingly—it would've been easier to get information out of her if she thought he was trying to help her. I'm sure he was shocked when she didn't, so he must have gotten reinforcements."

There was no arguing with his reasoning. My hope deflated like a pricked balloon.

"I don't like this. I'm leaving now to get Charlotte. We'll meet you back here," Billy said.

"Will you be able to find us?" I asked skeptically.

Billy rolled his eyes, but I wasn't so sure.

Henry opened his backpack. "Well, then I'm glad I thought to take this," he said, removing a filthy blue pup tent. "It was right next to my feet last time I was squatting under the shed window. I had a feeling it might come in handy. Oh, and while I'm at it, here," he said, rummaging around inside the backpack and tossing a bag at each of us. "This is the tracking material— if anyone comes, try to spill some of this and walk in it, or better yet, put it on your shoes. I'll be able to find you and maybe even track the people after you. And here's the insta-key, and—"

I couldn't believe the backpack could hold anything else. He reminded me of Mary Poppins.

"Don't tell me I forgot the healing ointment!"

Suddenly, he looked up, his face horror-stricken. "Oh no, I don't know what's the matter with me."

Ally winked at me. "We can get by without it."

"No, it's my experiments! I left them all in my room. If those formulas fall into wrong hands…I have to go back!"

I shook my head vehemently. "It's too dangerous, Henry."

"Don't worry," he said, although he looked delighted that I was. "I'll be careful."

"Henry, don't let Grogan see you," Billy said. "The rest of you should get back before curfew. I'll get Charlotte and come back as soon as I can, but I don't like the idea of you alone in the woods, Claire, knowing these people are after you." He suddenly looked much older than seventeen.

Winny cocked her head. "It's okay, I don't think they'll find her. They can't search the entire forest. There are hundreds of acres of woods surrounding the school, and then acres of conservation land. This could be the safest place. It's just…"

I was happy to have Winny's support, but I knew something was nagging at her. "What's bothering you, Winny?" I asked.

She sighed. "I know I keep saying it, but you should be the safest one. If Wilder has school files, he'd know you don't have a special, so why does he want you?" And then her mouth fell open, and she stared at me in disbelief. "Wait a minute—it's *you*! She had long, wavy auburn hair. And there was something familiar about her, but I couldn't place it." She paused. "Until now. Oh my God, Claire! The girl with the hawk is *you*."

I felt every pair of eyes on me.

# CHAPTER 24

# a Night with Ferana

Although she didn't ask a question, I still felt compelled to give an answer. "Yes."

"Why didn't you tell us?" Winny didn't accuse me; she sounded betrayed, which made me feel even worse.

"In a dream Nana Marie told me not to tell anyone," I said in a small voice.

"Oh." She smiled, as if that explained it. Then a shadow crossed over her face. "But ... you're going to die."

Ally took in a quick, sharp breath.

Anger flashed across Billy's face. "No, she isn't. My parents sent her to Lakeville High so the predictions wouldn't come true. She's never been formally trained. And she has us to protect her. She isn't going to die."

"Of course not," Henry agreed forcefully. "But maybe this camping thing isn't the best idea. Why can't you just go far away until this is over? I have some money—"

"He'd find me. He knows about the prophecy. He was a professor here, remember? He'd track me down. And he kidnapped Jane Morse—she may see me in the woods, but that isn't going to help much. You're right, Winny; I'm safer out here. And besides, I'm not leaving my parents. Billy, I know you're worried. I know you all are. You can't imagine how much it means to me...." I paused, struggling to keep my composure. "But I'm staying, and my decision is final."

Ally sighed in acquiescence. "But how will we find you if you need to move?"

As I was trying to work out a plan for communicating, I felt

Ferana's presence nearby. I looked up—of course. *Ferana!* I called as I stood up and put my hand out in front of me.

She hovered overhead. *Is it safe?*

*Yes, these are my friends.*

Cautiously, she glided down and landed lightly on my finger. I stroked her soft back. It was strange—I had worked so hard to be able to communicate with animals, and now talking with Ferana was like second nature to me.

"Ferana," I said out loud for their benefit, "this is my brother, Billy, and this is Henry, Ally, and Winny." I pointed to each in turn.

Everyone but Winny stared wide-eyed at Ferana.

Winny took a step forward. "Nice to meet you, Ferana," she said, waving, as if she met giant birds every day. "It's very nice of you to help us."

I translated. Ferana nodded her head once.

"The bad man I told you about—Timothy Wilder, the one who has my parents—is trying to get me, too. I'm going to hide in the woods. Can you show my friends where I am if I need to move?"

*Of course.*

"Claire, what if we need to contact you, but can't get here?" Ally asked. "Is there a place we can meet Ferana and give her a note or something?"

I thought for a moment. "Maxwell's Hole! It's not too far from the school or Ferana's nest. Wait there if you need to reach me." Again I translated for Ferana.

She nodded. *I can see the pond from the nest. I will fly to Shadow Mountain again with Talrin—he is now strong enough for the journey—and question the animals.*

*Thank you so much for all of your help. Wilder has to be there somewhere. I just know it.* I did not say this out loud.

Ferana spread her wings and carefully lifted off from my finger, straight up like a hovercraft, and then with one great flap soared above me. I watched her until she was swallowed by the darkness.

Winny stared at me. "You truly are amazing, Claire."

Me? I had never thought of myself like that before.

Ally looked anxiously at her watch. "We better get going before we miss curfew."

She was right. "Go—don't give Grogan a reason to expel you."

Ally hugged me, looking as if she was going to burst into tears. Winny rested her head on my shoulder, and then grabbed my hand and squeezed it. "Be careful."

Henry and Billy set up the tent in the thicket. I had to admit, it was pretty well concealed.

"Billy, don't come back tonight—it's too risky. Grogan could expel you and Charlotte for being out after curfew. Wait till morning. I'll be okay, really."

"Are you sure about this, Claire?" Billy asked, his voice strained.

I nodded.

Henry put his arm around my shoulder. "Look," he said in a gruff voice, "don't do anything impulsive. Think it through. Listen to the animals for any sign of danger, and stay hidden—all the time."

I nodded. How well he knew me. He was so kind, and smart, and loyal, and honest....Why didn't I like him instead of...I wouldn't even allow myself to finish the thought. Then I remembered what Uncle Dan had quoted when we were studying *Wuthering Heights*. "The heart has its reasons, which reason knows not of." My heart certainly was not listening to reason, and I was going to end up a lot worse than Cathy if I wasn't careful.

"I'll be back soon, and we'll keep you safe. Take this, just in case." Henry removed a flare from his pocket, handed it to me, and kissed the top of my head.

As my friends said one final good-bye, I studied each of their faces, people I had known only a few months risking their lives to protect me. For a second I thought about Tom and imagined how he would think we were all freaks, and perhaps we were. The funny thing was, I didn't care. Tom and the dance seemed like a lifetime ago.

I walked over to the tent, but I couldn't bring myself to go inside. I sat down on a rock and listened to the animals, watching as heavy clouds swallowed the moon and stars, surrounding me with a sea of darkness.

Ferana and Talrin returned just as a gentle rain began to fall. Talrin landed on my shoulder, Ferana on my finger. *I could sense something strange at the base of the mountain, on the western side, close to the lake. It is a barren place, Claire, a dangerous place. Must you go there?*

I nodded. *I have to save my family.*

*When will you leave?*

*Tomorrow.* My insides were churning as I thought it.

*Will you be all right here alone?*

I smiled feebly. *I'll be fine.*

She regarded me with her wise eyes. I was sure I didn't have her fooled. *Talrin, I'm going to stay here with Claire tonight.*

*You don't need to.* I tried to sound strong, but I wasn't sure I pulled it off.

*Mother, does that mean I can hunt and fly through the forest alone?*

*Yes, you are ready. Be careful.*

In his enthusiasm he set off a little too quickly, piercing my shoulder with his long, sharp talon. I winced in surprise.

*Talrin!* Ferana chastised.

*Sorry, Claire!*

*Don't worry about it,* I called, waving at him as he flew in an arc above me. *Thank you for staying, Ferana.*

*I'll be right outside the tent. I'll call if I sense any danger.*

I lay down under the blue plastic canopy, thinking about the last time I'd used it. Every summer my dad and Uncle Dan took us camping up in Maine. We hiked and swam during the day, and ate hamburgers (veggie burgers for me) and made s'mores at night. The highlight of the trip was always Uncle Dan's ghost stories, which he wrote himself. Last year, to his delight, I surprised him and wrote my own. I would give anything now to be under this tent with them instead of here alone, not knowing if they were all okay.

After a while, the heavy air exploded with thunder and rain pelted the tent so hard, it looked like the roof was moving. My thoughts turned to Ferana, out in the thick of it with no nest. *Ferana*, I called, *come in here with me.*

She swooped into the tent, landing lightly on my shoulder.

*I was worried about you out in the storm.*

*I'm used to storms.*

*Would you like to stay in here with me?*

She didn't answer but nestled in a corner of the tent.

I lay down next to her, happy for her company. Eventually the storm receded to a distant grumbling. Sleep did find me, but it was not a restful one, and when I woke, I didn't know where I was. Then I looked around the empty tent and panicked. Where was Ferana? I bolted through the opening, almost knocking her over. She was waiting right outside, guarding the entrance.

*Oh, I was worried about you.*

*I've been listening, and you're safe, Claire. Now I must check on Talrin and hunt, but I will return.*

*Thank you.*

She opened her wings, exposing her soft white stomach with the golden center.

*You have a heart of gold, Ferana.*

She cocked her head to one side.

I smiled. *Your beautiful golden markings, where your heart is. We have an expression to describe someone who is very generous—we say they have a heart of gold, like you.*

I could see her eyes soften. *Like you.*

With a graceful wave of her wings, she soared above me into the golden sunrise, her wings glimmering in the fiery light.

And then she was gone, and once again I was alone.

It was a hot and sticky morning; the storm had done nothing to clear the air. Winny had left me with a bunch of snacks, so I ate a granola bar and followed the stream down to a small pond to wash off. I lay down on the rock, letting the sun dry me as I struggled to figure everything out. The different clues were swirling around my mind like pieces of a puzzle—I just had to figure out how to put them all together.

My thoughts turned to Uncle Dan. Why did he have my mother's file about the anipathic girl—and why did he show it to Grogan? Why had he given us watches with tracking devices? Dylan had known all about the watches. Could Uncle Dan be working for Wilder? But Uncle Dan hated Wilder—he'd killed his wife, Josephine!

And then there was Dylan. He could have easily kidnapped me by now, but he hadn't. And he did take the watch so I couldn't be tracked. But there was no escaping that he'd lied about almost everything. And it had been *his* voice leading the charge to find me.

Frustrated, I jumped down and headed back to the tent to wait for Billy and Charlotte.

*Danger! Stranger in the forest!*

I stopped dead in my tracks as the animals hurried past me. I had a horrible feeling that I was not the stranger they were worried about. I was frantically looking for a hiding spot when the clatter of an engine pierced the stillness. I sprinted toward a fallen oak and dived behind it, squishing myself against the decaying tree.

The roar grew louder, and then suddenly stopped just feet from me.

I took in a sharp breath and held it, listening to heavy footsteps against the crunchy pine needles. They were coming this way.

# CHAPTER 25
## Surrender

"Look—here's her tracks! She went this way!"

I shuddered. Once again Dylan was leading the search. I lifted my head ever so slightly, peering over the log, and saw two men follow Dylan—but for some reason they were headed away from me.

The loud *vrrrrrm* of the dirt bikes roared through the clearing, and then it was quiet. I waited a few minutes to be sure they were gone before carefully lifting my head. The woods were empty—the only sign that they had been there was the air, still thick with dust from the bikes.

*Claire, Claire, where are you?*

I could hear Talrin before I could see him. I leaped to my feet, waving my hands. *I'm here!*

Talrin swooped down between two trees and landed unceremoniously on my shoulder. *Are you okay?*

I nodded. *That was close. Is your mother all right?*

*She told me to check on you*, he said proudly, puffing out his chest as he did, and bouncing over to my finger.

*Thank you*, I said, stroking his feathers with the back of my hand. His stomach had turned from pearly gray to mainly white, with streaks of golden-brown and black.

*Were those men on the bikes looking for you?*

I nodded, imagining Dylan's face. Just thinking about him made me clench my fists.

*If I see them, I'm going to claw them to pieces!*

*Talrin, no. These are really bad men. Stay away from them.*

He hung his small head down, his back hunched up above it.

*You are very brave,* I quickly added, *but your mother wouldn't want you to go after them. I can read her thoughts, so I know how much she worries.*

He stood up tall again. *She doesn't want me to grow up.*

My thoughts turned to my own mother and the lengths she went to trying to keep me safe. *She doesn't want anything to happen to you, because she loves you.* I stroked his head and his back. *I don't want anything to happen to you, either, Talrin, and I would never forgive myself if you got hurt. There is something you can do, though. Can you ask your mother to look for my brother and sister? They should be coming now, but I'm afraid Billy won't remember the way. If she can't find them, ask her to please check the kettle pond.*

*I'll be right back.* Talrin gently lifted off and soared above me, disappearing into the trees. I looked down at my shoulder—not a mark.

I approached the tent carefully, listening to the animals for signs of danger, but it seemed safe. I poked my head in between the pines, and what I saw gripped me with terror. The tent was slashed to pieces, little bits of blue plastic scattered across the ground. The cylinder with the flare to contact Uncle Christopher was smashed and Henry's bags trampled. With a heavy heart I turned around. There was nothing left for me there.

I walked for a few minutes, and then climbed up on a rock to wait for Ferana, hoping she would come soon. Suddenly, I could hear her frantic thoughts. She soared overhead, gliding along the light wind, and then dove right toward me, landing on my outstretched hand.

*I flew to the pond and saw Billy running through the woods with a small girl I did not recognize. They were followed by men on fast machines. The men took them away.*

I felt the bottom drop out of my stomach. *Did the girl have dark hair and look like Billy?*

*Yes.*

*That was my sister, Charlotte. Where did they take them?*

*I followed them to the mountain, but they entered a cave and disappeared.*

Disappeared. Like my parents, Uncle Dan, Maggie, Nik, Chey, Jane, and Jay. All gone.

Ferana watched me sadly. *What can I do?*

I wiped my eyes with the palm of my hand. I didn't have time for tears. I was the only one left, and I had to find them myself. I couldn't continue to put the lives of my family and friends in jeopardy.

*Ferana, I'm going to the mountain now. Can you please show me the cave?*

*Yes. I will tell Talrin, and then find you.*

I nodded my thanks and started walking through the woods. I needed a plan. Was the lab in the cave? How was I going to save them?

Ferana soon returned, watching over me as she flew. I walked in the hazy sunshine, grateful for her company. And then it came to me: I would simply surrender. I would find Wilder's henchmen, who would bring me to my family, and then I'd find the black tube. It was the only way.

Now that I knew what I had to do, I picked up my pace, ignoring my exhausted legs and grumbling stomach. I had walked most of the day, stopping only for water and to eat another granola bar, but if I kept going, I'd be there by nightfall. I looked out over the horizon toward the mountain and saw black clouds gathering, swallowing each other up in the oppressive heat.

When we reached a stream, the sun was sinking behind the trees. Ferana dove down and landed on my shoulder with incredible gentleness. *I will hunt quickly. Rest here for a few minutes.* Then she stretched out her wings and flew into the setting sun, a fiery orb in the midst of black clouds.

The forest seemed charged with electricity from the approaching storm. After I drank the cool mountain water and ate the last of the snacks Winny gave me, I found refuge in the shadowy trees.

Within seconds the sun disappeared and I was engulfed by darkness. My heart thumped loudly as I listened to the animals, but they were quiet, the woods completely still. I was wishing Ferana would hurry back when suddenly I felt someone watching me. Slowly I turned around.

A man stepped out from behind a tree, only feet from me, his face shrouded in darkness. I fought the urge to run.

And then I saw that it was Dylan. My mind was telling me to go, but my feet weren't moving.

"Claire, I know I lied to you, and there is no reason you should trust me," he said softly, inching closer to me. "But do you?"

I swallowed hard. Of course I didn't. I knew I shouldn't. He had tried to find me in the basement, had led the search for me this morning, had lied about everything, but—

"Yes."

He didn't say anything at first, clearly surprised by my answer. "Would you come with me?" he asked, sounding hopeful.

"Another time I would have gone with you anywhere. Tonight I'll only go with you if you bring me to my family."

There was a long silence. "I can't do that."

"You know where they are."

His voice was quiet when he answered. "Yes."

"You were sent here to get me, too."

"Yes," he admitted. "But I'm not going to....I'm going to hide you. That's why I wanted you to come with me before."

I was stunned. "Hide me?"

"It's *you* they want, Claire," he said urgently. "But I can save you! I knew you were close by this morning, so I sent them in the opposite direction. But no matter what I do, he'll get you eventually, and then...." He paused, his voice barely a whisper. "Please, trust me—before it's too late."

"I know Wilder wants me, and I know why—because of the predictions that I'll be the one to stop him."

"For a long time he's been looking for a girl who could communicate with animals. He said he wanted to try to recruit her, since obviously it's a very powerful gift. It was my job to find her. It never occurred to me that it was you—you don't even go to specials! But when I realized you wrote about animals...I had to put my mind at ease, which is why I kept trying to read your notebook. Then that day you fell asleep, I finally read your stories. That's when I knew the girl was you."

"And then you told Wilder."

"No. I swear I didn't."

"Then how does he know it's me?"

His lips pursed into a thin, straight line. "I don't know. All he said was he *extracted* the information, I don't know from who." He shuddered. "Claire, Wilder ordered me to search the school records for references to a girl who could communicate with animals. I got lists of everyone and their specials, but there was never a mention of an anipath. Then he had me break into your house and scan all your mother's files. There was a whole folder on an anipath, but no name. Later, when I realized it was you, I was frantic it might be documented somewhere else. So," he continued, "I broke into Grogan's office, then your mom's, but I couldn't find anything."

"We were in Grogan's office that night looking for a computer chip, and we heard you break into my mother's office!"

He smiled weakly at me. "I saw you run across the quad that night. So the records were on a computer chip in Grogan's office? I looked everywhere."

"It was tough to find. Who trashed my house? Was that you?"

He nodded. "If there was anything that would give you away, I had to find it—before Wilder did. I shredded all her files, but I was worried your mother's desk had a secret compartment or something that I missed, so I just destroyed it. Sorry," he said, looking up at me sheepishly. "Then yesterday Wilder told me you were the anipath. That's when he sent me—and the others—to get you. He ordered us to search your house. I made sure I got there first, and it was empty, but then I realized you were probably in the basement. I know you can get in and out of the house through the shed."

I looked at him, shocked.

"I've been following you," he admitted, "as often as I can, but only to make sure you're safe. Anyway, I went to the basement and yelled to give you time to get away."

"Why didn't you tell Wilder it was me when you first figured it out?"

He paused. "I don't know, I guess I was worried about his motives for talking to you. I really did leave right after I said good-bye to you. But I had to come back. I couldn't just leave you here unprotected. I never would have forgiven myself if something happened to you. I didn't know what he had planned at first, I swear. I would never have gone along if I knew—" He stopped.

"That he was going to kill me."

His voice was rough and angry when he answered. "I promise you I won't let that happen." He reached his hand out to me. "I'll hide you—"

"No."

"Claire, you have to listen to me! Wilder built a death machine! It's so dangerous, it has to be operated remotely—just being near it destroys brain cells! I don't know much about it since it's top secret, but he tested it yesterday on this guy, Scott. He was in too deep, like me. He tried to leave, and they caught him. Wilder had a big demonstration in the lab to warn everyone what happens to those who betray him. He put Scott in the machine." Dylan shuddered. "I could hear him screaming, and then...silence. He was vaporized." It took him a minute before he could go on. "I keep breaking it, so it's taken him longer than he planned to get it up and running, which has kept him from giving you his full attention. But now that it's working, he'll stop at nothing to find you. We have to leave, *now*."

"I can't! This death machine is all the more reason why I have to do this!"

"You're putting everyone in jeopardy—even your friends! He's rounding all of them up to find out where you are. He has powerful truth seekers who'll know if they're lying. Don't you see? He's going to put *you* in that machine!"

I took a step closer to him. "Listen, my parents tried to save me from this, too, but it's my fate. I'm the only one who can save them—all of them. I have to do this. Nothing you can say will change my mind."

When he spoke again, his voice broke. "You'll die."

I swallowed hard. I wanted to sound brave. "I know." I felt my eyes well up. He really did care about me; it hadn't all been part of the plan. "If I don't go, Wilder will kill them and the school will be destroyed."

"I don't give a damn about the school," he said harshly. He moved closer to me; we were almost touching. "I don't care about anyone. Only you."

I leaned forward, closing the space between us, and touched his rough face. "I care about you, too; but I can't go, leaving my family to die, knowing I could have stopped it. My mind's made up. If you don't take me to them, I'll find another way. I'll surrender. And if you try to stop me, I'll never forgive you."

He didn't answer at first. "Then I am going to save *you*," he finally said. His voice was hard. He pulled my body in to his, nuzzled his face into my hair, and then kissed me. I could have stayed like this, wrapped in his strong arms, kissing him, forever.

And then I heard Ferana's angry cry, jolting me back to the present. Difficult as it was, I gently pulled away from him. I couldn't afford to be distracted. "Take me to them."

He nodded and reached his hand out to me. I looked up at Ferana, but I couldn't hear her thoughts. "Ferana," I yelled out loud, but she didn't fly down.

Dylan followed my gaze. "Are you trying to talk to that hawk?"

"Yes, but for some reason I can't."

"Because of me."

"What do you mean?"

"I have a really rare special: I can block other people's powers. In fact, that's sort of my natural state. I had to be trained *not* to block powers."

So that's why I could never hear the animals when he was nearby. It all made sense now.

"Your mother's the only person who knows. She noticed it when she examined me at my interview and taught me how to block my power so no one else would know. It's been hard to keep it from Wilder, though."

"Why didn't you tell him?"

He looked off into the trees for a moment. When he looked back at me, his eyes were filled with regret. "Because of your mother. At my interview she warned me that I should choose who I tell very carefully—there would be people who would want to exploit me. She told me my abilities could one day make me the most powerful person alive, which was both a blessing and a curse."

We were both quiet for a moment. "You know, she fought for you when you were expelled."

His voice was rough when he answered. "I didn't know."

Just then Ferana swooped down, heading straight for Dylan.

"Unblock my special!" I yelled just as she reached out at his face with her deadly talons.

*No, Ferana! He's trying to help me! I was wrong!*

At the last second she veered and landed roughly on my shoulder. I put out my hand and she jumped onto it, never taking her hostile eyes from Dylan. It was strange to see her look so ferocious. Dylan tentatively lowered his arms, which had been shielding his head.

I took in a few deep breaths to calm myself. "Dylan, this is Ferana. She's been helping me. She's my friend." I turned to Ferana. *This is Dylan—he is bringing me to the mountain to save my family.*

She leaned her head forward and squawked at him in warning—an angry, high-pitched scream—spreading her wings out wide.

All the color drained from Dylan's face as he watched her.

*I couldn't hear you.*

*I know. He can stop us from communicating, but he didn't mean to.* I stroked her back gently. *Don't worry about me, really. Thank you, for— for everything.*

She flew straight up, hovering overhead. *I'll be very close.*

He watched her fly away with relief. "I should be grateful to her. She's how I found you."

"What do you mean?"

"I've seen you with her before, and today I saw her flying

toward the mountain. I hoped she would lead me to you, and she did."

"How long have you been following me?"

"For a few hours. My plan was to kidnap you myself. I was sure you'd never come with me willingly. But…"—he hesitated—"I just couldn't do it."

"I'm glad for that. Now we need to hurry, before…" I couldn't even think about my family in that machine, much less say it. I turned away, struggling to keep my emotions in check.

Just then a flash of lightning illuminated Shadow Mountain, silhouetted against the black sky.

"Are you sure about this, Claire?"

I nodded.

"Ready?" he asked. I placed my hand in his rough, injured one, and he pulled me in close to him. He placed his other hand around my waist, as if we were about to slow dance. "Hold on," he warned, a hint of mischief in his eyes.

Suddenly, I felt like I was on a roller coaster flying at breakneck speed, and I'd left my stomach behind me. And then we stopped. I looked around; we weren't in the same place anymore. "What just happened?"

"I can do telekinesis."

"I know."

"On myself."

# CHAPTER 26
# Journey to Shadow Mountain

I was speechless. I opened my mouth to ask a question, but then we began moving again. It all made sense now, of course—how he could appear and disappear so quickly. I began to notice that we traveled at an uneven speed; when the trees were close together, he went much slower; when they spread out, he could move faster. After several minutes his breathing became labored. We moved again, but this time I could see the trees blur past us. "Dylan, you need to rest," I whispered in his ear.

He stopped, releasing me from his tight grip. I looked around at the unfamiliar surroundings as thunder grumbled in the distance. We were on the shore of the lake, miles and miles from school. Suddenly, I saw something shimmer on the water; the moon had temporarily won its battle with the clouds, illuminating the shore for just a moment. Then the moon disappeared, and we were once again surrounded by a sea of darkness.

Dylan stood hunched over, his hands on his knees. I steered him toward a large rock. "Rest," I said, leaning him against it.

"It drains me to go so far, but I'm fine now. Can't keep me down for long," he added with a wink.

"Are we almost there?"

He nodded slowly. "Wilder built an underground facility in Shadow Mountain," he said, gesturing toward the dark purple peak in the distance.

"So close to Cambial." It was shocking what he was able to accomplish right under everyone's noses.

"He stayed nearby because of you. He once told me some woman named Josephine had a vision about a very powerful anipathic girl. Yesterday I found out the rest of the prophecy—that this girl would destroy him."

"How long has he known?"

"I don't know. He's had Grogan's records for a while."

I shook my head. "Grogan. I knew he was involved with Wilder."

He chuckled. "No, it's not what you think. Wilder had someone hack into Grogan's computer and install a program that transfers all of the information back to him. Grogan doesn't have a clue. He knows something's up, though—that's why he's out all the time investigating, and why he's expelling the Exceptionals. He's trying to get them away from here to protect them."

I couldn't believe how wrong I'd been about so many things. "Why's Wilder kidnapping the Exceptionals?"

"Two reasons. First, he's building an army with the best in each special—it will make him the most powerful person alive. He wants the students to join him."

I shook my head. "Never."

Dylan looked away. "He can be…very persuasive."

I didn't buy that. "What's the second reason?"

"If they don't join him, he doesn't want them against him."

"So—join him or die?"

He didn't answer.

"My brother almost won the TT."

"I know. I was there. Wilder sent a few of his followers to kidnap the winners. I was worried when I heard your brother was in it, and I…I heard he wasn't very good"—he looked up at me apologetically—"but if he won, Wilder would have had his mind read, and I was afraid he'd know you're anipathic. I was the one who pulled that bat down to the log."

I thought back to that day. "I saw you in the woods through the fog!"

"The fog was courtesy of Grainer, Wilder's number two. He can affect the weather by sending molecules into the clouds."

I couldn't believe what I was hearing. "He can control the weather?"

"No, not control, influence. It was a rainy day anyway—he just made it worse."

My head was spinning. Death machines, weather control…I shuddered, wishing more than anything that I'd never heard of the prophecy.

"I'll be ready in a minute." Dylan leaned down on the narrow bank of the lake and splashed water all over his face.

I closed my eyes and listened to the gentle waves lapping against the shore. I inhaled the smell of moist earth and lilies growing with abandon between the weeping willows, and once more felt calm. I opened my eyes and saw Dylan standing before me, his tall, perfect body bathed in moonlight. I watched him eagerly, trying to imprint him to memory.

"Do exactly as I tell you. There are two entrances: I'll take you in through the back one, closest to your family, as my prisoner. We'll rescue everyone, and then I'll disable the system."

"What about security?"

"It's pretty tight, but nothing I can't manage. The problem is the electromagnetic field he has around the lab. You can't get in or out without the code to deactivate it. Getting in will be easy, since I have the code, but unless we can get out undetected"— that sounded extremely unlikely—"he'll change the code, and we'll be trapped. The field also blocks clairvoyants from seeing in. It's like everything within the field doesn't exist. There're even a few ghosts down there, some of your relatives, and they can't get out."

I immediately thought of Nana Marie—no wonder she couldn't reach her brother, Christopher! All of my grandparents must be trapped within the field. "Where's the power source?"

"I don't know. Somehow he's capturing the electricity from lightning strikes on the mountain and using it to create the field. The electricity is converted in his lab."

"How do you disable it?"

He frowned. "I don't know that, either. It's really high voltage, so you can't just disconnect it. I tried," he said, holding up his scarred hand. "I loosened it enough so it was off for a few seconds, but then my hand began to burn—this jolt of electricity ripped through me, and then I went flying."

"So that's how Nana Marie sent me the message not to tell anyone about my special—she must have projected herself when the force field was off."

His face lit up. "I'm glad it did some good. I thought Wilder would kill me. He's completely paranoid, but I told him I wanted to make sure the current was strong enough to keep the prisoners in and others out. Good thing I can block powers. His truth seekers couldn't tell I was lying, so he believed me—thinks I'm his number two with Grainer." He absentmindedly traced the dead skin on his hand with his finger.

"What if he catches us?" I asked in a small voice.

"Hopefully we'll have freed everyone, and it will be them against us."

I smiled, thinking of my family and friends. "I like our chances. And I've heard you're pretty good."

He smiled a wicked grin, "You ain't seen nothin' yet."

My heart skipped a beat. That, I was sure of.

"Ready?"

I had to ask the question that had been gnawing at me. "One more thing—Dan McAllister. Is he..."

"With Wilder? No."

"But, the watches—he gave them to us."

Dylan scowled. "Wilder's been keeping an eye on him for a few months. He found out that McAllister was trying to trace who bought the materials he used to build his death machine. Wilder knew McAllister suspected that he was still alive, so he told me to follow him. When I saw him buy the watches and have your names engraved on the back, Wilder told me to install the tracking devices."

"But Wilder didn't know I could hear animals then. Why did he want to keep track of us?"

"He knew your parents would come after him eventually. He wanted to know where you were in case he needed...leverage."

Dylan leaned toward me and scooped me in his arms again,

his hand on the small of my back. I inhaled, breathing him in as he leaned in to me, kissing me urgently. I wanted to have this, to remember it, to take it with me.

And then the woods around me swirled together in a blur, and we were gone.

Finally, on the far side of the lake, we stopped.

As we did, a gust of wind whirled around us and the heavens roared in anger, fingers of lightning reaching down as if to grab us.

Dylan held me even tighter, resting his chin on the top of my head for what I knew was probably the last time. Tucked within his arms, I felt safe, and then, all too soon—

*Vrrrrmmm.* The noise cut through the night like a knife.

"Change of plan. Follow my lead," he whispered in my ear.

He gave my hand a little squeeze before grabbing my shoulder roughly. "Move it!" he yelled. I knew it was for show, but his sudden harshness still startled me.

"Hey—Ed!" He waved at a huge man on a dirt bike. "I've got her!"

The man rode over to us immediately. He cut the engine and eyed me hungrily, his tar-black eyes cold as steel.

"It's about time, too—the boss was getting anxious," he said in a voice as greasy as his face.

"It wasn't easy."

Ed grabbed my face with his big, dirty hands. "Slippery little minx, aren't you?"

I pulled away. When he wouldn't let go, I spit in his face.

He jerked his hand away.

"Don't touch me!" I yelled.

Ed raised his hand and slapped me, hard, across the face.

Almost at the same time I felt the sting, Dylan's body flinched. I stumbled backward as Dylan punched Ed square in the jaw. Before he could get up, Dylan moved his left hand slightly and sent him flying into a massive oak. He landed at the base with a thud, blood streaming down his face. Dylan closed his eyes again and Ed sailed farther through the trees.

I had never seen anything like it.

"He won't be bothering us anymore." He flourished his hands, covering Ed with leaves and branches.

"Is he—" I couldn't bring myself to say the words.

"Dead? No. Not that he doesn't deserve it. He's unconscious—hopefully until tomorrow, or at least until we get away. Either way, he won't be found any time soon."

I took a deep breath to steady myself. "Can anyone else do what you can?"

"Wilder. But I've been training, and he doesn't know what I'm capable of. I think we're pretty well matched," he said.

I smiled. "Well, my money's on you."

He laughed. "It better be." He paused, and the smile disappeared from his face. "We better go before patrol finds us again," he said, wrapping his arms around me. The bottom dropped out of my stomach, and a few seconds later we were standing on a narrow ledge partway up the mountain, in the middle of a raging thunderstorm. The rain pelted down on us as an angry wind slapped our bodies back against the rough boulders.

My ears popped as I looked down at the valley spread out beneath us. Another bolt of lightning zigzagged across the sky, and I spotted Ferana below. "Dylan, unblock my special."

*I'm here*, I called to her silently, waving my arms.

She landed on my shoulder, eyeing Dylan angrily.

*Please don't do this, Claire! This is an evil place.*

*I have to. He's holding my family under the mountain. If I don't see you again, I want you to know how much you and Talrin mean to me. I love you both so much.*

She nuzzled her soft, wet head next to my cheek. *I'll be waiting for you.*

She dove downward, and then embraced the raging wind with her wings, flying faster than seemed possible. I envied her; how I longed to ride the storm alongside her instead of face my destiny in the depths of the mountain.

Finally I took a deep breath. I wanted to be done with it. "Let's go."

Dylan took my hand, and we followed the ledge to the mouth of a cave. It was as sinister as a black hole. "Don't tell me we're going in there."

He chuckled softly. "I don't believe it—*you* scared?"

I bit my lip.

"Well, you'd be a fool not to be. Come on." As we stepped into the abyss, I felt all the warmth drain from my body.

Dylan pulled out a flashlight and turned it on, directing me past a narrow cleft in the rocks and into a small opening in the cave. Feeling along the wall for something, Dylan whispered, "It's a steel door made to look like part of the cave."

He removed a small section of rock, exposing a keypad, and punched in a series of numbers. The door slid open to reveal a passageway.

"Sorry," he whispered as he again pulled me in front of him. We followed the descending tunnel in silence, our footsteps echoing in the dimly lit chamber. I could see a man up ahead in a black jumpsuit walking toward us.

"That's Murphy. Don't worry, he's more afraid of Wilder than you are."

I found that hard to believe.

"Hey, kid, you finally got her, huh?" He was big and burly, about my height, with a wide face and a crew cut. He certainly looked menacing—even more so than the guy outside.

"I'll be glad when this is over. I can't take it much longer." Murphy suddenly jumped as if he was pushed from behind. "Stop it, damn it! There's nothing I can do! I told you that!"

I looked around the passage, but we were the only ones there.

He ducked his head under his arm, and spun around. It was as if he were a puppet and someone without much skill was controlling the strings.

"Damn ghosts," he muttered. "I'll help you, kid." He was about to grab my elbow when he staggered back, spooked.

"That's okay, Murph. I got it," Dylan said kindly, and put his free hand on Murphy's shoulder. "This will all end tonight. Hang in there." He paused, and then added under his breath, "Later, if you see me, follow my lead. I'll take care of you, Murph—remember that."

Even though the man was much older than Dylan, he obviously admired him. He nodded, puzzled. "Thanks, kid."

"Don't tell anyone I have her. I'll see you later," he whispered.

Murphy looked even more confused, but again he nodded.

As we continued along, I could hear the echo of his sobs. I couldn't help but feel sorry for him. "What's up with that guy?" I whispered.

"He sees ghosts, and some of them are your relatives. They're hounding him."

"Good."

He stopped, pulling my back in closer to his chest. When he spoke again, I could barely hear him. "Some people follow Wilder because they're rotten bastards. Others," he paused, "have gotten themselves into a situation they can't get out of. Wilder is evil—but not all of his followers are."

I knew he wasn't just talking about Murphy. I reached back and squeezed his hand.

A moment later we reached another dead end. Again Dylan removed a section of rock. "Now listen, we're going to try to slip in and out without being seen, so no matter what you see, don't make a sound," he whispered.

"Is that where they are? Behind that door?"

"Shhh." He nodded.

I wanted to yell out *I'm coming! I'm here!*

"Once I open the door, wait here until I disable the camera," he said as he furiously pressed the keypad. The door slid open, and with a quick flick of Dylan's fingers, the camera came crashing to the ground.

I ran past him into the room.

Nothing could have prepared me for what I saw.

# CHAPTER 27
# The Death Machine

My breath caught in my throat. All along the cave's walls were glass cubicles—cages, really. Inside were my mother and father, Billy, Charlotte, Uncle Dan, and Jane. My mother stared at me, horrified, her face bruised. "Dylan's helping us!" I said, running over to her. I pressed my hand against the glass wall, as did she. Tears streamed down her face.

Dylan rushed to the door on the opposite wall and made sure it was locked.

"Claire, listen to me," my mother urged. "It's you Wilder wants; he's going to kill you."

"Claire, you have to leave, NOW!" my father shouted.

"No, I'm here to save you."

My mother looked at Dylan. "If you really are helping us, take her out of here—I am begging you!"

He shook his head. "I've tried, I swear. She won't listen. We have to hurry. Someone will notice the camera down, if they haven't already."

I noticed Jane's eyes flash to Dylan's. She looked thrilled to see him, but then she quickly looked away. Everyone else looked at Dylan like they could rip his head off.

"How are we going to free them?" I asked, taking in the thick glass doors, seamless except for a small pad on each.

"Only Wilder can open them. The pads scan his eye and thumb. I've thought about it, and I'm going to have to break them with those boulders." He motioned toward the far wall.

Billy shook his head. "No one can move those, and even if you could, there'd be no way to control them—they'd crush us."

Dylan sighed, clearly annoyed, and didn't bother to respond. "All of you, stand back. Claire, get behind me and cover your face."

He turned toward the rocks, deep in concentration. He slowly lifted both hands, and a huge boulder rose into the air as if it was made of Styrofoam. "Professor Crane—you first," he said, his voice strained, "I'm going to hit the side. Ready…now!"

The boulder slammed into her glass cage and smashed it into a thousand pieces before coming to an abrupt stop. In an instant she was by my side, her arms around me.

"You"—he motioned to my dad—"get ready." A moment later there was a thunderous boom as the boulder broke the glass.

Dad rushed to me, too, as Dylan freed Jane and Uncle Dan, which only left Billy and Charlotte. Before he could raise his hands again, we heard voices on the other side of the door.

"Please hurry!" I whispered.

Dylan moved his hand. The rock crashed through Billy's enclosure and, without stopping, went straight through to Charlotte's, the roar reverberating through the room. Dylan leaned forward, his hands on his knees, and then the door flew open. He had a shard of glass to my throat in less than a second.

I didn't need to pretend to look terrified. Two men were pointing guns directly at me.

Suddenly, Charlotte screamed and ran toward me. Billy grabbed her, turning her in to his chest. "Calm down, Charlotte," he said firmly.

Dylan pushed the glass a little closer to my throat. "All of you—against the wall. I don't want to hear a sound out of you or she's dead." I caught my breath; he spoke with no emotion whatsoever, as if my life meant nothing to him.

My mother walked quickly to the wall. The others followed, except for Charlotte. She looked at Dylan, her eyes huge.

"I said move!" Dylan said, his voice as hard and sharp as the shard against my skin.

My father quickly pulled Charlotte behind him, shielding her. Uncle Dan's face was filled with loathing as he glared at Dylan.

"Hey—what the hell are you two doing? Weren't you

supposed to be monitoring the damn cameras?" Dylan yelled at the men. One was about the same age as my parents, horsefaced with pasty skin, and the other was about Dylan's age, African American, with small, dark eyes that quickly took in the situation. Both wore black one-piece jumpsuits.

The pale man's expression rapidly changed from confusion to terror. "We were watching them, but you know, nothing ever happens, and so we were talking, and…" His voice trailed off.

"How did you get here in time to save the day?" the younger man asked shrewdly. "Wilder told you *not* to come in the back way—to bring her in the front with Ed."

"Let's get something straight. I don't answer to you, Jay. Don't ever forget it." The threat in his tone was unmistakable. "Ed wasn't where he was supposed to be—probably drunk again—so I came in the back. Good thing I did, too. I caught them trying to escape. That one is telekinetic," he said, gesturing toward Billy.

The older man eyed Billy. "I thought he was no good."

I cringed.

"What do you think, Clay? He's a Crane—of course he's good." He laughed darkly. "He's just never been properly motivated before. Now, Clay, stay here and help me keep an eye on them. Jay, go get Murphy."

Clay smiled smugly at Jay, who walked over to the keypad.

"What are you doing?" Dylan asked.

Jay pushed the buttons furiously before answering. "Disabling it. I'm not taking any chances. No one's getting in or out that door."

My heart sank. Getting out that door quickly had been Dylan's plan. I shouldn't have dared to hope.

Jay turned back to us and shook his head slowly. "Something's not right here. I know this kid from school," he said, motioning to Billy. "No way he could break the glass. I'm getting Wilder."

"But Billy almost won the TT!" Charlotte cried. "He could—"

"Charlotte!" I glared, hoping the men didn't pick up on the *could* instead of the *did*.

"Jay, just shut up and do what I tell you," Dylan seethed.

200

Jay looked like he could breathe fire as they stared each other down. Then he turned to leave.

Dylan chuckled. "You know what? Go ahead. Tell Wilder I got a piece of glass to the girl's neck to keep her very powerful family in line because you weren't doing your job, so you missed it when they tried to escape. And if I hadn't come in when I did, they'd be long gone. But do me a favor, when he kills you try to hang on long enough so I can say I told you so."

The color completely drained from Clay's face. "H-Hey—Dylan," he stammered, "can you not tell him about the camera? Can you tell him we ran down right away and the three of us stopped them together?"

I realized this was what Dylan wanted all along, since Wilder would be suspicious of Dylan's story. "I don't know, Clay, lying to Wilder?"

"Come on. He'll be furious with us if he finds out."

"And we all know what happened yesterday when he was furious," Dylan said darkly. "Sayonara, Scott."

Jay looked at him with utter hatred in his eyes, but Dylan's bluff worked. "We'd appreciate it—and we'd owe you one."

Dylan smirked. "I guess I could say that to Wilder. If you hurry your ass out of here and get Murph."

Jay threw Dylan a malicious look before rushing out the door. Then with a quick movement of Dylan's free hand, Clay sailed through the air and landed with a thud where the boulder had stood. Dylan released the glass from my neck and shut the door. "Stay right there and hold the glass—I'm going to need to have it to your neck when Jay comes back with Murphy."

"Okay," I breathed.

"Hey—Charlotte, you're doing great, but play along, okay? I swear I won't hurt any of you, and I would never hurt Claire."

She smiled warily at Dylan. "Are you going to rescue us?"

"I'm going to try."

"The ghosts will help, too."

"Good, we can use all the help we can get. Now that we can't leave through that door anymore, we're going to have to go out the main exit. It'll be tough to do that undetected." He moved his arms like a conductor, and the boulder rolled over the shattered glass and stopped in front of Clay, blocking him from view.

I heard the door squeak open. Dylan had the glass next to my neck before I could blink. In the doorway stood Murphy and Jay.

Murphy's eyes were huge as he took in the situation.

"I'm fine, Murph. Remember what I told you earlier?" Dylan said.

Murphy nodded.

Jay looked suspiciously from one to the other. "What did you tell him?"

"That's none of your damn business! Question me again, and I just might let it slip to Wilder how we ended up in this situation."

Jay scowled. With his beady eyes and mouth that seemed to be fixed in a sneer, he reminded me of a hyena. "Where's Clay?"

"He had important work to finish for Wilder. It's on a need-to-know basis," Dylan said smugly.

Jay looked as if he might explode. "I do know about it! I even invented part of the machine!" He paused, composing himself. Then he walked slowly toward me until he was so close, I could feel his hot breath on my face. Dylan's hand tightened around my shoulder. "Well, together we came up with a solution. I don't want to ruin the surprise; but needless to say, after Claire goes into the machine, she will never pose a threat to us again."

"What are you talking about?" my father asked, unable to keep his voice steady.

My knees buckled, but Dylan held me firmly. Then I saw the gleam of pleasure in Jay's face at my fear. I would not give him that, too. I summoned my strength and stood tall. "The prophecy *will* come true—*I* will make sure of it," I said evenly.

"Cling to your delusions," he snickered, "if it makes you happy in your last remaining minutes before we throw you in the machine."

"Over my dead body." My mother was near hysteria.

"That's the idea!" Jay laughed. "You'll be right behind her."

"To think we went looking for you, worried you were abducted," she continued.

Of course! Jay was Jay Burke. He hadn't been kidnapped at all.

"At first I was just trying to arrange a recruitment meeting with Clay's son, Henry, but he wouldn't come. He just ran and told you."

"Henry would never work for Wilder!" I yelled.

I glanced back and saw the jealously on Dylan's face, but I had no way of telling him there was no need. I shook my head ever so slightly, and then winced as the shard grazed my neck.

"You see what happens when you don't shut up? Next time it'll be more than a drop of blood," Dylan said so coldly I caught my breath. "I'm sorry," he whispered, shoving me in front of him.

"And then," Jay continued, clearly enjoying this, "I thought, why not draw Professors Crane and Walker away from Cambial? Pretend I was being recruited. That, combined with Chey's disappearance, should send them out investigating, and then it'd be easier to find the anipath. Oh, we knew all about the prophecy," he said, turning to my mother, "ever since Dylan broke into your house and scanned your files."

I could feel Dylan's body stiffen. I ached to turn around and comfort him, but all I could do was stand there and watch while my mother, father, and Uncle Dan turned and glared at him, their eyes blazing with hatred.

Jay looked around the cave suspiciously. "Who moved the boulder?" he said, walking over to it.

My heart raced—if Jay looked behind it, we were done for.

"I made the Crane kid move it back. Jay, take Professor Walker and Professor Crane, and Murph will take the others. I'm keeping Claire with me. The rest of you—remember, anything funny and I'll slit her throat."

"Harm Claire, and you'll pay with your life," Uncle Dan seethed.

Jay turned around. "You're in no position to threaten anyone,

McAllister." And then he shoved my parents out the door. We followed behind, into a long, narrow passageway. It was dark and damp, and I could hear things scurrying past us. After a few minutes the tunnel split; we veered off toward the right, away from an earsplitting, high-pitched hum. I winced and hunched up my shoulders, then suddenly thought of Winny's vision—she said I covered my ears because of a terrible noise. That must be where the black wire was! At least I had found it.

In the distance I could make out a large cavern. Dylan stopped. "Jay, I need you to go find Clay while Murph and I take them to Wilder. There's something important I need him to do."

"No," Jay said, looking very disgruntled. "There's something fishy going on here. I'm going with you and there's nothing you can do stop me."

Dylan smiled his most charming smile. "I think there is." With a quick flick of his hand, he sent Jay into the air, and then slammed him against the far wall. Jay collapsed in a heap.

Murphy stared at him, looking thunderstruck, his eyes wide and his mouth open.

"Murph, Wilder is an evil bastard—you know it. We're going to do the right thing and fight him. The best and the brightest are right here. That includes you, Murph, or Wilder wouldn't want you."

"But look what happened to Scott. He'll catch us, and then..." Murphy looked terrified.

"I won't ask you to risk your life," Dylan said softly. "But don't stand against me."

"I could never do that." Murphy was quiet for a moment, and then nodded. "Okay. But why do we need to fight him? Why can't we just all get out of here?"

"That was the plan, but then Jay disabled that door."

"There's a way around it, a secret passage. Follow me!" Murphy whirled around and charged back the way we came. As we followed him I was flanked protectively by my father and Uncle Dan, keeping me from Dylan. "I don't trust him, Claire," my father whispered.

"I don't, either," Uncle Dan said. "This could all be a trap."

I shook my head no, and ran ahead with Murphy. I noticed he didn't swat the air once. Maybe, just maybe, we'd all get out and I wouldn't have to pull the wire.

All of a sudden a loud beeping noise echoed against the walls. The alarm.

My hope vanished as quickly as it appeared.

"Damn it!" Dylan said, hitting the cave wall.

My father pulled him roughly aside. "If you really are helping us, you'll get my children out of here while we fight Wilder."

"I really wish I could. But I can't. There's a huge force field around the lab—no one can get in or out without the code, which automatically changes when the alarm is sounded. I need to disable the field or we're all dead."

The words hung heavily in the air.

Suddenly, we heard footsteps clamoring toward us.

Dylan turned around. "This way—run!" he yelled, holding his hand out for mine. Without looking at Uncle Dan or my father, I grabbed it.

"We're going to come out into a cavern," Dylan said. "On my count, Billy, we'll attack anyone in there. I'll disable the force field and then you'll all need to follow me out. There are tracks and carts to move the heavy materials; if we get separated, follow the tracks to the far side of the cavern—to a tunnel that leads outside. Once you're out, keep running. I'll go back for the others."

Before I could ask where Maggie, Nik, and Chey were, we ran into the enormous cavern, and then stopped dead in our tracks.

There, in the middle, stood Wilder. He was tall and thin, but he didn't look like the photographs I'd seen of him. He was almost handsome, but the *almost* made all the difference. There was something odd about him, like he was made of plastic. I remembered what Dylan had said—that he had been badly burned by the fire. He must have had plastic surgery, but he didn't look...well, he didn't look human.

# CHAPTER 28
# Timothy Wilder

Stationed behind Wilder were a dozen men and women dressed in black jumpsuits, all carrying guns. Wilder raised an eyebrow. "Well, well, well, what do we have here?"

I looked over my shoulder, hoping to turn back, but the people who had been chasing us now blocked the entrance to the passageway. We were surrounded.

Wilder took a step toward me, but Dylan jumped protectively in front of me.

"I assume this beautiful young lady is the famous Claire, the anipath? Yes, I can see the resemblance, Maura. She does so look like her grandmother Marie. Pity she didn't suffer long when she died." He emphasized *died* ever so slightly. "None of them did. They were incinerated within seconds. I knew they were coming, of course; so when I saw the plane, I just snatched it from the sky with a flick of my hand."

The rage boiled up inside me, taking hold as I stepped out from behind Dylan. "You evil murderer!"

He smiled wryly. "You dare to face me? You are a very brave girl—I can see that. Unfortunately, history does prove that the brave die young, and often painfully."

"What do you know about bravery?" I spat out. "You have your henchmen kidnap students while you hide out in a cave!"

"I have no interest in appearing noble. I do not care about the means—only the ends." He spoke with restraint. "The timing is perfect, really. It's as if the stars aligned: the machine is finally operational just as you join us, Claire." He paused. "Naturally, I've been concerned about the prophecy for some time—it has overshadowed all I have accomplished. The anipath needed to be eliminated as soon as possible, and it proved most difficult to determine that the anipath was you."

"Claire was never named in the files," my mother seethed. "You have the wrong girl—she has no special."

Wilder smirked. "Smart not naming her, Maura. It did take some time to determine her identity. But I have ways of *extracting* the truth. Isn't that right, Jane?"

All eyes turned to Jane. "I only had the vision a few days ago, Claire, and I swear I never told him. I didn't even think it was true—I mean, you don't even have a special, and you're so…ordinary. But then yesterday he made me drink a serum, and…I *had* to tell him that I saw you talking to a hawk, and then you pulled a thick black wire, and then you died. I had no choice!"

"You told him all of it!" I said incredulously.

"It's not your fault, Jane," my mother said. "Wilder's the devil himself."

"You flatter me, Maura. But then another problem presented itself—what if the prophecy referred to you as a ghost? It never specified. I couldn't take the chance that even after I killed you, Claire, you could still somehow fulfill the prophecy," he hissed.

"What are you talking about?" Dylan raged.

"Until now Claire's ghost would have been trapped down here. But the new and improved machine kills all forms of life—both seen and unseen." He looked me in the eye. "You will be vaporized in a nanosecond. Then there will be *nothing* left of you."

I closed my eyes and swallowed hard, trying to keep the terror at bay. I couldn't imagine anything so horrible. I had clung to the knowledge that once I died, I could still communicate with Charlotte, Uncle Christopher, and my grandparents, and watch Dylan, even if I couldn't talk to him. If Wilder destroyed my spirit, I would be worse than dead. I could hear the outraged screams of my family in the background, but I couldn't focus enough to hear the words.

"I'll never let that happen. Mark my words, you will pay for this," Dylan threatened. As he held me closer, I felt my courage start to return.

Wilder took another step forward, and his henchmen did as well. He put up his hand to stop them. "Stay in position; they pose no threat. Where would they go?" He laughed and his tight skin looked as if it would split. "I have a few things to discuss with Dylan before he dies. How dare you challenge me when you know I am the most powerful person alive?"

My mother shot a quick glance at Dylan, remembering, I was sure, that she had called him that.

Dylan took a deep breath and stood taller. "No, you're not. They defeated you before, and *we* will this time."

"We?" Wilder scoffed. "WHEN DID YOU DECIDE TO BETRAY ME?" he screamed, suddenly very angry.

"When I discovered that you had lied to me! You told me no one would be hurt, and when I asked if you had anything to do with the missing students, you denied it. And then you ordered me to bring Claire to you for questioning—but your plan all along was to kill her!"

Wilder cocked his head to one side, wearing a look of dawning realization. "How stupid of me. Of course, you've fallen in love. I should have known, since love was my folly as well. It was the beautiful Josephine—"

"How dare you say her name!" Uncle Dan screamed, "I know why you want to destroy the ghosts. I'm sure she haunts you day and night, you bastard!"

An evil smile flashed across Wilder's face, but his eyes remained as hard and cold as iron. "As a matter of fact, she doesn't. I know things about Josephine that you'll never know."

"That's a lie!"

"Is it? Since you are about to die, perhaps I should tell you what happened to her. Would you like that?"

"I wouldn't believe anything you said. And if you're right and I'll be dead soon, I'll ask her myself. Then we'll both haunt you."

"Oh, I don't think you'll find her," he smirked, as if laughing at a private joke. "And besides, you'll go through my divine new machine and *Poof*! No more ghost. I will *obliterate* you—all of you. Then *I* will take over Cambial. Who would be strong enough to stop me? Chetan has proved especially defiant; I think I will use him to illustrate my point to the remaining professors and students. Soon everyone will know that those who do not join me will suffer a fate far worse than death."

"Why? What do you want?" I said. "To rule the world?"

"No. I couldn't be bothered with the complications. But those in power will answer to me. They will do *exactly* what I order or suffer the consequence." He opened his arms, emperor of this underground kingdom. "You have no idea what I have already accomplished. I have just touched the surface of discoveries that will change the future of mankind. What do I want? WHAT DO I WANT?"

I stepped back, catching my breath.

"I want FREEDOM! A basic right denied to me. I want to test my powers unchallenged! Crane's Commandments—HA! They are mere shackles for the weak-minded. Even forced into hiding, I am more powerful than all of you *combined*! I can harness the weather! Lightning will strike where I order it! I can—"

My mother came forward. "Still playing God, Timothy," she said, shaking her head as if she were scolding a child. "As I've warned you before, things never bode well for those who do."

Wilder paused, collecting himself. "Perhaps I'll keep you in your cage, Maura, just so you can see me prove you wrong. Then again, why go to the trouble to keep you alive?"

I was so angry, I could taste it. "If you fear no one, why go to so much trouble to capture me? Which, incidentally, you couldn't even manage, so maybe you're not as powerful as you think. I sought *you* out and discovered your secret location. Why are you so afraid of a fifteen-year-old girl who can talk to animals?"

"Claire," my father warned, pulling me back toward him.

Wilder's face contorted. "YOU WILL FEAR ME NOW!" He released his fury like a tidal wave, running at me with outstretched hands. But Dylan met him, blocking whatever he was attempting to do. Then Wilder's guard moved, cutting off our escape path on the other side of the cavern.

"Claire!" Dylan yelled, his voice strained. "Get out! Do it for me—it's what I'm fighting for." Before the words could sink in, before I understood that he was going to sacrifice himself for me, he ran straight at Wilder. But Wilder was too fast. He sent Dylan flying backward, slamming him into the cave wall, and an instant later an enormous boulder hurtled straight at his head.

"Get the girl!" Wilder yelled. "Throw her in the machine!"

"NO!" Dylan cried out furiously, throwing both hands up to block the boulder and pushing it back at Wilder.

Wilder laughed maniacally. "Is that all you can do? I over-estimated you." The boulder was suspended in midair as they wrestled it. But then Wilder's henchmen advanced toward me, and Dylan tried to block them, as well. I watched in horror as Wilder began to prevail.

I stood there, helpless to save Dylan, when I remembered what I had to do, what I was meant to do: pull the wire. I ran back toward the passageway that led to the dreadful machine.

"DON'T LET HER GET AWAY!" Wilder screamed behind me.

Shots echoed through the cave. Billy spun around and blocked the bullets directed at me. They ricocheted against the walls, disturbing the bats hanging high above us. Hundreds came swooping down, circling all around the cave in a state of utter confusion. I had to concentrate to block out their thoughts.

"SEDONA, GET THE GIRL!" Wilder roared again.

A petite woman with long red hair threw her gun to the ground and ran straight for me, her hands outstretched in gleeful rage. My legs moved faster than I thought possible, but just before I reached the passage, I felt myself rise off the floor. I fought with everything I had—it wasn't my time to die yet.

My mother grabbed Sedona's gun and sprayed bullets at her, but Sedona easily deflected them with a flip of her wrist.

"BILLY!" I screamed. I was ten feet in the air and headed

straight toward a cluster of razor-sharp stalactites. I was going to be skewered. "Billy! Help!"

Billy tried to move me back down, but he was outmatched. As Wilder's guard raced at him, Uncle Dan ran to his aid, grabbing loose rocks and hurling them. My mother continued to fire Sedona's gun furiously while my father did the only thing he could—threw some serious punches.

But still I inched closer and closer to the ceiling.

A second later Dylan was below me, challenging Sedona in a struggle for my life...while my mother fired at Wilder, who easily deflected the bullets.

"Oooh, you've been practicing, but you're not as strong as I am," Sedona taunted Dylan.

"I wouldn't be so sure," Dylan growled.

I watched the scene from above, lying prone like a rag doll. My body was pushed up and pulled down in succession. Then as Dylan's eyes narrowed with a combination of fury and concentration, I slowly moved away from the ceiling.

"*Arrgh!*" Sedona shrieked, trying in vain to spear me, but the closer Dylan got to her, the more he blocked her powers. Suddenly, Dylan moved in a blur, closing the distance between them quickly and shoving her to the ground. Instantly, I fell to the cave floor with a thump, landing hard on my arm.

At that moment Wilder came at me, making the ceiling tremble as stalactites came loose and flew like daggers. Dylan blocked them just in time. Once again, he charged Wilder, backing him into a corner of the cave near the passage we had come from.

Billy grabbed my hand protectively as Wilder's fighters surrounded us. Wilder had turned the tables on Dylan, and now it was Dylan who was trapped in the alcove. Try as he might, Dylan couldn't get past Wilder.

I stood with my parents, Billy, Uncle Dan, and a whimpering Jane near the center of the cave. I couldn't see Charlotte anywhere. I barely registered that I'd lost track of her when Wilder's followers started moving in. Billy telekinetically catapulted smaller rocks past me like a pitching machine, right at Wilder's henchmen, while my mother fired at anyone who came near us. But it was only prolonging the inevitable; we weren't going to last much longer.

I had failed.

# CHAPTER 29
# Secret Passage

All of Wilder's guards moved in at once.

"Claire's mine!" Sedona yelled, and I felt myself jolt forward toward her. Wilder still had Dylan trapped, and everyone else was fighting.

I would be in Sedona's clutches in seconds. I closed my eyes.

But all of a sudden, I moved backward.

"Oh no. Ye won't be hurtin' my friend." I would recognize that brogue anywhere. With a graceful flick of her wrist, Maggie pinned Sedona to the wall with several huge stalactites.

"Maggie—"

"Charlotte and Murphy freed us! Now go, Claire! Ye can't help us, and it's you the bastard's after."

My eyes scanned the dimly lit cave, and sure enough, there was Nik using telekinesis to hurl rocks at two of Wilder's guards, and behind me was Chey, furiously fighting three of them himself, and winning. If they could just hold on long enough for me to get to that machine...

While everyone was fighting, I seized the opportunity and serpentined through the cavern, dodging both Wilder's fighters and my family—both would try to stop me. I darted through the tunnel and was almost at the fork when a thunderous noise reverberated throughout the cave. I looked back over my shoulder and saw Wilder ripping up the tracks that bisected the tunnel and hurling them at Dylan, still trapped in the alcove.

I watched in desperation as Dylan swooped and swatted like a boxer, dodging the jagged metal pieces while frantically trying to get closer to Wilder to block him. But it was clear that Wilder was going to prevail and—I knew with chilling certainty—kill Dylan.

I ran back to the edge of the cavern—I had to do something! But what?

"How long do you think you can last?" Wilder shouted. "I hate to kill you, with your talent. I saw you transport yourself *and* block Sedona's powers. Don't you see what we can do together? Come back to me—we'll put this all behind us."

"You don't forgive or forget," Dylan said, struggling. "You used me, like you use everyone. I'd much rather die than join you."

"They'll never forgive you after everything you've done."

Dylan didn't answer as he struggled to block everything Wilder was throwing at him. He was no longer moving forward or hurling anything back, he was just trying to block Wilder, and it was obvious he wouldn't be able to do that for long.

"Claire already has forgiven me," Dylan panted. "She's the only one I care about. Besides, I'll never forgive myself."

My stomach twisted as I realized what he was doing—trying to hold on long enough for me to get out, and then *he* would pull the wire. He'd never planned on getting out alive. Well, I wouldn't let that happen! I couldn't let him die in my place.

I looked around urgently for some way to help. A small black bat flew past me, and suddenly, I realized that I *did* have a talent I could use. I closed my eyes and concentrated with all of my might. *The strange man in the middle and the people in the black suits are bad. Please, please, help us! Fly at them, distract them, especially the man in the middle.*

The bat eyed me warily, thinking, *Why should I help you?*

*That man is evil. He's a danger to the forest and all the animals who live there. He is the reason they're fleeing. He must be stopped.*

The bat just flew away, back into the cave.

*Damn it!* That was my last hope.

"Claire!" Billy yelled, running up to me with Jane in tow. "What are you still doing here? Run!"

"I have to help Dylan. Wilder has him trapped!"

"If you stay here, you'll kill him. He can't fight Wilder when he's worried about you. He made me promise him that I would get you out, and that's a promise I intend to keep! Now come on." He roughly grabbed my arm.

"But the vision—I have to pull the wire!"

"It's changed!" he said, exasperated. "Dylan changed it— don't you see? He's on our side now, and he's going to stop it."

"But he can't if he has to keep saving *you*," Jane simpered. "And I, for one, want to get out of this hellhole. Now, come on!"

I couldn't. I just couldn't leave him there to die. But to my amazement, a moment later hundreds of bats swooped at Wilder. It worked! Dylan seized the opportunity and charged at Wilder in a blur of fury. As I let Billy and Jane lead me out of the cavern, I turned back for a fleeting glance at him, knowing it might well be my last.

Once we were back in the tunnel, Murphy and Charlotte ran to us, grinning broadly. "The ghosts told us to stay back so Wilder wouldn't know I'd betrayed him," explained Murphy.

I was so relieved to see Charlotte that I threw my arms around her. "Thank God you're okay."

"I was so worried about you guys," Charlotte said to me and Billy. "And guess what? Nana's here!" she cried. I looked at the spot she stared at and put out my hand, trying to connect with what I couldn't see.

Charlotte paused, then nodded. "Nana says you're doing great, but we have to follow Murph."

Billy swallowed hard. "You've done great, Charlotte," he said, giving her a quick hug.

"Touching. Really, just moving. Now can we leave this filthy place?" Jane scowled.

"Nana says there's another way out!"

Murphy nodded. "Like I said before, there's a secret chamber where Wilder is holding a prisoner, and it leads to the back exit."

"Someone else from Cambial?" Billy asked.

He shook his head sadly. "Been his prisoner for years."

"Years? That's so awful. There are worse things than dying and being a ghost," Charlotte said.

Murphy stared at her. "You're a very wise girl, Charlotte."

She was right. There were worst things—like watching the people you love die. Now I no longer feared for my own life, but Dylan's. What if Billy was right? What if Dylan changed the future when he joined us, and now it was he who would pull the wire and die?

Murphy led the way to the secret exit, stopping at a large boulder. We climbed through an opening behind it, barely big enough for Murphy to squeeze through, and came out in a passageway that opened to a small cavern.

"Nana Marie's going to go first and tell us how many guards are in there," Charlotte said.

Murphy smiled at her. "You're very talented. I couldn't communicate with ghosts that well until I was much older."

"I knew you weren't all bad, even when you helped them put me in the cage." She paused. "Do you know why the ghosts bothered you the most?"

He shook his head.

"They knew it, too."

Even in the darkness I could see him grin.

A moment later Murphy nodded. "Yes, it should work." Then he turned to me. "There's only two guards—one's a medium. Marie's going to get help—the ghosts will take care of him. I'll handle the other one, then we'll run outside as fast as we can."

"Let me help," Billy said.

I was waiting for him to tell Billy to stay there with us, but he didn't. "Yeah, you're good at telekinesis—really accurate. I could use you. I'm going to pretend you're my prisoner, and when we get close, take the gun and knock them out."

"Why not just shoot them?" Jane asked.

Murphy stared at her. "Because it's wrong, and because the only ghosts down here are good ones. But there are bad ones, too, let me tell you that. We don't want those men as ghosts. People can be more powerful in death than in life."

Charlotte peered down the passageway. "The ghosts are standing by. Good luck."

"Billy," I whispered, "be careful!"

We pressed ourselves against the cave wall and watched as Murphy pulled Billy in front of him, holding the gun loosely.

"Hey, Grady, Cole—I caught this one. What are you doing here?"

Grady, who looked to be in his early forties, with sallow, pock-marked skin, answered, "The girl's loose. She'd never find this exit, but Boss stationed us here, anyway—no one gets past us."

Just then a tall man came through a door concealed in the stone. He was holding a thin, frail woman with long, dirty blond hair and vacant blue eyes. Her mouth was gagged and her arms bound.

"Where are you taking Josephine, Victor?" Murphy said.

Josephine! She wasn't dead after all.

"Boss wants me to get her out of here. He doesn't want to chance anyone seeing her. Who do you have there?"

"I got one of the Walkers," Murphy said. "Bringing him to Wilder."

Josephine's eyes darted to Billy, and she suddenly sprang to life. She started to scream something from behind the black gag.

"Well, look who woke up." He laughed again.

Josephine kicked Victor, frantically trying to get away. He pulled her roughly down the passageway and out of view.

All of a sudden, Cole, the tall man next to Grady, started to swat at the air. "Stop it. Go away!"

"What's your problem?" Grady said.

In the commotion Billy flexed his palm, and in one quick movement the butt of the gun came down hard on Grady and then Cole. They fell to the ground.

"Nicely done," Murphy said. "Now follow me." We ran though the cavern and down a passageway, slipped behind another boulder, and eventually ended up at the first keypad. As I feared, it wouldn't open. Murphy tried every combination he could think of, to no avail.

"How are we going to get out?" Jane cried desperately.

"We have to wait for Dylan to disable the system," Murphy answered. He put his hand on my shoulder. "Don't worry—he'll do it. That kid can do anything."

I smiled. "I know."

"You really care about him, don't you?"

I nodded. A sob caught in my throat.

Billy gave me a twisted grin. "He's a pretty good guy."

"Well, love isn't going to get us out of here." Jane scowled.

"Have *you* seen anything that might help?" Billy asked.

She shook her head. "I've hardly seen anything since I've been down here. I usually just sit and talk to Dylan," she said wistfully. "He even comes when Wilder interrogates me." As soon as the words tumbled out of her mouth, her expression changed as she began to make the connection. I realized it then, too; Dylan only sat with her to block her powers so she couldn't make any predictions about me to Wilder.

Her eyebrows narrowed together and her lips twitched into a hard line. "Not that I care about that loser, but he couldn't stay away from me," she said with a flip of her dirty hair. "And incidentally, Claire, he never mentioned you, not once. Not that it matters now—we're all going to die in here because Dylan's never going to be able to disconnect the force field."

"He'll do it. I know he will." I tried the door again. Nothing. Frustrated, I slammed it with the fist of my good hand.

I heard a responding knock.

"Dylan?"

I could barely hear the answer, but it sounded like *Claire*.

I pounded and pounded against the door.

Jane yanked the arm I had landed on. "STOP IT!" she screamed.

"Owww!" I yelled as a searing pain traveled all the way to my shoulder. "Don't touch me again!"

"Are you crazy, Claire? Or just stupid? That could be one of Wilder's men."

"It isn't! I can tell. Now do me a favor and shut up." Ferana had told me to trust my instincts, and that's what I was going to do. I continued pounding with my good hand. "There's a keypad in a rock!"

"We're coming," a voice called back. After several long minutes the door finally slid open. Standing before me were Henry, Ally, Winny, and Principal Grogan.

"Claire!" Henry beamed. Then a look of horror crossed his face at the same instant a guttural scream escaped from Winny's lips.

I whirled around to see Sedona standing behind Murphy, grinning triumphantly as she sent a huge dagger toward my chest.

"I'VE GOT YOU NOW!" she screamed.

Henry pulled me to the side, but even then I knew it was too late.

# CHAPTER 30
# The Black Wire

"NO!" Murphy yelled.

To my horror, I watched as he leaped in front of me. The knife went straight through his stomach. For a second he stood there as if nothing happened, and then he slumped to the floor.

"Murph!" Charlotte yelled, running over to him.

"You're right, Charlotte, there are worse things than death. Run," he whispered, his voice raspy.

Sedona blew the whistle that hung from her neck. "Seal the exit! They're getting away!" she shouted, raising her hands toward me.

And then several things happened all at once.

Grogan yelled, "No you don't!" and ran past me into the cave while Henry pulled me out of it. Billy grabbed Charlotte and was out the door with Jane in an instant. Ally disabled the keypad, and the door slammed with a resounding crunch.

I could scarcely believe it—we had made it out.

A moment later I realized Grogan was sealed inside. I stood there in the dark tunnel, dumbstruck. Grogan was in terrible danger, and Murphy had saved me, but it had cost him his life.

Charlotte began to sob hysterically, snapping me into action. I grabbed her hand and rushed behind Henry as he turned on his odd flashlight. It cast an eerie glow on the cave walls and illuminated blue footprints on the ground, which, I realized, were mine. We followed them out through the cleft and into the cave that led outside. I could hear Sedona's shrill voice behind us.

The cave was lighter than when I'd entered it, but it was

menacing nonetheless. We dashed outside in single file and carefully made our way across the narrow ledge, clinging to the side of the mountain for dear life. I looked up at the sky, lapis blue as night surrendered to day. It was hard to believe that just hours ago I had stood here with Dylan.

"Where're Chey and Maggie and Nik?" Winny asked, frantic.

"They're still inside, fighting alongside my parents and Dylan. They'll make it out. I'm sure of it," I said, trying to convince myself as much as her.

"Chey's amazing—he took out a bunch of Wilder's guards," Billy said. "He'll be fine."

I held Charlotte's hand tightly as we made our way over the rocks.

"Murphy," Charlotte sobbed. "Is he going to die?"

The image of the knife ripping through him ran through my mind. "I think so," I said softly.

"Are they going to put him in that awful machine?"

My stomach lurched at the thought. "No. Dylan will stop them."

Henry stiffened next to me. "So you trust him now?"

I nodded. "He's fighting Wilder. He helped save us." I was still amazed to see them all there. "How'd you even find us?"

*Claire!*

I looked up and saw Ferana soaring above me. Of course, she had led them to me. *Thank you, Ferana! You saved my life!*

I surveyed the dirty, exhausted faces of my friends. "I don't know how to thank you—all of you—for saving us."

Winny shook her head. "We knew we had to come and rescue you, and that changed the prophecy, so now you won't die," she said very matter-of-factly.

I felt a lump in my throat. Relief washed over me as the truth sank in. I had braced myself for so long; now I realized how happy I was to be alive. A gift Dylan and my friends had given me. But we still had to save my parents and the others.

I quickly explained about the machine and the force field,

hoping one of them would come up with a rescue plan, or at least a place where we could hide until we formed one.

We were in a fairly open area, but up ahead I spotted a ridge of pines that would conceal us while we figured out what to do. Adrenaline surged through my body as we ran through the thick underbrush, Ferana watching from above.

"How did you guys keep up with Ferana—and how'd you get here so fast?"

"I had a vision of Grogan helping us," Winny explained, "so I told him everything. He got his hands on a few dirt bikes, and then we waited for Ferana at Maxwell's Hole. We couldn't understand her, but we followed her, hoping she'd lead us to you. She had to hold a flashlight in her talons so we could see her."

"And I thought you might get noble on us." Henry grinned. "So I put a liberal dose of powder on your shoes and the tent floor. Once Ferana brought us to the cave, we followed your footsteps down the tunnel to the keypad."

"Believe it or not, I broke the code to open it," Ally said.

"I'm sure glad you figured it out! I couldn't stand being locked up in there." Billy shuddered.

"Oh, stop complaining," Jane snapped. "My hair is greasy, my face is breaking out.... I haven't had a hot shower in weeks! Just a gross pail of water and a bar of cheap soap. And the food? Bread, bread, and more bread. I never even eat carbs!" She paused, then added in a small voice, "It felt like I would never leave."

"Poor Murph won't get to," Charlotte said through tears.

We were almost at the ridge. Even though we were all exhausted, we hurried on. Just as we reached the pines two people suddenly stepped out from behind them.

I froze; I swear my heart stopped beating. There, not ten feet from us, were Wilder and Sedona. Wilder barely moved his hand, but I went sailing to him as Charlotte flew to Sedona.

"I'd advise everyone to stay right where they are," Wilder threatened, his large hand encircling my neck. "It's over. Your family and friends have all been captured and will soon be quite dead. This has been amusing, Claire—I will give you that. I knew that you would try to disconnect the power source, but of course, I would win in the end, as the talented Jane foretold." His voice was as cold as ice. I couldn't stop myself from trembling as he tightened his grip. "So I knew exactly where to wait for you."

What? The wire was inside, in the lab. Was he really crazy? Or was Jane trying to throw him off? My eyes darted to Jane, but she looked confused.

Sedona smirked. "It did take Jane an *annoyingly* long time to tell us that. If we pushed too hard, her mind would crack"—she snapped her fingers—"and then she'd be useless to us."

"Yes, that's what happened to Josephine." Wilder's face hardened as he said her name. "I don't tolerate betrayal. That's why Dylan is on his way into the machine as we speak."

I felt the hatred surge through me. I would *not* let that happen. Wilder had been waiting here because the power source must be nearby, and not in the cave as I had thought. I scanned the woods frantically for some sign of it, but I didn't know what I was looking for—except someplace dark. I glanced up just as the sun climbed over the mountain, and a glint of metal caught my eye. There above the next ridge, in the shadow of tall pine trees, stood a shed surrounded by a tall electric fence. That must be it.

"So you figured out how to harness lightning?" I asked, stalling for time.

He laughed. "I discovered that long ago. The trick was finding a way to make it strike a specific spot."

"The spot in the shed."

"Precisely."

I had to pull that wire—but how was I going to get away from Wilder? And then I heard her cry above me.

*Claire, what can I do?*

*Attack them! Please, hurry!*

*When I get closer, duck!*

Without a noise Ferana dove straight at Wilder. He saw her

at the last second and, in his bewilderment, let go of me to shield his face. I ducked and rolled out of the way in time to see a large hawk attack Sedona. I thought it was one of Ferana's friends, but then I read its thoughts.

*Run, Claire!* It was Talrin.

Charlotte sprinted to Billy, and I ran, faster than I ever had, up the mountain to the shed. For a fleeting moment I wondered how I could get over the fence, but then I realized Winny could fly me right over it. It was ironic, really, how I tried to keep everything from my friends, yet in the end I couldn't pull the wire without them.

"Winny—help me!"

She hurried to my aid, quickly realizing what I was asking her to do. She hesitated, and then with tears streaming down her face and a flip of her hand, she sent me sailing over it. The last glimpse I had was of a flare soaring over the trees.

I darted into the dark shed, immediately covering my ears. The buzzing was so loud and high-pitched that I fell to my knees. I pictured Dylan writhing in pain, and I forced myself forward. The black wire, at least a foot thick, was pulsing. It was attached to some sort of metal disk on the ceiling, and then it ran into a huge contraption in the ground. I thought of Dylan's hand. Would I have the strength for this? I scanned the dirty room; there was a greasy old towel in the corner. I grabbed it, wrapped it around my hands, and pulled with all of my might.

The pain was like nothing I had ever experienced before. Every inch of my body shook and thrashed as I felt the energy surge through me, burning everything in its path. My brain kept screaming *STOP* and then sent a message directly to my hands: *LET GO.* But I didn't. With every bit of strength I could summon, I pulled and pulled, until I finally fell backward.

I felt the wire drop from my hands as they lost their ability to hold on to anything. The pain gradually lessened as everything went from blindingly bright, to gray, then slowly faded to black. I had done it. Even though it was going to cost me my life, I wouldn't have changed a thing. Well, maybe one thing. I wish I had written it all down in my journal, so everyone would know how much I loved them and that I had no regrets. Especially Dylan; he was going to blame himself for my death, of that I was certain. I worried for a moment that I hadn't pulled the wire in time to save Dylan and my family, but then a warm peace covered me like a blanket.

They were going to live.

# CHAPTER 31

# The Exceptionals

I was floating, sometimes in my body, sometimes above it. Winny was with me, holding my hand, sobbing. I could see everyone else running up the mountain toward us. I was so filled with relief and happiness that they were all alive. Poor Winny—I wanted her to feel like I did, warm and safe and serene. The only thing that bothered me was that I didn't see Dylan.

And then I realized my Nana Marie was sitting next to me, stroking my face. Christopher was there, too, along with Grandpa Paul and my other grandparents, Edmund and Jillian, and Murphy. I could see them all clearly now, while my family and friends became transparent, as if they were the ghosts. Marie held me in her arms. "You were so brave, darling."

"Don't be afraid—it's nice being a ghost," Murphy said, looking happier than I had ever seen him.

"You saved my life," I said, taking his hand in mine.

He shook his head. "You saved mine."

"Where's Dylan? Did I pull the wire in time to save him?"

Murphy smiled. "You sure did. Wilder had six guards ready to take him into the machine. But once Wilder and Sedona left, Dylan was able to block their powers and get everyone else to safety. Before he could get out, though, Jay came to and locked him in the tunnel. He wouldn't have lasted long with the machine on—but then you pulled the wire and it stopped."

My Grandpa Paul beamed at me. "You saved everyone here, even us spirits! We are so proud of you."

A tall man walked into the shed, full of authority. I had never met him, but I would recognize him anywhere: William Crane. He sat by my side. "Well, you're a chip off the old block. The most famous Crane—and that is saying something, indeed. The girl who saved the school, her family, the ghosts, and who knows how many others."

"Were you down in the caves, too?"

He nodded. "A dreadful place."

"Is Wilder dead?"

"No, he got away. They let him," he said, motioning to everyone clustered around my body below me, "to try to save you."

My mother and father were there along with Charlotte and Billy, Uncle Dan, and my friends. Everyone was crying. Ally was holding my arm, gently stroking my skin. Nik sat by her side, looking at her as if she were the most beautiful girl in the world. Chey was holding Winny, who was sobbing uncontrollably. I had done it; I had saved them all.

I wondered where Dylan was, though. I wanted desperately to see him one more time before he became completely transparent to me; then I heard him. He ran into the shed and screamed like a tortured animal. I wanted to go to him, to tell him it would be all right, but I couldn't move.

Dylan rushed to me, but my mother held him back. I wished I could tell her to let him go so that I could see his face.

Then Henry leaned over me, kissed my cheek, and rubbed something cold and slimy all over me.

Ally continued to touch me, her hands becoming warmer and warmer. I started to feel uncomfortable, an ache growing in my chest.

Dylan struggled against my mother and finally ran to my other side.

"I love you, Claire. Please, don't leave me," he said, his voice somewhere between a whisper and a sob.

My Nana Marie continued to hold my hand, but then she began to fade. "Nana? Don't go, please! I'm scared."

I could face death with my loved ones there; I wasn't sure I could face it alone.

She smiled, and the dark and dismal shed lit up with a bright, glorious light. "It seems you are not ready yet, my darling."

I looked at Christopher, Murphy, and my grandparents. They were all fading, and the pain in my body was growing. "I don't understand. I died."

Nana Marie stroked my cheek. "Many forces have saved your life—the power of medicine, the power of healing, and the power of love. It is not your time, but know that the ones you love are always here watching over you, and we will never leave you."

She shimmered like a star, and then disappeared.

The pain became unbearable. I heard someone scream, an ear-shattering shriek. And then I realized it was me.

I slept for what seemed an eternity. At times I could hear voices—my family, my friends, and, of course, Dylan. I wanted to talk to them, but I couldn't. My body wasn't doing anything I told it to. But I had several dreams, and despite everything, they were all wonderful. I dreamed I walked with Nana Marie through the forest and then we flew through the air with Christopher.

When my eyes finally opened, the first face I saw was Dylan's.

"Hi, there," he said, his gorgeous face lined with worry. He was sitting on a chair next to my bed, holding my hand. I looked around—I was in the school infirmary. "How are you feeling? Are you in any pain?" he said anxiously.

I smiled weakly. "You're here." I was so relieved to see him, it didn't even matter that my head ached and every muscle in my body throbbed.

He nodded. "You did it."

"We did it, all of us." I looked around the empty room. "Where is everyone?"

"Your parents are talking to the doctors, and everyone else is still at specials. They'll be here soon."

"Specials?" It seemed strange that life had just carried on. "How long have I been here?"

"Almost a week. You've been in and out of consciousness

because of the pain meds they're giving you," he said, gesturing to the IV tube in my arm.

With his injured hand he lightly traced circles on my wrist. Seeing his scarred skin made me think—was I burned like that all over? I immediately touched my face; it felt smooth, but… "Can you get me a mirror?"

He laughed lightly. "You're still beautiful—don't worry. Not that it would matter to me."

"But your hand—how was I able to pull it, not die, and not be…"—I could barely say the word—"disfigured?"

"You have pretty amazing friends. You were in bad shape when I got there. You were…"—he paused, and took a deep breath—"dead. No pulse, no breath."

After a few moments he turned back to me, his beautiful green eyes composed. "Ally was able to heal your injuries, but your heart wouldn't start. She worked so hard to save you, her whole body convulsed like she was having a seizure. I sat with you—"

This I remembered. "You told me you loved me."

He smiled. "So you remember that? Well, I do love you. You're everything to me," he whispered.

I felt my heart surge. "I love you, too."

He leaned forward and kissed my lips very lightly.

"So I'm not burned?"

"No." He got up and walked into the bathroom, removing the round mirror from the wall. "See?"

I looked at my reflection. It was me, but I looked different somehow. The person staring back at me looked older, confident. Something I wasn't accustomed to seeing in my face.

"But you were hurt," he paused again. "Every inch of you was burned from your neck down. The current went from your hands, up your arms to your chest, and then down to your feet. Henry put the cell accelerator all over you, and your skin sort of re-grew. All of your scars faded—well, all but one."

He pulled down gently on my hospital gown, and there, right above my heart, was a pink star. I smiled, remembering Nana Marie's glow before she left me.

"That's from my nana."

He looked at me, slightly confused, but he didn't say anything.

"I promised I'd get your parents if you woke up," he said, getting up. "I just wanted you to myself for a few minutes."

I smiled. I liked the sound of that. "How's it going with my parents?"

He shrugged. He returned a minute later with my parents and Uncle Dan. They crowded around my bed, showering me with gentle kisses and hugs. My mother sat closest to me, on the edge of my bed, stroking my hair. "The prophecy we tried so hard to protect you from came true. You saved us all, Claire, but we were so worried we had lost you! To think what could have happened—"

"I know, Mom."

She didn't answer; she just kissed my forehead. I couldn't help but smile. I was sure there was a lecture in my future about keeping myself safe.

"I saw everyone—Nana Marie, Grandpa Paul, Grandpa Edmund, Grandma Jillian, even Great-Grandfather William. I saw Murphy, too...." I turned to Dylan, "He's happy now."

Dylan smiled sadly. "He's the closest thing I ever had to a father."

"Oh—Uncle Dan, Josephine's alive! We saw her." I also remembered what Wilder said about her mind snapping. I couldn't bear to tell him that part.

"I know. Billy told me. I should never have given up," he said softly, the pain raw in his voice. "I'm leaving soon to find her. I'm just trying to narrow down where to look. Christopher and Murphy are helping me—they'll tell Charlotte what they discover."

My mother patted his arm. "We'll find her."

Dylan inched closer to me, but my father blocked his path. Clearly, he had not come around.

I opened my mouth to protest, but before I could, Billy, Henry, Ally, and Winny burst into the room.

"Finally you're awake!" Winny said, as if I had overslept for class. I couldn't help but laugh. She squeezed in next to Billy, who still seemed oblivious to her feelings. I noticed she only wore one necklace, a leather rope with a talon dangling from it.

"Nice necklace."

She laughed, fingering it. "This is Talrin's talon! It was lodged in Sedona's face! She's going to have a nice scar. Boy, that Talrin's tough. Anyway, I have loads to tell you—and school's out in two days! But we're rooming together next year!"

I must have looked stunned because she quickly backpedaled. "I mean, if you want to."

"I'm boarding?" I said to my mother.

"Well, I don't think you need to take the entrance exam to prove your abilities!" Principal Grogan chuckled from the doorway, Charlotte by his side. "I think I can vouch for you."

I looked into his kind eyes. "Thank you for saving my life."

He nodded curtly, turning crimson. Both my parents turned and stared at him in surprise; he obviously hadn't told them about his role in my rescue. "And to you for saving mine. I was sure I was going to die in that godforsaken cave," he said, suddenly becoming very serious. "And not even to live on in spirit."

The smiles disappeared from everyone's face. Although we had much to celebrate, Wilder was still out there somewhere, undoubtedly plotting his revenge as we spoke.

I grabbed Ally's and Henry's hands. "How can I ever thank you both?"

My mother smiled warmly at them. "How can I?"

Ally reached behind her and unexpectedly grabbed Dylan's hand. "We all did it together."

Charlotte jumped up on the side of my bed next to my mother. "Guess what? I've been accepted in the Exceptional Society! Principal Grogan just told me. I'm the youngest in Cambial's history!"

I looked over at Billy, who rolled his eyes. We weren't going to hear the end of it from Charlotte.

My mother kissed the top of her head. "Well, she's got you

beat by a couple of weeks, Dylan. Her birthday's in March. Dylan was also accepted a year early at Cambial, and won the TT his first year, so he was the youngest Exceptional at Cambial," my mother explained.

"Until now!" Charlotte exclaimed.

Dylan laughed. "Congratulations, Charlotte."

"Actually," Principal Grogan continued, "it hardly seems important considering what you've all done, but...you've all been accepted into the Exceptional Society."

Billy's face lit up. I was so happy. I knew what this meant to him.

"Congratulations, you guys! When's the ceremony? Will I be outta here in time to go?"

Principal Grogan put his hand on my shoulder. "Claire, when I said everyone, I meant you, too. None of us would be here without you and your special."

Me? An Exceptional? I searched for something to say, but the words got caught in my throat.

The doctor came in a moment later and ushered everyone out to examine me. He changed the bag on my IV, and before long I started to drift off.

After he left, I felt someone hold my hand. I could tell from the rough, scarred skin that it was Dylan. I squeezed, and he squeezed back.

# CHAPTER 32
# Good-bye

I was still stuck in the infirmary when school finished for the year. I had only been sprung once—to be inducted into the Exceptional Society. I still had a hard time believing it. (As did Jane; the look on her face was priceless.) When I said good-bye to all my friends at a party we had in my room, the nurse had a fit, but since Principal Grogan came, there wasn't much she could do.

Once I went home, some things were the same, and some weren't. My mother seemed to trust me more but also worry more, if that was possible. I decided to cut her some slack, for now. Dylan visited every day. (I don't know where he went when he left me. I hoped he wasn't sleeping on the hard forest floor, but when I told him that, he only answered that he'd slept in worse places.) And although I could tell my mother liked him—mainly because you really knew when she *didn't* like someone—it was very obvious my father and Uncle Dan didn't.

Principal Grogan came over quite a bit to talk with my mother about Cambial's new security policies, and it was nice to see them getting along. Charlotte and Uncle Dan spent a lot of time with Murphy. He watched over Charlotte all of the time, and Dan questioned him—through Charlotte—over and over again about Josephine. Everything was going better than I could have hoped—except for one thing.

Although I spent most of my time with Dylan—usually in the forest, but also doing normal things like watching movies and going for ice cream—I knew in my heart he wasn't staying. I almost asked him at least a dozen times, but I was too afraid of the answer.

One night at the end of June, we celebrated my sixteenth birthday. My whole family was there, along with Principal Grogan (I was having a hard time calling him George, like he asked) and Dylan. My father and Uncle Dan were trying their best to hide their disapproval, which I was grateful for.

It was a wonderful celebration, with a terribly dry, lopsided cake my mother made herself, several pineapple pizzas from Tony's, and Almond Joy ice-cream sundaes. After dinner we played Scrabble with Charlotte, who always won because Murph helped her—and, I suspected, told her our letters.

It was perfect.

After I opened my gifts, Dylan and I went for a walk. The night was beautiful, warm with a light breeze that rustled my white sundress. The moon and stars sparkled like diamonds above us. I held his hand, and when we reached the meadow, it was bathed in moonlight.

We sat up on the rock, listening to the water churning in the brook and the song of the tree frogs.

"You're so beautiful," he said, tracing the contours of my face with his finger. Then he placed something cold around my neck. "Happy birthday."

I looked down. It was a necklace, a golden star. "It's gorgeous!"

"I know how much you love that ring, so when I saw the necklace, I knew it would be perfect."

"Thank you." I wrapped my arms around him and looked into his dazzling green eyes, trying to memorize everything about him.

He leaned forward and kissed me like he never had before, without holding any part of himself back. But his intensity frightened me. It was a kiss to remember. It was a kiss good-bye.

He pulled away from me and said what I knew he would. "I have to go."

His eyes were warm, filled with regret, but they were set. "I can't stay here, Claire. I've made too many mistakes for anyone to overlook."

"That's not true. You saved everyone—"

"No, *you* saved everyone from a situation I helped create. I am not innocent in all of this. McAllister let me go, but he's not going to let me just hang around Cambial."

This was true. "They'll come around. My mother already has, and—"

He shook his head. "Your mother always saw something in me no one else ever did"—he paused—"except for you."

"I can—"

"No. I can't let you do that," he said, as if reading my mind. "Leave your family, for what? I don't know where I'm going—what I'll do. I can't let you come with me."

I held his gaze. "Can't, or won't?"

He smiled, exposing his dimple. "Is there a difference?"

"All the difference in the world."

He kissed the top of my head. "I'm sorry. I won't do that to you. I care too much about you." He stood up and pulled me into his arms. "I love you, Claire. I always will. But you need to be here. You have two years of school and training you need to finish, and there's no place for me here. But there are other things I can learn, things I can do to try to make up for some of the mistakes I've made. Please try to understand."

The worst part about it was, I did. He needed to wrestle with his demons away from Cambial, and that meant away from me.

"Will you come back?"

"Just try to keep me away," he said, circling my waist with his arms. "But I don't know when, and I'm not asking you to wait for me. If you met someone else, I'd understand." He looked away. "Henry's a pretty great guy."

"He is," I agreed. "But he isn't you. I love you. I'll work on my special, and you do what you have to do. I won't be waiting for you—I'll be waiting for us to be together again."

He kissed me again, his lips full of longing. I inhaled his woodsy smell, running my hands across his broad shoulders.

And then he pulled away.

I felt my heart plummet. Letting him go was the hardest thing I've ever had to do. I took a step toward him, but he retreated, disappearing into the forest.

*  *  *

Sitting up on the rock, I let the tears come freely now. My heart ached more than it had when I was electrocuted. After a long while, a shadow crossed over the moonlit meadow. I didn't need to look up to know who it was.

*Hello, Ferana.*

*Claire, what's the matter? Why are you so sad?*

*Dylan had to go away.*

She swooped down and landed gently on my shoulder, nuzzling my face.

As I stroked her long, beautiful feathers, another shadow passed overhead. I looked up, surprised to see Talrin, now bigger than Ferana. He flew down and landed on my outstretched arm. *Your mom is out looking for you, Claire.*

I sighed. I had lost track of the time, and of course she would be worried.

*Thank you, Talrin,* I said, still amazed at his breadth. *I'm not used to seeing you so grown-up.*

*Neither am I,* Ferana agreed.

*I'm sorry you're so sad,* Talrin said.

*Are you going to be all right?* Ferana asked.

I took a deep breath, brushed away a tear, and answered her truthfully. *I will miss him, but I'm going to be fine. I better get home, but I'll come and see you both again tomorrow.*

Ferana gently lifted off my shoulder, followed by Talrin. I watched them soar into the sky, glistening in the moonlight, and saw that Talrin now had a glorious red tail.